BANGING NOISES FROM THE BACK HAD TO COME FROM MARINA, OR SO BARRY DESPERATELY WANTED TO BELIEVE.

Then she called him. Then she started shooting. Barry freaked, his hand almost reflexively yanking the trigger before he stopped it. Her bullets glowed with an intense white heat, burning into his retinas. The goggles only made it worse. When he heard something else, something closer, he swung around to try to see it but ghost images from her bright rounds in his eyes half-blinded him. And it was dark against dark, just a rustle of motion passing from one shelving unit to another. Could have been a big rat.

Or something else.

He blinked, afraid to leave his eyes closed longer than a fraction of a second. While they were closed he heard something else, louder and closer. Marina's voice sounded very far away. He opened his eyes again. The ghost images had faded a little, allowing him to see better through the goggles.

He wished he couldn't, wished he was blind.

Instead, he saw a horrible thing charging him. Its forehead was swept back, tiny eyes bright, nose jutting forward. Below that a gaping mouth held jagged teeth, way more teeth th␣ ␣␣thing needed.

Enter the terrifying world of

30 DAYS OF NIGHT

Novels available from Pocket Books:

30 Days of Night: Rumors of the Undead

30 Days of Night: Immortal Remains

30 Days of Night: Eternal Damnation

30 Days of Night: Light of Day

Graphic Novels/Comic Books available from IDW Publishing:

30 Days of Night

30 Days of Night: Dark Days

30 Days of Night: Return to Barrow

30 Days of Night: Bloodsucker Tales

30 Days of Night: Dead Space

30 Days of Night: Spreading the Disease

30 Days of Night: Eben and Stella

30 Days of Night: Beyond Barrow

30 Days of Night: 30 Days 'Til Death

30 Days of Night Annual 2004
(featuring "The Book Club," "The Hand That Feeds,"
"Agent Norris: MIA," "The Trapper")

30 Days of Night Annual 2005

30 Days of Night: "Picking Up the Pieces"
(featured in IDW's Tales of Terror)

30 DAYS OF NIGHT™

LIGHT OF DAY

JEFF MARIOTTE

Based on the
IDW Publishing graphic novel series

POCKET STAR BOOKS
New York   London   Toronto   Sydney

Pocket Star Books
A Division of Simon & Schuster, Inc.
1230 Avenue of the Americas
New York, NY 10020

This book is a work of fiction. Names, characters, places, and incidents either are products of the author's imagination or are used fictitiously. Any resemblance to actual events or locales or persons, living or dead, is entirely coincidental.

First Pocket Star Books paperback edition October 2009

POCKET STAR BOOKS and colophon are registered trademarks of Simon & Schuster, Inc.

For information about special discounts for bulk purchases, please contact Simon & Schuster Special Sales at 1-866-506-1949 or business@simonandschuster.com.

The Simon & Schuster Speakers Bureau can bring authors to your live event. For more information or to book an event, contact the Simon & Schuster Speakers Bureau at 1-866-248-3049 or visit our website at www.simonspeakers.com.

Cover design by Alan Dingman, art by Justin Randall

Manufactured in the United States of America

10 9 8 7 6 5 4 3 2 1

ISBN 978-1-4391-2227-3
ISBN 978-1-4391-6476-1 (ebook)

This one's dedicated to Ed.
Because really, it's overdue, isn't it?

Great thanks go out to Steve Niles, Ben Templesmith, and the gang at IDW Publishing; to all the fine folks at Simon & Schuster; to Dianne S. for the webwork; and to Howard and Katie, who take care of me.

I

LORD, HE WAS HUNGRY.

He groaned and his eyes flickered open, shifting from the darkness of unconsciousness to the literal but less complete darkness of his surroundings. It took him a few moments to remember where he was. As the gauzy cobwebs fell away from his mind, he recalled that he had been attacked in the common area of his housing unit. The scientists at this research facility lived in apartments, eight units per building, each with a lobby area, common recreation facilities, and a secure room in the basement. When the warning klaxons had sounded—almost simultaneously with the first explosions from the attacking force—he had stumbled out of bed and headed for the hallway, bound for the secure room. But he had dithered, taking time to pull on a robe over his cotton pajamas, wondering whether he should try to grab a laptop or any other personal objects, and by the time he made it to the recreation room, another blast blew in a window and part of the wall, showering him in glass and debris.

He fell behind a couch, hoping its bulk would protect him from further attack.

It was an ugly beast, that couch. School bus yellow, with red, orange, and green stripes on a diagonal, staggered about three and a half feet apart, with a solid wooden frame and what seemed like eighteen inches of foam padding. He and the other scientists laughed about it sometimes, because the couch hadn't just shown up here. Every building had one just like it. Some government procurement officer, probably sitting back in DC, had decided that this particular couch would work well for this particular facility. They wondered what kind of kickback the manufacturer of hideous couches could offer a procurement officer, figured he probably had a houseful of equally ugly chairs by now.

But it was a heavy son of a bitch, that was the thing. All that wood, all that padding. He could barely move it. So when he realized he would never make it to the secure room, he went behind the couch instead. The thing should've have been heavy enough to shield against a nuclear blast. It could keep him safe.

Except it hadn't.

He dragged himself from behind it now, his guts churning. He was cut and bruised, but he didn't think anything was broken. And he was so hungry. There was food in his apartment, and he needed to get something in his stomach. He took a couple of steps when a sharp pain in his left thigh almost dumped him back on the floor. With effort, he made it back to his door and pushed inside. The whole building reeked of smoke and burned electrical wires. He would have to find out if there were any other survivors. Later, though. First he had to eat.

His kitchen appeared intact. He opened the refrigerator. A couple slices of leftover pizza sat on the top shelf, enclosed in a zippered plastic bag. His stomach flipped as he tore into the bag, then shoved the end of one wedge into his mouth and bit down.

As soon as the familiar taste hit, he choked and spat into the open refrigerator. Bile filled his throat. He spat again. Had the pizza gone sour? He had eaten the rest just that night.

There was some chicken in a plastic container, roasted with garlic and rosemary. It didn't sound any better than the pizza, but that furious hunger wouldn't let him go. He popped open the lid and snatched up a leg with his hands, bringing it toward his face.

He couldn't bring himself to bite into it. It smelled rancid, foul.

There *was* a smell present that made his mouth water, that kept the hunger stalking inside him like a wild beast, but it didn't come from the refrigerator.

He let the door swing shut and stood in the kitchen for a minute, trying to isolate the aroma. When he realized what it was, his stomach lurched again. He understood, finally, what had happened.

Rushing into the bathroom, he flipped open the toilet lid and tried to vomit. Nothing came out but a few drops of bile. He spat, ran some water in the sink, ducked his hands under the stream, and doused his face and hair.

Wet faced, light filtering in from the hall illuminating him, he looked at himself in the mirror. He thought he knew what to expect. Larry Greenbarger. Thirty-nine, he looked forty-five easy. He carried forty pounds more than he should have, on a small frame, with skinny legs and puny arms and sloping shoulders that bowed toward the center of his chest. His brown hair was curly, receding prematurely from a high, freckled forehead. His eyes were blue and clear, and he had never needed glasses. Not many of the scientists he knew could make that claim.

At the moment, he wouldn't have minded a little blurriness in his vision.

He was still Larry Greenbarger. There was a familiarity in his eyes, in the curl and cut of his hair.

But beyond that, all was new.

His face had gone gaunt, his chin distended, his forehead elongated. Ears that had once been small and tucked close to his head flapped out like bat wings. Skin that had been tanned by months spent in the Nevada desert—never mind that he worked indoors, just walking from the residence to the lab or over to the commissary or snack bar was enough to bake a man—had gone pale, almost as porcelain white as the sink he leaned on.

The worst was his mouth; once small and pursed, it gapped like a briefcase opened wide, filled with what seemed like hundreds of needle-sharp teeth.

The lacerations and bruises covering his body came not just from the glass and bits of wall that had struck him but also from the brief, fruitless struggle he had forgotten about until now.

He swung away from the mirror, unable to face himself any longer. He knew what he had become. He had studied enough of them to recognize it.

And he knew with utter certainty what it was he hungered for. He wouldn't find sustenance in his refrigerator, or anywhere in his apartment. Out there, though, in the hallways and common areas, maybe even in the so-called secure room that he suspected had proved more trap than salvation? Oh, yes, he would find it there, and plenty of it.

As he stalked from the apartment, he tried to remember his attacker. It had been dark, except for the uneven light cast by flickering flames, but it seemed that it had been a female, young—at least in appearance, if not years on this earth—slight. Black hair, cropped short, black clothing. Tights, he recalled, striped tights on her legs, pink and white, incongruous with the rest of her look. Little girl tights, he had thought.

He had been hiding behind that heinous couch, blubbering softly, even as he told himself that only steely silence could protect him. And he had wet himself, to his mortification. But he believed himself safe from harm just the same, as if the couch could cast some sort of force field around him. Then he felt an iron grip on his right ankle, just above his sock (Larry had always worn socks to bed, since childhood, although he had tried unsuccessfully to break the habit in college), and something yanked him from hiding as easily as he might have pulled a child's doll from the same location.

He remembered screaming, batting at the person— the young woman—who held him. Her claws had dug into his ankle and his thigh and she had pressed him down onto the couch, slithered into his lap like a lover, her breath fetid and hot, and she had slapped him once across the face, stinging him and silencing his cries, and then she had pressed her mouth against his neck, almost tenderly at first, again like a lover. He remembered swelling inside his soaked pants, the moment more erotically charged than any he had experienced in years, since college really (with Verna McFall, who had been the reason he'd tried to break the socks habit), and thrusting up against her. And then white-hot pain, blinding, and he must have passed out because there were no memories after that, nothing until he woke up, once again behind the couch.

Touching his neck, he found the slash there, the skin dried out, tissuelike, but he could shove the end of his index finger into the hole and wiggle it around.

Larry made it to the secure room and punched in the code on the keypad mounted beside the door. Beeping noises sounded and the lock ground open and he pushed the door in. A light inside blasted like full sun, so he slapped the wall switch, shutting it off. He didn't need it.

He could see just fine in the dark.

He went to the nearest body. Andrea Harmon, he remembered. Midfifties, thick around the middle, as smart as any human being he had ever met. She had published four books, three of them obscure scientific texts, but the fourth a popular science book about the biological similarities and differences of immediate family members, and how those things might influence family dynamics. She had even appeared on one of the morning news shows, a network, though he couldn't recall which one. He had always felt somehow inferior to her and to other, more well-known scientists he met. He wanted to make a difference in the world, to be recognized for his intellectual accomplishments.

Andrea Harmon wouldn't be writing any more books, though. She was dead, bled out through gaping wounds in her chest and neck. He put his hand in the tacky pool on the floor beside her, then brought it to his face, sniffed it, licked it.

The hunger raged harder, consuming him. He lapped every drop off his palm and fingers, then dropped his face to her body, to one of the biggest wounds, tearing it wider with his many teeth. He shoved his tongue into the opening. No use—she had lived long enough with her wounds to lose most of her blood onto the floor, and he could find only traces, enough to make him feel starved.

He grunted and shoved her aside.

"Who's there?" a weak voice asked.

He peered through the gloom. More corpses littered the floor, but behind them, tucked into a niche between a big stainless steel freezer and a shelving unit that held emergency blankets, first aid kits, and other supplies, a wounded man huddled, blinking against the darkness. "It's me."

"Larry?"

"That's right. Come on out, Ron."

Ronald Tapper, that was his name. He and Larry had not been friends, but they knew each other, all the scientists at the facility knew each other. He and Ron had often competed for attention, for the best assistants, the better lab space.

"I'm afraid, Larry. You're . . ."

"It's nothing, Ron. You're suffering from shock." His voice didn't sound the same anymore, the new shapes of mouth and tongue and throat altering it. But it must have sounded similar enough for Ron to recognize. "We need to get you some medical help."

He stepped over the corpses on the ground. Ron stayed in his niche, thrusting out a hand to ward Larry off.

Larry grabbed Ron's wrist and pulled (remembering the sensation of being tugged by the ankle, the terror that powerful grip had inspired). Ron burst from the niche into his arms. He opened his mouth and wailed.

And Larry hauled him to his feet, shoved his head

back into the wall hard enough to break plaster, and raked his fingertips (no, his claws, he realized, more than an inch long, jagged and strong) across Ron's exposed throat.

Blood sprayed from the wound. Larry clamped his mouth over the opening and drank deep.

At last, his hunger could be sated.

This, he knew, was the stuff he craved.

Larry Greenbarger had become *nosferatu*. A vampire. Undead.

Other people might have doubted their senses, questioned that conclusion. But Larry had known plenty of vampires, had studied them, undead and completely dead. He and the other scientists working at this former military base in northern Nevada's Great Basin country did so on behalf of Operation Red-Blooded, a top-secret government operation dedicated to the eradication of that awful species. He had been probing them for weaknesses, trying to find new ways to exploit their vulnerability to sunlight. Other weapons, crucifixes for example, had long since been proven ineffective, their power to harm vampires relegated to the stuff of mythology. He had been trying to understand what had come to be known as the "Immortal Cell," with hopes of turning that understanding against them.

Larry knew what he had become, and that realization told him something else: the attackers who had stormed the base had been *vampires*. Scouring the grounds, it didn't take long to discover that they had won, for the most part. They had destroyed most of the main lab. Red-Blooded Director Dan Bradstreet had been pleading for death, drenched in blood. Darrel Keating and some of the other top scientists on staff were dead, along with most of the soldiers tasked with force protection. They had blown up the power plant. They had almost totally crushed one of the American government's most secret facilities.

What they might not have known was that Red-Blooded's tendrils stretched far and wide. They had destroyed the on-site computers, but all the data from those computers was captured on servers buried deep beneath Virginia hillsides, in caverns that could withstand a strategic nuclear strike, and mirrored in still other sites. They had killed scientists, but they had not eliminated data, or science. Red-Blooded paid well and would have no trouble finding new researchers.

Larry loved science. And like many scientists, he was a realist, not a romantic. So then: he had become a vampire, and there was nothing he could do to change that. The temptation to lash himself to some immovable object that would greet the rising sun came and went with barely a moment's consideration. The urge to survive ran strong in him.

At the same time, he knew that he had access to something most other vampires couldn't imagine. All the knowledge that Red-Blooded had about his kind—his new kind—was here, at his fingertips. His allegiance was to science, to knowledge, not to humanity. Human beings had never been particularly nice to him when he was alive—they had tolerated him, they had valued the things his intelligence could do for them. But most people didn't understand science or scientists, thought of them as some sort of useful subspecies if they thought of them at all.

He couldn't stay for long. By now there would be choppers en route, fighters scrambling, convoys rolling across desert highways. Sunrise would find clean-up teams already scrubbing the place.

Larry found some laptops and started downloading. Someone in Virginia or elsewhere might clue in to the fact that classified data was being snatched. But that someone might not have heard about the attack, and even if he or she raised an alarm, soldiers could only get here as fast as they could get here. Since they were already on the way, he wouldn't be changing that. As long as they didn't shut him out of the system, he would get the data he wanted, spread across several laptops because no single one had enough memory to capture it all.

When he finally left the facility in a stolen truck, Larry still had just over an hour of darkness. Not a lot, but enough to get him safely away. He could hole up for the day, and keep traveling when the sun fell again.

Larry Greenbarger's world had been reversed in an instant; he had become that which he had worked against, his days had become nights, and hungers once repulsive to him were suddenly as familiar and mundane as a young boy's attraction to peanut butter and jelly.

He was nothing if not adaptable. It was all about survival.

With a couple of fresh corpses rolled in a tarp in the back of the truck, laptops safely in the foot well of the passenger seat, he pressed the accelerator to the floor and drove.

2

"DUDE, VAMPIRES ARE *REAL*."

Mitch stared at Walker as if he had just emerged, wearing a bikini, from inside a giant cake. Walker shuddered. He had seen himself naked since birth, but that was an image even he didn't want trapped inside his brain. "Yeah," Mitch said. "And the sun sets in the west and ninety-nine percent of the music played on the radio is utter crap. What else is new?"

Walker took his seat in front of a big computer monitor. The bank of equipment arrayed on the desk had cost more than everything else he owned combined, but he and Mitch made their living online, so being able to rely on their gear was paramount. "No, I mean yeah, we've always believed in them. But I mean *really* real." He slammed his palm down on the wooden desktop. "As real as this."

"You doubted?"

"Believing in something is different from *knowing* something, dude. That's why they have two different words."

"So you believed, but now you know."

"That's what I've been saying."

"Because of the stuff Andy sent?"

"Duh."

"It *was* pretty trippy, no shit."

It was more than that, but Walker let the understatement slide as he settled in front of the desk and started checking on the status of several auctions. He was distracted, though, thinking about the data Andy had sent out.

For months, Walker Swanson (and Mitch Morton, although less enthusiastically, but they were partners in business and best friends, so he went along) had been part of Andy's network. Walker had posted information Andy sent, monitored online chat rooms and message boards, watched the news for signs, and generally did whatever Andy asked, all in the service of informing the world about the reality of vampires. But until the massive data packet he had received three days before, he hadn't known that Andy was really Andy Gray, former FBI agent. He hadn't seen actual video of the vampire invasion of Barrow, Alaska, several years ago, or read *30 Days of Night,* the true account of that invasion written by Stella Olemaun, one of the area's sheriffs, who had been one of the few survivors. He hadn't been exposed to still photographs of the victims of vampire attacks, or of vampires themselves. Some of the pictures Andy had sent showed close-ups of vampire skeletons, horribly mutated skulls, jaws that swung open wider than any human's could, jammed with awful teeth.

The distinction he had made for Mitch had been accurate. He had believed what Andy had said about vampires because he had wanted to, and because Andy made a convincing case. But that belief had been centered in his brain, in his imagination, not in his gut. That's where it was now that he had seen the pictures and video, read a PDF of the book. Those things had changed belief into certainty, and certainty meant reconsidering everything he had ever thought about the world.

Walker hadn't slept much over the past few days and nights. He had spent a lot of time thinking. He took a Snickers bar from his shirt pocket and peeled the wrapper back, took a bite.

"Breakfast of champions," Mitch said.

"Eat me." He suppressed a shudder—he would have to be more careful about saying things like that in the future.

"How's the utility belt doing?"

"I'm checking!"

"Okay, chill. Geez."

"Sorry, dude. Guess I'm just a little tense."

"I guess."

Walker took another bite of the Snickers, washing it down with a swig of Diet Coke. He recognized the hypocrisy: diet sodas wouldn't help him lose weight that he packed on with terrible eating habits. Every now and then he felt like he should do something about his physique, which was more or less that of a snowman with legs. That feeling usually passed quickly, swept away by bingeing on pizza or burritos or burgers and fries. He was twenty-five, and figured he would be lucky to reach fifty. On the other hand, life was essentially a long, boring chain of disappointment and heartache, broken occasionally by minor tragedies, so he didn't really see much value in extending it through healthy living.

"Utility belt is at two thousand bucks. Little over. Seven hours to go."

"Sweet," Mitch said.

"Yeah." The belt had been made by IDEAL! and sold in 1966 to cash in on the Adam West TV series. The one they had on eBay was in its original packaging and included a batarang, batcuffs, batrope, bat message-sender dart, bat flashlight, bat grappling hook, and for unknown reasons, a gun. Batman never used a gun on the TV show, so Walker didn't understand why it was there. It was supposed to shoot the message-sender dart, but it was still a gun. Maybe IDEAL! hadn't trusted kids to buy any play set that didn't involve firearms. Bidding would get furious in the last hour or so, he expected, and the belt would likely fetch more than five grand.

"So what's the matter?"

"What makes you think something's the matter?"

"Walker, look at you. You're acting like your mom died again."

"That's nice."

"I'm just saying."

Walker let out a sigh. "It's the stuff from Andy."

"The stuff you were supposed to send out immediately."

"Yeah."

"Three days ago."

"Dude, I know, okay?"

"So what's up?"

"I don't know if I can do it."

"Didn't you always do whatever Andy told you to?"

"Yeah . . ."

"So what makes this different?"

"It's . . . like I said, now I know they're real."

"And?"

"There really are vampires. It's not a myth anymore. It's for real, and . . . and they're bloodthirsty monsters. They kill, they feed, they show no mercy. They're killing machines, superior to humans in almost every way."

"Yeah?"

"So that fucking rocks!"

Mitch just looked at him, silently.

"I mean, don't you want in?"

"Meaning what?"

"Dude, don't you want to *be* a vampire? Wouldn't that be better than sitting around this house selling old toys on the internet and eating candy bars?"

"I guess so."

"You guess so."

"What do you want me to say?"

Walker couldn't believe he had to ask. "Prowling the dark streets, hunting for our meals. Knowing that people cower in fear of us. Seeing that look of terrible recognition in their eyes when they know their lives can be measured in seconds. How could you not want to be part of that?"

"I guess it sounds pretty cool, when you put it that way."

"Of course it does." He had known Mitch would come around. He always did.

"So in all that info Andy sent, did he tell you how to find any vampires who could turn us?"

Andy turned to another auction, a 1965 Gilbert Oddjob action figure, from the James Bond movie *Goldfinger*. Most of the best stuff had been released before he was born, but that didn't keep him from buying and selling it. This one still had a couple of days to go, and had just passed four hundred bucks. "No," he said. "Plenty of advice on how to protect yourself against them, but nothing about how to find them."

"There are still those message boards and all. I mean, if you're serious."

"Yeah," Walker said. "Always hard to tell if there are any real vampires on those, or just wannabes. But I'll keep an eye on them."

"You got any other ideas?"

This question, more than any other, was what had prevented Walker from sleeping during the night. He had rolled around in bed, going over and over the options, trying to tease out the pluses and minuses of the plan that had occurred to him. "I have one," he said.

"What?"

"If we want to become vampires, we have to bring vampires to us."

"And how do we do that?"

"We attract them," Walker said, "by acting like vampires. Starting right now."

3

IN HIGH SCHOOL, Walker had asked Missy Darrington to two dances. The first time, during sophomore year, she had turned him down and gone with Chad Benson, who was on the football and track teams and who had, three years after graduating, taken a dozen Ambien tablets, downed a fifth of Jim Beam, and gone for a drive in his father's restored vintage Thunderbird. Even if the pills-and-alcohol combination had not done him in, the collision with the utility pole did the trick. The second time Walker asked Missy out (and that had been excruciatingly difficult; although it was senior year and he had enjoyed a couple of dates with other girls by then, he still remembered her earlier rejection like it had happened only days before), she not only spurned him, but she talked about it online.

She still lived in her parents' old house, off 155th in Harvey, Illinois, where they had both grown up. She was still one of the most beautiful girls Walker had ever seen outside a porn site. Her shiny dark brown hair hung past her shoulders and curled up gracefully at the ends, which were healthy enough to be used in shampoo ads. Her eyes were big and brown, her lips pink and perfectly shaped, her cheekbones just right, her nose small but exceptional, all of it contained in a face that was almost perfectly oval. Her body had inspired many an emission, nocturnal and otherwise, beginning during his fifteenth year.

At the moment, she was tied up in the basement of Walker's house.

He and Mitch had gone back and forth about it for a couple of days. Walker had been trying to figure out the best approach, but Mitch still needed convincing on the idea as a whole. Walker had pressed, knowing all the while that Mitch would give in.

"We aren't vampires yet," Walker had said. "Which leaves us with some disadvantages. So we'll just have to go with our strengths. We can walk in daylight. We can blend in with other people. Nobody can tell by looking at us that there's anything different about us."

"Because there's not."

"You don't feel it yet, dude? I do."

"Feel what?"

"I feel stronger already. Determined. Like I've finally found my purpose, after all these years. I know what I was meant to do."

"I guess I'm not there yet."

"You will be. Trust me."

Rather than seek out a random, nameless victim, which might have exposed them to law enforcement or observation by witnesses, they decided to start with someone they knew. Missy Darrington had come immediately to mind, since Walker knew where she lived and had spent many hours sitting in his car outside her house over the years, watching for any glimpse of her through the windows. He knew who all her neighbors were, and that the old busybody living on her left went to bed early.

Plus, he was still mad at her.

They had gone to her place at ten o'clock the night before. She would still be up, but most of her neighbors would be asleep. Walker sent Mitch around to watch the back door while he knocked on the front. She came to the door, suspicious at first, but opened it when she recognized Walker. She even managed a hesitant smile.

"Walker? This is a surprise," she said. "I haven't seen you in ages."

"Hi, Missy," Walker said.

"It's pretty late, Walker. But—"

"I know. Can I come in, just for a minute? I wanted to apologize, but I feel kind of exposed standing out here."

"For a minute," she said. She had already dressed for bed, in loose gray sweats with nothing on underneath, and fuzzy red socks. Her hair was pulled back into a ponytail. She backed away from the door and let Walker in. Walker's breath caught as he passed close to her, inhaling the fresh scent of her soap and toothpaste. "Apologize for what?"

He pushed the door closed with his foot and reached under his coat. The gun he drew out was fake, but it was a replica snub-nosed .38 Police Special from 1975, and the casual observer would never know it wasn't the real deal. Especially staring into the barrel. "For this."

Missy gave a little shriek and brought her right hand to her mouth. "Oh my God, Walker, what are you doing with that? What . . ."

"Just stay quiet, Missy. I don't want to shoot you."

"Then put that away."

"I can't. Not yet."

"Is it real?"

"What do you think?"

Tears brimmed her eyes and started down those perfect cheeks. "But . . . why . . . ?"

"Turn around. Hands behind your back."

She swallowed but complied, shuffling around on legs that threatened to give way beneath her. Trembling hands offered themselves behind her back. Walker couldn't help enjoying her terror, her sense of helplessness, as he snapped handcuffs around her wrists. They had come from a sex shop in the city, but they were the real thing.

Beside her door there was a short section of wall, blocking the view of the dining room from the doorway. Three sections of textured mirror were hung on it, her parents' idea of style, Walker supposed. But Missy hadn't taken them down when her mom had finally moved into a nursing home, so she was just as much to blame. He pressed her up against the wall, leaning into her with all his weight.

"Walker, I'm going to scream if you don't cut this out."

Holding her in place with his bulk, he opened the glass bottle of chloroform that he had made following directions he'd found on the internet, and he doused a rag with it. Then he shoved the gun back into his pocket and clamped the wet rag over her nose and mouth. She bucked against him, making spitting and gagging noises, but he held it in place. It seemed to take a very long time, but finally her knees buckled and she went limp in his arms. He lowered her to the floor, checked for a pulse by pressing his hand against her left breast, which he knew wasn't the best way to find one but which satisfied a long-held desire. She was alive, breathing softly, but unconscious.

Walker let Mitch in. They got her out to the car and drove her back to Walker's house. Walker had a garage there with an automatic opener and a doorway to the inside, so nobody watching would have seen them take her from the car and carry her in. Then it was down to the basement, where she was securely bound and gagged.

"What are you waiting for, Walker?"

It was about the fiftieth time Mitch had asked that question. Missy had awakened downstairs—they could hear her struggling, kicking and writhing in her bonds. Walker's answer wasn't any better than it had been. "I don't know! I just don't know if this is the right thing to do."

"You said if we act like vampires, we'll attract them."

"I know what I said. But how will this attract them to us? We made sure nobody saw us, nobody knew what we did. How will they know what we did, or where to find us? If they're even real, that is."

"If? Man, I thought you were sure!"

"I was!"

During the time they had been considering their plan, the media had run with the vampire story. Walker knew from the online forums and vampire blogs that he wasn't the only one to receive the data packet. It had been big news, but mostly in a mocking way. Cable news channels and tabloid papers covered it nonstop, but nobody seemed to take it seriously. Law enforcement and other government officials had pushed back hard, saying that Andy Gray was a rogue agent who had suffered a mental breakdown, murdered his own family, and then used his computer skills to play out his sick fantasies on a big stage. Rumors had spread that the whole thing was a viral marketing campaign for a low-budget vampire flick, shot *Blair Witch*–style, and the video that had seemed so convincing was just bits of the movie.

All of it had since shaken Walker's confidence. Not enough to get him to call off the plan, because once he had settled on Missy Darrington as their first victim, nothing could have dissuaded him. Now, though, faced with the reality of what he had done, and what he had yet to do, his certainty had turned to ice water in his guts.

"Well, you can't ever let her out of this house," Mitch reminded him. "She knows you."

"I know that!"

"So one way or another, you have to get it done. You might as well go through with the original plan."

"I will, dude. Just . . . give me a few minutes."

"You want to still be at it when the sun comes up?"

"No . . ."

"Then you're running out of time. Let's get this done. The first step on a great journey, that's what you said before."

"Yeah."

"Claiming our heritage, you said. Right?"

"That's right."

"So let's do it."

"Okay," Walker said.

"For reals?"

"For reals."

His mind made up again, Walker went into the kitchen and got the sharp knife he had had in mind the whole time. He wanted to act while the desire still raged inside him, before he had a chance to think too much again. Knife in one hand and empty glass in the other, he rushed down the stairs so fast he nearly lost his balance. But he reached the bottom. Missy was there, hands behind her back, heavy ropes lashing her to wooden support beams in the unfinished room. She was still in her gray sweats, almost the same color as the concrete floor. A rag had been stuffed into her mouth, held there with duct tape, but the fear in her eyes spoke loud and clear. She was sexy, like the hot girl victim in a horror movie, breasts prominent against the sweatshirt, sweat adding a sensual glow to her skin.

Her fear gave Walker strength. She had refused him, humiliated him, taunted him. She would never do that to anyone else.

She bucked and twisted as he approached her. She couldn't get away, though, couldn't break the ropes or the beam. "Don't worry, Missy," he said. "It won't hurt for long. And you'll be making history. That's pretty cool, isn't it?"

"Just cut her," Mitch urged.

Walker moved quickly to her side and just cut her.

It was harder than he had expected. Slicing through the skin was no problem, but muscle offered more resistance. And what else, he wasn't sure, cartilage or bone or whatever. He worked at it, though, and in moments he had opened up her throat. Blood spewed from her like water from a burst pipe. Her eyelids fluttered and her eyes rolled back in her head, and a series of racking shudders coursed through her body.

Walker held the empty glass under her neck. Blood splashed his hands, his clothes, spattered on the floor. But it went into the glass, too. He kept it there until it was half full.

Missy slumped forward in her bonds, small aftershocks still twitching her body. Her feet, tied at the ankles, beat out a tap dance on the floor.

When she finally went still, Walker held the glass up toward Mitch. "Cheers," he said.

"Bottoms up, man," Mitch said. "Do it!"

Walker sloshed the liquid around in the glass, willing it to taste like strawberry-flavored milk. He held the rim to his lips and tilted. His mouth filled with thick, warm blood.

He swallowed.

First, he gagged, spraying blood all over Missy's already blood-soaked body. Trying to fight it back, he dropped the glass, which shattered on the floor and drenched his shoes. He clapped a hand over his mouth.

But his stomach heaved and he bent forward, vomiting on the woman he had just killed. He dropped to his knees and kept it up until his guts were empty and nothing but bitter strings of bile would come out.

"That's attractive, man," Mitch said. "Nice going."

"Fuck you!" Walker cried. He wiped his mouth, his runny nose. "I didn't know it would be like that."

"It's not that bad," Mitch said.

"Did you even have any?"

"While you were busy puking on her, yeah. I had what I could get that didn't have your chunks in it."

"Well, aren't you badass?"

"Hey, Walker, ease up. It's just the first time. It'll get better."

Walker swallowed. "You think so?"

"I know it. Come on, we've got to empty her out."

The concrete floor had a drain in the center, and they had already brought a hose down from the front yard. The idea was to empty as much blood as they could from her body, wash it into the sewer system, then dump her someplace where she would be easily found. The appearance of a bloodless corpse, while the vampire controversy still raged in the media, would be certain to draw attention. They would keep it up until the real bloodsuckers found them, and then they would ask to be turned.

The plan should have been foolproof. It wasn't as easy to carry out as Walker had hoped, but that didn't mean the concept was bad.

He spat on the floor and knelt beside her, trying to avoid broken glass, and he started to cut.

4

"YESTERDAY ON THIS BROADCAST I told you that the vampire scourge—if it exists, and isn't simply a fiction made up by a liberal administration forever looking for new ways to spend your hard-earned tax money—is the inevitable result of a secular society that has turned away from religion and conservative values in favor of an anything-goes approach to governing and to life. When people ignore the teachings and tenets that have brought America so far and focus only on their immediate gratification and self-satisfaction, the results are dire.

"Needless to say, I got a lot of email from viewers. Some of it was complimentary, and some, mostly from the usual haters on the left, called me the usual names. People, you can save yourselves five minutes—I've heard them all before and nothing you write can shock me anymore. And if you are going to write, please consult a dictionary, because with some of you it's hard to tell exactly which word you're trying to use. Four-letter words aren't that easy to misspell, but the lefties always seem able to manage.

"The point I want to leave you with tonight is this: the liberals and secular humanists among us have once again made America less safe. To make things worse, you can be certain that in the weeks and months to come, we'll be hearing card-carrying ACLU types telling us that vampires have rights, too, and so-called progressives telling us that we can't tap their phones or imprison them without trials or use intensive interrogation techniques to find out where vampire cells are or what plans they have. It'll be up to us, the citizens of Real America, to protect ourselves and our families, because we can't count on big government to do it for us.

"Until tomorrow night, this is James Callahan, Mayor of Real America, saying God bless the USA—but keep your powder dry, just in case!"

Callahan snatched the earpiece from his ear and dropped it on the ground. A tech was there unclipping the unit from his belt as he rose from the chair. "Great show, Mr. C," she said. Callahan ignored the comment. The tech had a decent rack, but she would be gone by next week, if history was any guide, so he wasn't going to bother learning her name or conversing with her.

He brushed past Louis Orszag, the show's producer, who was feeding him a variation of the same line. Of course it was a great show; he didn't do bad ones. He had heard it all before, just as he had the insults from the unthinking, unimaginative leftists in the audience. As he had tonight, he liked to mention those degenerates from time to time; it worked them up, kept them from tuning out, and Nielsen didn't differentiate political leanings when its ratings were reported. He meant to hit management up for a hefty boost when his contract was up for renewal. His dressing room was just across the hall from the set, so he thanked Louis for the feedback and let his door swing shut.

In his dressing room, he wiped his face down with cold cream to remove the makeup, then took off his jacket and shirt. He hung them on the rack. Someone would come in later and take them away to be laundered. He pulled on a ribbed turtleneck and a leather coat from Barney's and called Serena to make sure she would be at his place when he got there. Sometimes Callahan needed a little rough sex to come down from the buzz of a show, and she was the best there was, always willing and ready.

In the studio hallways, he had to run a gauntlet of well-wishers, the kind of people who needed a moment's contact with a celebrity to validate their existence. He allowed a couple of them to slap his palm as he rushed toward the parking garage.

James Callahan was the self-proclaimed Mayor of Real America, and as such he felt he had to take seriously the responsibility to be a man of the people. As a result, he declined the limo that the network would happily have provided him, and drove himself to and from work each day. It cut into his free time, but instead of reading or writing his show during the trip, he spent it listening to talk radio to get a sense of the public's mood.

The parking garage was quiet. It was guarded at

all times, of course, and well lit, and his reserved space was only steps away from the elevator. He climbed into the H2 and started the engine. He loved the sense of power the big machine gave him, the steady growl of its motor, the elevation from the street. Callahan was not a tall man, although he had broad shoulders and a deep chest and he was a man people noticed when he swept into a room, so he liked being able to look down on pedestrians and most other motorists as he made his way to his Upper East Side Park Avenue brownstone.

By the time he got there, Herman would have let Serena in and closeted himself in his quarters. She would have some candles lit, the bed turned down, a few toys out, and she would be wearing silk, or maybe leather, and not much of it, at that.

He heard the first thump on the roof as he passed 60th. Callahan glanced at the ceiling. Maybe some punk had thrown a water balloon or something. It hadn't sounded like a rock, fortunately. But if it was a paint balloon, or anything that would have caused real damage to the SUV, he would have the network's security people all over that corner until they found the culprit. As soon as he was safely parked in his private garage, he would stand on the running board and take a look.

A few blocks farther on he heard another noise. This one was softer, but unmistakable. Maybe he'd been wrong at first—maybe a squirrel or some other varmint had fallen from a tree and managed to hang on to the roof. He sped up a little, hoping to shake it off. He could handle another speeding ticket, if it came to that. Most cops gave him a pass, sometimes in exchange for an autograph, and those tickets he did receive he just handed over to a producer to be paid.

Between 66th and 67th most of the street lamps were out. He would have to have Herman call the mayor about that. He liked the sidewalks to be well lit when he drove past—a person never knew who might be skulking around in the dark.

Callahan recalled with fondness a cocktail party at the mayor's home. He had met Marcella there. Submissive, slender, sexy Marcella had been one of his favorites. He was thinking about the way she used to shrug out of an evening gown when something darted from the shadowed sidewalk.

He stomped on the brake. The Hummer fishtailed slightly as it lurched to a sudden halt.

And a face appeared before the windshield, upside down. It stared in at him with malevolent eyes. Not a squirrel, then, or any other kind of urban wildlife. No, this was some sort of freak, a drug addict, most likely.

Then he noticed the figure pinned in his headlights had a similar look. They both had long faces, open mouths full of teeth, flicking tongues. More of them scurried out of the darkness. Crackheads? Callahan always drove with the doors locked, so when they pawed at the handles, the sturdy SUV forbade them entry. He took his foot off the brake and pressed down on the accelerator. He would just have to run them down if they didn't get out of his way. The street was empty for blocks—he would find if the creep on the roof could hang on at eighty or ninety miles per hour.

But as he started to move forward, the driver's door opened—no, that was the wrong word, the freak outside didn't open the door but *ripped* it off, hinges and lock giving with a horrendous scraping, snapping sound. Callahan batted at clawed hands reaching toward him. He let go of the wheel but kept his foot on the gas, and the vehicle surged ahead, drifting toward the sidewalk.

By the time it hit a shop on the next corner, he was out of the seat and sprawled on the cold hard pavement of Park Avenue. He was screaming, but his screams grew ever weaker. He was surrounded, men and women, or males and females anyway, barely human, holding him down while a couple of them opened his veins with those gnarled hands. James Callahan smelled his own blood and knew what it was, and as the klieg lights of life's soundstage were shut off for the last time, one by one, he knew that he should not have taunted the damn liberals so often, because they had finally had their say, and they weren't nearly as peace-loving as they had always claimed. . . .

5

"LEAVE HIM!" ROCCO ORDERED. Already traffic was piling up on Park, cars screeching to a halt, headlights stabbing toward them. Sirens wailed in the distance, but headed this way. "We don't want to be caught!"

"Right," Caleb said. He drew away from Callahan's body. Blood slicked his chin and cheeks. "Let's go." He touched a long finger to his right cheek, drew some of the blood to his mouth, leaving a pathway where it had been. "He's a little on the sour side."

"I thought so, too," Dragon Lady said. "Bitter." She was always the most critical of them. Her constant carping was hard for Rocco to take sometimes, but he loved her in his way, as he did all those in his den.

Shiloh, Valentine, Brick, and Lothar left the corpse more slowly, reluctant to leave a meal only half-finished. But that had been the plan all along: the very public death of a noted figure. And with much more of the same yet to come.

Rocco led them down the block, up an alley, over a fence. They had a long distance yet to cover, but they owned the shadows, and it would be a while before anyone went from the shock of finding Callahan's drained husk to searching for his killers.

Callahan had been the perfect target. They had settled on the plan, then stalked him, learning his habits, studying the route he invariably took home from the studio each weeknight. What made him ideal was not just that he was the host of a top-rated cable news program, but that he had started talking about the *nosferatu* on the air every night. Once the circumstances of his death were revealed—and they would be, the media couldn't resist such a delicious story—panic would set in.

Callahan had to die, not because he threatened to expose the existence of vampires, but because his death, carried out in just this way, would confirm their existence for that segment of the public still determined to deny them.

Some of the undead wanted their existence to remain a secret, the stuff of whispered legend and pulp fiction. Rocco and the others in his den, though, wanted the world to know them, because to know them was to fear them. Other dens had started similar efforts, stepping up their attacks and trying to do so in very public ways. He had heard about actions in Pennsylvania, North Carolina, Oklahoma, and Idaho, and even in other countries: France, Ukraine, Colombia, and more. They longed for general panic. They knew how humanity would respond, once their existence

became common knowledge. People would stop trusting one another, if they ever had. They would leave
their homes armed, if they left at all. In their paranoia
and suspicion, they would set upon one another. Vampires could never kill as many humans as humans did
themselves, and without a good old-fashioned war
under way on American shores, rampant terror would
have to do.

They made their way downtown at a brisk pace,
avoiding the busiest streets, taking to the rooftops
when they had to. At 43rd, they went underground,
ducking into an unused subway tunnel, and they raced
along the old tracks, full of vitality from their meal,
laughing at the clockwork precision of their plan. "If
only you could have seen his eyes!" Lothar declared at
one point. "When I looked down from roof of his car,
so wide were they!" He had lived in the United States
for most of the last century, but he still spoke the ac-
cented, stilted English of the Balkan peasant he had
once been. But he was lithe, light on his feet, and could
jump like he had springs for legs.

"I wasn't positive," Shiloh said, "because his mouth
was full of blood bubbling up from his throat, but I
could have sworn he called us hippies. Who talks about
hippies anymore?"

Rocco could understand his error. Shiloh had been
a *real* hippie, turned in 1969, and she still tended to
wear patched jeans and loose cotton tops and beads.
Sometimes she even stuck flowers in her hair, but they

always wilted quickly, so she didn't try that often these days. She was a chunky girl with long wavy blond hair and football-shaped breasts that she still liked showing off, and she had often told Rocco that those free-love days of the late 1960s had been her favorite times, alive or undead, despite the fact that one of the many men who had tasted her pleasures had also killed her and turned her.

"He deserved what he got," Rocco said. He unlocked the passageway that led from the subway tunnel up into their den on the Lower East Side and started up a narrow, winding staircase. "He was an idiot, and the world is better off without him. The good news is that once he and a few more like him die, no one will be able to escape the conclusion we want them to reach. We're undead . . . underfed . . . and we *love* the red!"

Men were nothing but dogs.

Marina Tanaka-Dunn took pride in her appearance, but she made the effort only for her own satisfaction. She believed that most women could have virtually any man they wanted—they didn't have to be stunning, just readily available. Men might talk as if they had standards, but how many of them would turn down a woman who was standing in front of them?

Marina *was* stunning, though: coltish and limber, with perfect features framed by a sleek black mane. Her father had been a Japanese scientist, one of that rare breed of playboy scientists with movie-star looks and the social skills to go with them—and criminal connections that helped finance his research but demanded much in return. Her mother had been a beautiful American journalist who went to Japan to interview him and had never left his side. Marina was a living testament to the power of good genes mixed with a troubled upbringing.

For years she had thought that nothing could be as fun as sex, particularly those variations typically frowned upon by polite society. That was before she learned to kill. Since then—especially since she began killing bloodsuckers—sex had taken a backseat to dealing in death. Her brains, combined with her bloodthirstiness, had carried her to the top ranks of Operation Red-Blooded, where her title, since Dan Bradstreet had taken up permanent residence in a hospital bed, had been Director of Field Operations.

Her new assignment, she'd been troubled to learn, entailed plenty of meetings and inter-office politics. She was based in Washington, DC, which she had always hated because the gray- and black-suited men who worked its corridors kept their desires so buttoned up, rather than out in the open where she preferred it. But she was told that she would have leeway to pick her own strike teams, and because she intended to spend as much time as possible in the field, she made sure that she could read the emotional and sexual nature of each of the people on the team she would work with most often.

She wound up choosing eight agents for her team, seven men and one other woman. Of the men, three wanted to fuck her, and one wanted the team's other woman (blond and corn-fed, she had the kind of body that would look lush until it went to fat in a few years). One was gay and out: Dan Bradstreet, disturbed or threatened by the man's homosexuality, had never utilized him to his full potential, but Marina had trained and worked with him and thought he was one of the best field agents in the agency. Another was gay but suppressing it. Marina believed he would be her best asset, because she could channel that suppression into action. The last man was completely asexual, his only passion the destruction of others, and he was a potent if unpredictable weapon. Some of them would require shorter leashes than others, and the men might even become problems if their lust got control of them. Marina would have to keep a close eye on the blonde, too, because Corn-Fed wanted to fuck her as much as any of the guys did, and Marina thought that just might turn out to be an enjoyable idea, at the right time.

At the moment, instead of being out with her team, she was stuck in a conference room with no windows and pale green concrete block walls and a bunch of bland bureaucrats trying to make her think their jobs were important. It was everything she hated about DC closed up in a single stuffy space.

". . . facility has been completely inventoried," one of them was saying. His name was Zachary Kleefeld.

His head was bald, except for a fringe of curly gray hair that cupped the back of his head. He was Acting Director of Operation Red-Blooded, the Director of National Security having removed the last director immediately upon receiving news of the devastating Nevada assault. But he was a numbers man, all about facts and figures but with no passion or real sense of the mission, and Marina doubted he would last a month in that position. "All assets are accounted for except one."

"That's what you call counting the corpses of our co-workers?" Marina asked. "Taking inventory?"

"With all due respect, Ms. Tanaka-Dunn, the task is much larger than that. Yes, our people on the scene had the unenviable job of counting corpses, as you so inelegantly put it. But they also performed heroically, rescuing sixty-four survivors. There were hard assets to be inventoried, equipment and experimental subjects—"

"You mean the vampires," Marina interrupted.

"Well, among other things, yes. Vampires, and the remains of vampires. The Nevada plant was a biological research facility first and foremost and had to have specimens to study. As I was saying, the team brought out survivors and prepared a thorough report of hard and soft assets, of which you've all been given a summary."

"But you said something's missing, Zach? What is that?" The questioner was Lowell Rudin, a pale man with spidery limbs, lank dark hair, and a pinched face. He managed the agency's relationship with the rest of the national security apparatus, and as a result was barely trusted by many, who saw him as a sort of spy in their midst.

"Not a what, but a who," Kleefeld said. "One of our top researchers. I think some of you have met Dr. Lawrence Greenbarger."

"Good old Larry," Natalie Kakonis said. She represented Human Resources, or something like that, but the department had some other name Marina could never keep straight. Marina was brilliant, but preferred not to use precious brain cells memorizing stupid government acronyms. There were three other agency drones in the room, keeping silent for the most part. "I always thought he was . . ."

"Crazy?" Marina asked. She had met Greenbarger, and that had been her initial estimation of him. Something was not quite right about him, but she hadn't had an extended enough time with him to narrow it down further.

"Let's just say he's very smart, but he's lacking in certain social abilities."

"The question is," Rudin said, "is he a traitor? Did he leave with the attackers, and if so, was it willingly? Have there been any ransom demands made?"

"I don't think he left with them," Kleefeld said. "After the alarm was raised, we repurposed a satellite and we had eyes on the base within the hour. Several hours after the assault force left, a single military truck drove away. We believe Dr. Greenbarger was driving it. We found the truck two days ago in Salt Lake City, with traces of a somewhat grisly cargo—a cargo that helped to complete the inventory, in fact. But we haven't yet found Greenbarger."

"So we don't know if he's a traitor," Rudin said.

"That's correct. We don't know why he hasn't made contact. But he seems to be on the run, for whatever reason."

"We're working on finding him," Marina said. She and Kleefeld had been talking about the problem for days, but this was the first the others had heard about it. "We'll bring him in."

"I should hope so," Rudin said. "I'd hate to have him running around out there telling who knows what to who knows who. Someone like that . . ."

"He knows too much, is that what you're saying?"

"That pretty well sums it up, Ms. Tanaka-Dunn. I would certainly expect a serious attempt to—"

Marina cut him off. He didn't believe her capable of *serious,* because of the way she looked and the proclivities she liked to indulge. She didn't know how he could walk, sleep, or sit with a two-by-four up his ass, but she didn't question him about it in front of their peers. "We'll find him. We've also got other operations in the works." She made a show of turning to look at the clock on the wall. "In fact, I've got to run—we have a situation brewing in New York that I have to look into."

"Attend to it, Marina," Kleefeld said, effectively shutting down any protest from the others. Marina rose from her seat and let them watch her ass as she left the room.

Dan Bradstreet's focus had meshed smoothly with the agency's—research the bloodsuckers, understand them scientifically and sociologically so you could apply old-fashioned intelligence principles against them. Marina was more basic than that. She wanted to destroy the bastards. Every last one of them.

In New York, she would be going up against an active cell with her new team of hardcore, balls-to-the-wall killers, their first time in action together. This was going to be more fun than that gangbang with a Russian Army brigade, back in her postgrad days, and which still lived on as one of her favorite memories that didn't involve killing anything.

There would be killing this time. Lots of it, she hoped.

Killing gave her a reason to get out of bed every day. And getting paid for it?

That was even better.

6

LARRY GREENBARGER WAS A man of science, not a spy or some sort of action hero. He didn't know much about how to disappear, how to elude professional pursuit. He had seen a few movies, but those guys always made it look easy and seemed to be able to rope a beautiful woman into helping them. Even human, he wouldn't have been able to pull that off.

But he knew he had to stay hidden. Letting Operation Red-Blooded find him now would be suicide. He had driven the stolen military truck to Salt Lake City, feeding en route from the corpses he'd brought along. He dumped it there, in an airport parking lot. During the drive, he had experimented with warming his skin, using the power of his will to restore something close to a human appearance. He could only keep it up for short periods, but it was enough to get a cab from the airport to a cheap motel on the city's outskirts. The next night he went on the hunt for the first time, catching a woman between a bar and her Jeep. She was drunk, unsteady on her feet, laughing quietly to herself. He waited until she had the driver's door open, so he could see which vehicle was hers, then attacked.

She could barely defend herself, and killing her was no problem.

After he fed and threw her in the back, Larry used her keys to start the vehicle. He found her address on the Jeep's registration and drove it to her house. She lived alone, which was what he had been hoping for. He carried her body inside and put it in her bed, in case he got hungry again later. She had some cash in her purse, not a lot of it but enough to help pay for expenses on the road. She had a couple of credit cards that he would be able to use for a few days, he figured, at gas pumps and the like. He also realized that to someone with no qualms about killing, much came easily.

Repeating that basic pattern, Larry traveled by night to Denver and then to a suburban house on that city's fringe, one surrounded by thick evergreens that blocked the view from any neighboring properties. It was a lucky find, and he knew he wouldn't be able to stay indefinitely. But he had found it by killing a widower, on his way home from a bowling alley where he had bowled alone, and Larry guessed the man didn't have a lot of friends who would be checking in on him.

What the old geezer did have, stashed in various boxes and jars in his pantry and freezer, was more than forty thousand dollars in cash.

A lucky find, indeed.

Spring had come to the Rockies, and Larry found that with his new strength he didn't need a coat, except perhaps on the most arctic of nights. He hunted in shirtsleeves and jeans. His body hadn't changed much in appearance—a little leaner, a little longer, although still recognizably him, to his eyes—but his strength was multiplied many times, and all his senses were far sharper than ever before.

He used the widower's Buick to drive into the city after dark. He parked someplace crowded—he liked the lot across the street from the Tattered Cover, a bookstore that did business well into the night—and struck out on foot in one direction or another. He kept to the shadows, he never attacked if there were witnesses around, and he only chose victims who were by themselves. He wished the vampire who had turned him had stuck around to teach him the rules; these he had made up by himself, because they seemed to be common sense. He knew more than a lot of other newbie bloodsuckers would, he was certain, because of his exposure to vampires as a researcher. But he couldn't help wondering if there were more steps he should be taking, other ways to protect himself that he hadn't considered.

During the days, Larry kept up his researches as well as he could, given his limited resources. Sure that he was being hunted, he made sure to keep away from Operation Red-Blooded's private computer network. He figured that as long as no one knew the old man whose house he was using was dead, he could use the years-old desktop he had found in the house, and the man's internet account, to do some rudimentary work online. Mostly, he sat at the man's kitchen table working out calculations, letting his thoughts race along as they had always done, and jotting down notes that would remind him later what he'd been thinking of. Having set up the most basic lab imaginable using things found in the man's house and a chemistry set he bought at a 24-hour discount store in the city, he used drops of his own blood and saliva to carry on with his previous studies.

As a human being, he had been one researcher among many, and for the most part he had been fine with that. Pragmatic enough, anyway, to understand that it was the way things were, and trying to change the way things were was a fool's game.

But now he was one of one, in a class by himself, or so he suspected. What were the chances that any other scientist with his background had ever been turned? The opportunity was unparalleled—to study his primary subject from the inside? No biologist studying animals or plants had ever become one. He alone was qualified to uncover the secrets of the vampire lifeform, the ones that had been invisible to him before.

Rather than try to study everything—an impossible task—he had narrowed his focus down to what he thought most immediately crucial: the reaction vampires had to sunlight. He had experimented with it, walking out the back door into morning's soft daylight. The response was immediate and agonizing. He felt like a human might when walking into a room superheated to eight hundred degrees. He thought his blood would boil in his veins, his hair would burst into flames, his skin would dry up and peel off in flakes. He could stay out only for seconds, and when he raced back inside, his flesh was literally smoldering. The pain lasted for hours, but by the next morning, after feeding once during the night, he was whole again, with no lasting effects.

Operation Red-Blooded had done enough research to understand that it was the ultraviolet component of sunlight that vampires couldn't bear. They had used that knowledge to make weapons, called TRU-UV lights, that mimicked that ultraviolet spectrum exactly. What he needed to find out was why vampires reacted that way, what in the physiological nature of the species made them vulnerable to it.

Vampirism, Red-Blooded had determined, was caused by the presence in the body of the Immortal Cell. It could be transferred by the intentional exchange of fluids, although it didn't pass from a vampire into every victim—a new vampire had to have enough blood remaining in his or her body, Larry believed, for the cell to take hold. Most of the people vampires fed from died almost immediately, drained as completely as possible. Larry wasn't sure why he had been turned instead of killed—another question for that young woman bloodsucker, if he ever found her. Maybe she had been interrupted at the task and had left him inadvertently. He supposed he would probably never know.

The Immortal Cell only needed to be a single cell at first, but in the new host body it divided and mutated, overpowering any resistance the body's other cells offered until it had taken over. It mimicked those other cells' individual functions, but imperfectly, and it added new twists to the mix. Hence the need for blood, the physical changes in the body, the incredible strength, and the aversion to sunlight.

Any cell could be altered, though; modern medical science had shown that. It could be taken apart, understood, controlled. Once altered, if introduced into a new host body, that body's changes would not match the traditional vampire physiology. It would become something new, something altogether different.

If he could eliminate the harshly negative reaction to sunlight, it would be something virtually without limitations.

To accomplish that, however, he needed a better lab. He had already reached the limit of what he could do with makeshift equipment.

It was time to go hunting again . . . but not for a meal this time.

What he did next, he would do not simply for himself, but for all of his new species.

7

A LITTLE ONLINE SLEUTHING confirmed that the University of Colorado at Denver had a medical school. The Anschutz Medical Campus in Aurora would doubtless have the items Larry needed.

He went on a Sunday night, figuring that the campus would be at its most empty then. He parked in the Georgetown visitor parking lot, which had a couple of vehicles in it. It was unlikely that campus police would notice one more, and it wouldn't matter that he didn't have a permit. Anyway, he didn't plan to stay for long. The lot was adjacent to the Bioscience Park Center, a rose colored modern building with plenty of glass. He left the trunk ajar and stole across a grassy lawn to a locked glass door.

The hard part would be the alarms. He was a biologist, not an electrician, and had not the slightest idea how to circumvent them. The door wouldn't pose a problem—Larry had yet to encounter a circumstance that pure muscle could solve that he wasn't strong enough to master—but he was sure that as soon as he broke in, an alarm would sound, or a silent alarm would go off in campus police headquarters. Probably both.

He could go around the building looking for an open door. But that would increase his chances of being spotted. In a building like this, which contained administrative offices as well as lab space, there might be a guard on duty in the lobby all the time.

Maybe this hadn't been such a great idea after all. He could almost sense the equipment inside, calling out to his experienced hands. He needed a scanning electron microscope, a centrifuge, more, and the computers to run it all. He couldn't carry it all to the Buick in one trip, even if he could fit it all in. He was certain, though, that it was all sitting around, just inside.

Larry stood outside the door, undecided. Go in? Or give up for now while he tried to formulate a better plan? Maybe he could buy the stuff online, have it shipped to the old man's address. He couldn't use the house indefinitely, though—sooner or later a neighbor would come by or a package would be delivered by someone who knew the old widower, and Larry's hideout would be compromised.

No, he had to take whatever he could tonight. If he needed more he would come back, or find a different lab and raid that. Larry would rely on his phenomenal strength and speed to get him in and out safely.

He grabbed the double door's two handles and pushed. The lock held for a moment, then gave, breaking with a loud pop, and the doors swung inward. An alarm began to whoop almost instantly, the noise nearly deafening to his newly sensitive ears.

Wasting no time, Larry ran inside and started kicking in doors. All the rooms on this floor were offices, it seemed. He took the first staircase he came to, running up to the second floor, then passing that and going to the third and top floor. He could smell chemistry being practiced on this floor, the faint, familiar odors as strong to him now as the smell of roaring flames would have been to a human being. Again, he kicked in doors.

Behind the third door, a rangy young man in a lab coat waited with a steel rod in his fist, held back like a billy club. "What the hell, man?" he asked.

Larry looked past the man. His gaze landed on exactly the things he sought. "I'm just looking for this place," he said.

"You're . . . not a student here."

"In a way."

The man fumbled in his pocket for a cell phone. "I'm calling the cops."

"You don't think they heard the alarm?" Larry asked. Instead of waiting for an answer, he charged the man. The steel rod swung toward him, but Larry batted the man's arm aside, crushing the bones in his forearm, and the rod flew into a glass-fronted case containing supplies. The man screeched in pain. Larry silenced him by jabbing his palm into the man's chin. The man's head snapped back, flesh tearing, spine snapping, and he dropped to the floor with a wet thump.

The scent of blood filled the air instantly. Larry's

stomach tightened. He needed to feed, but not here, not yet.

He grabbed what equipment he could carry in two strong arms, and without further thought, jumped through the window, landing awkwardly amid a rain of glass on the lawn outside. Sirens wailed in the near distance. He ran to the Buick, loaded the stuff into the trunk, and ran back. There might have been security cameras in the parking lot, but the campus police were already distracted and probably not paying much attention to that.

This time, a campus cop waited for him in the hall, an automatic pistol gripped in an unsteady fist.

"Stop right there!" the cop commanded. The hand holding the weapon quivered with fear.

"No," Larry said. "No, not gonna do that, sorry." He kept going toward the cop. The man didn't know how to react. Larry could see indecision in his eyes, a trembling of his lower lip.

"Freeze!" the cop said.

Larry kept going, speeding up, from a walk to a jog to a sprint.

The cop fired.

Larry braced himself. This, he had not experienced before.

The bullet tore into him, passing between the second and third ribs. It no doubt ripped open his left lung. It hurtled through his back and continued down the hall.

The pain was intense, as severe as being stabbed with a hot poker might have been a couple of weeks ago. Larry winced, cried out.

But it didn't stop him, barely even slowed him down. By the time the cop had recovered from the gun's recoil and brought the barrel down again, Larry was on him, sweeping him aside with a powerful right arm. He drove the cop's head against the wall, where it collapsed like a melon hit with a hammer. Larry was halfway up the stairs before the cop finished sliding to the floor, the faint jingle of his keys mostly obscured by the alarm and approaching sirens.

Larry made it back to the car with another armful of gear, and then had to give up. The campus was coming to life. People hustled toward the building, emergency vehicles racing across pathways and lawns with their lights flashing. Larry guessed that less than two minutes had passed since he first broke through the doors. No one paid any attention to the bland Buick in the parking lot as it started up and pulled from its space. All eyes were on the building, and no doubt on the grisly scenes waiting inside.

The expedition was not a complete success. Larry could have used at least one more trip into the lab. But what he was able to patch together at the old man's house was a thousand times better than what he'd had before.

Encouraged by his progress, he redoubled his efforts over the next several days, sleeping only when he absolutely had to, leaving the house just long enough to grab a quick, convenient meal wherever he found one. He worried less about witnesses, knowing he could escape quickly enough even if he was observed.

He had stolen a small ultraviolet light, and although it pained him to do it, he experimented with it on isolated cells taken from his own blood. At first, the cells shrank from the light, dying quickly when exposed to the UV. But he manipulated them, carefully recording his efforts, and finally he managed to create some that didn't shy away from the light. Time was passing, and he knew he would have to move on soon . . . but not yet, not while he was locked in the white heat of scientific discovery.

He needed a living test subject, though. Until he tried it on a sentient being, it was all just theory, nothing more than informed guesswork.

Larry found a small wooden box in the old man's bedroom closet and took it out into the nighttime city. Standing in an alley behind some restaurants, he listened until he heard the distinctive scurrying sounds of rodents, the clicking of tiny claws on pavement. He peered through darkness that would have been almost absolute to his human eyes, and when he saw one of the creatures, he swooped.

An hour after leaving his temporary home, he was back with three captive rats.

He caged two of them and held the other in his left hand, close enough to the head that it couldn't bite him. He didn't know what damage it could really do—he doubted that vampires could be brought down by rodent-borne disease, even if it carried rabies or bubonic plague, but why take that chance? He had already prepared a syringe with his specially manipulated cells inside it, in a glucose solution that was as pure as he could make it.

Larry injected the little beast, put it back into the wooden box, and waited.

The rat raced around in circles for a few minutes, but it grew steadily weaker. Finally, it lay down, evacuated its bowels, and stopped breathing.

Larry sat in the old man's easy chair and closed his eyes. In minutes, he was asleep.

He woke again when he heard a furious skittering coming from the wooden box. When he opened it, the rat was busily gnawing and clawing through the wall.

Its teeth were almost an eighth of an inch longer than they had been before, its snout reshaped by jaws that no longer fit where they once had.

By injecting it with the Immortal Cell, Larry had created a vampire rat.

Larry had to find out what happened to it in UV light. He exposed it to his small ultraviolet, which didn't seem to disturb the creature in the least. He played the light across his own hand, to make sure the spectrum hadn't changed somehow, and had to yank his hand away when the skin started to burn.

His achievement brought a smile to his face. He

loved science, loved the process of experimentation and discovery. Losing his humanity hadn't taken away that pleasure.

He now waited for the day to break. In one of the old man's kitchen drawers, he found a ball of rough brown twine, and he tied a loop in the end, fed the rat through the loop, and tightened it around the creature's middle. With the string on it, he could feed the rat enough to walk out into the sun, and could reel it back in if it tried to go where he couldn't keep an eye on it.

Opening the back door, he stood back from the encroaching sunlight and let the little guy go.

The rat darted out so fast Larry almost lost the ball of twine. He fumbled with it, hung on to it, and slowed the rat's progress by feeding string out at a more measured pace.

The rat twitched its whiskers, glanced up as if checking to be sure the sun was high enough in the sky, and kept going. Its fur didn't burst into flames, or even smolder. Larry could feel the grin spread across his face as he watched the rat go farther and farther into the light.

Then the rat froze with its front paws elevated just off the ground. An instant later, Larry heard the reason why. A dog, snarling and barking, bounded toward it with teeth bared. The rat held its ground as the dog neared, and at the last second, when it looked as if the dog would chomp into him, the dog hesitated. Larry had the twine taut, ready to yank the rat back if need be, but he was curious now. What had given the dog pause? The fact that the rat hadn't tried to retreat?

Larry gave the rat a little slack, and the rodent charged the dog, a spaniel easily three or four times its size. The dog yelped and then launched into a snarling, crooning wail, shaking and pawing at the rat, but the rat had a grip on its throat and wouldn't let go. Larry fed it as much twine as it needed.

A minute later, the dog was still, lying on its side in the grass. Larry gave a gentle tug on the twine, to bring the rat back so he could look it over.

The rat pulled back. Larry tugged harder, but the rat jerked the other way with enough force to snap the twine. Suddenly free, it tore off faster than Larry's eye could even follow.

You've earned your freedom, buddy, he thought. *Go and prosper.*

You may be the first of your kind, but I'm guessing you won't be the last.

8

THE NEXT MEDIA PERSONALITY to die was Marlene Beljac, an editorial writer for *The New York Times* who had, the day after James Callahan's death, published a piece entitled "If They Walk Among Us, Why Don't We Know It?" She argued that the uproar about vampires was almost certainly manufactured by some human faction—subtly suggesting, although not outright claiming, that Islamic terrorists were to blame. Had vampires existed all along, she reasoned, they couldn't have remained hidden from the world's mainstream population. Therefore they weren't real and the only thing to get worked up about was finding out what set of thugs had actually murdered the TV pundit.

Beljac's husband, who slept in a separate bedroom, found her when she didn't get up at her usual time in the morning. Her legs and hips were on her bed, torso and arms hanging off. Her head had been savagely torn from her body. The room should have been flooded with blood but there was hardly any there.

After that came Madison Keller, a liberal news show host who had invited four vampire "experts" on her show, but then shouted down the right-wing guest who called vampires "Dempires" and claimed they were led by undead members of the Kennedy clan. In return, Keller suggested that someone exhume Prescott Bush and make sure he was still in his grave. Keller's drained body was left in the walk-in cooler of an all-night grocery in SoHo, discovered by a clerk who had fallen asleep at the front counter during his graveyard shift and then wondered why the cooler door was ajar when he woke up.

A late-night radio jock made a crack about vampires sucking, and barely made it a quarter mile from the studio after his shift before persons unknown opened up his body and removed all the blood, leaving him draped across a couple of newspaper boxes on a street corner. A popular blogger who riffed on the topic was found dangling upside down from his third-floor balcony.

Naturally, the blogosphere was melting down over speculation, half-truths, and conspiracy theories. Andy Gray's data pack had made waves everywhere. His videos were posted to YouTube and distributed at file-sharing sites, and as fast as they were pulled down, someone else put them up. If someone was killing media personalities to quiet the chatter, it wasn't working.

But that didn't mean they didn't have to be stopped. Operation Red-Blooded had access to the world's best forensic science labs, and bits of trace evidence, hairs and fibers and some soil with a particular sort of mold mixed in, led Marina's team to a row of abandoned houses on the Lower East Side, just blocks from the river.

Marina had the NYPD close off the block at both ends at high noon, figuring the bloodsuckers would all be inside at that hour. Zachary Kleefeld had arranged things with the mayor and the NYPD brass, making sure they wouldn't try to interfere no matter what they saw. She and her team drove to the site in a converted cargo van, its walls lined with high-tech weaponry. More of the same filled the containers beneath the bench seats. It wasn't made for comfort but for utility, and could carry an eight-person team and enough gear to win a small war. They would go in carrying specially configured Barrett Arms M82A1s mounted with TRU-UV lights and loaded with special .50 caliber phosphorous rounds designed and built in Red-Blooded's armament labs, grenades, and long-bladed knives.

She sat in the back, wedged between Spider John, who she called that because of the spider web tattoo covering most of his body (all the spiders living on the web tattoo currently hidden by his black tactical clothing, but there were many), and R.T., a massive bald man with skin so dark it looked like a starless night sky. Spider John was the man who she believed had no interest in sex whatsoever, but who had directed those energies instead into all manner of mayhem. On R.T.'s other side was Monte, a rangy guy from east Texas whose criminal record Operation Red-Blooded was willing to overlook because his talents were so suited to the work.

He was the one who wouldn't come out of the closet, and the one Marina had the highest hopes for.

On a bench across from them were Kat, the team's other woman, a onetime Olympic powerlifting contender, and Tony O., an Army Ranger who had been recruited into the FBI, and from there into Red-Blooded service. Up front were Tony H., behind the wheel—his background was law enforcement, and he had spent years on L.A.'s SWAT team—and Jimbo, the out gay man, a veteran of two wars in the Persian Gulf and several years of mercenary work around them. Tony O. thought he had a future with Kat, and maybe he did as long as it didn't interfere with his duty to Red-Blooded.

". . . so I always did. From the time I was little," Kat was saying. Marina had been trying to ease the tension, while keeping them focused on the mission, so she had asked the others when they had started believing in vampires. Kat's had been an extreme case, brought on by watching the vampire movie *The Hunger* on TV when her parents thought she was asleep.

"My old man was a Master Sergeant in the United States Army," Monte chimed in. His accent was Southern, but not the mellifluous sophisticated Southern that Marina found charming. More redneck than Kentucky colonel. He wasn't stupid, but sometimes, she thought, he came off that way verbally. "I was raised to believe in three things: rules, him, and the flag. In that order. If I had believed in anything like vampires he woulda broke my fuckin' nose. In fact, I think that was one of his rules—no believin' in shit you can't see, touch, or kick the crap out of."

Before anyone else could reminisce, the van came to a halt. Tony H. killed the engine, but nobody budged. "We're there," he said. "As far as we can drive, anyway."

"Okay," Marina said. "We don't know which house it is—it's one of the first three on the north side of the street. So we'll enter all three at once. Teams of two, as we discussed, with me and Monte hanging back to support whichever team hits the jackpot."

"Right on," R.T. said. "Hope it's my team."

"These bloodsuckers have a rep," Marina reminded them. "They've been active and they're not afraid of publicity. So expect resistance. This could get as hairy as that battle in downtown L.A."

"Hoping for that, too," R.T. said.

"Who isn't?" Tony O. said.

"Let's do this," Marina said. She rose from her seat and opened the van's rear doors. They all piled out except Tony O., who stayed inside long enough to pass out weapons and ammo. Then he jumped to the ground and closed the doors.

The NYPD officers stared anxiously at them. They hadn't been told much about the mission, but knew they weren't supposed to get in the way. That was all Marina wanted from them.

There were six houses on the north side of the block, but the three on the far end had been ruled out by surveillance. The three on the near end were all seemingly abandoned, but structurally sound and yet free of the usual squatters, gangbangers, drug dealers, and whores who would otherwise have made use of them. Those people stayed clear for a reason, and Marina figured the most logical reason was that those who *were* using those houses were too bad to mess with. She also guessed the vampires were primarily in the center house, leaving the other two unoccupied as buffer zones. But they might know that someone would figure that out, and so use one of the others as their den. Thermal imaging wouldn't be much use in this situation, since the blood-suckers and their prey were all on the cool side.

The team fanned out, watching the windows in each of the houses (the police had evacuated everyone from the houses on the south side; anyone hiding out in the empties at the end of the block was on their own). Nobody moved inside. R.T., Tony H., and Spider John carried handheld battering rams and had their automatic rifles strapped to their backs; the others were ready to open fire at the slightest provocation. Marina and Monte stood a dozen feet back from the center house's door, watching Tony H. and Jimbo and hoping her guess was correct.

When everyone was in place, Marina took a deep breath and shouted, "Go!"

Simultaneously, rams crashed into three doors.

The door of the center house didn't buckle under the assault like the others.

"It's this one!" Marina cried.

Tony H. swung the ram twice more, putting his shoulders and back into it, and the doorjamb split. The door buckled open into the darkness.

By the time she and Monte reached the four steps up to the door, the agents from the other houses had joined them. The cops would watch the surrounding houses, but she really believed they were out of play. This center one was where the action would be.

It didn't take long to get started.

Tony H. dropped the battering ram and brought his weapon around as he took his first two steps into the house. Before he had the gun in place, though, a dark form dropped on him from above. Jimbo had gone farther into the house already—if he turned and fired, not only would he risk hitting Tony H., but his rounds would threaten the other Red-Blooded operatives charging the door.

"We're engaged!" Marina shouted. She clicked on the TRU-UV lamp mounted on top of her weapon as she rushed up the stairs.

The vampire hunkered on Tony H.'s back. It made a horrible hissing noise and gnashed its teeth, from which pink-tinged spittle flew. Marina caught it in the beam and it screeched. Jimbo got his TRU-UV on. Pinned between the two, the vampire dropped off Tony H. and curled on the floor like a bug on fire.

Tony H. aimed down and fired two phosphorous rounds into the creature's head. The phosphorus burned, bright and white-hot in the dark house, and the vampire writhed for only an instant before its brain was destroyed.

The phosphorus emitted a lot of smoke, but before the room filled up, its white glow revealed the real nature of the hell they had entered. The floors and walls were brown, caked in old blood. There were skeletons, bones, and body parts strewn here and there, with no real pattern or order. The bitter smoke couldn't cancel out the stink of death.

"We're in the right place," Marina declared. "Let's mop this up."

9

WHILE TONY O., KAT, Jimbo, and Monte went up the stairs, Marina, Tony H., R.T., and Spider John descended into the house's basement. It was impossible to tell from the odor which level got the most use, because the house was rank, disgusting from wall to wall, floor to ceiling. They should have been wearing Hazmat gear, Marina thought, not tactical, but it was too late to change. *Vampires must have been using this place for years.*

With every step down, the air seemed to grow thicker. The stairs were slick, some of the blood coating them still liquid, but even though her hands were gloved she didn't want to touch the walls to steady herself. Instead she took careful steps, knees flexed, bending over slightly to see what was coming. She didn't want anyone taking her out at the knees. Her TRU-UV light beamed out ahead of her.

There was no electricity on in the house, and before heading down the three of them had donned night vision goggles. The goggles relied on ambient light, although very low levels of it were needed, so in absolute blackness they wouldn't be any help. But the TRU-UV lights gave off enough illumination that Marina could see clearly, albeit with a greenish glow.

At the bottom of the stairs they found a narrow hallway. The bloodsuckers attacked as soon the agents were in the hall with nowhere to retreat to except back to the stairs. They swarmed the three agents, hissing and screaming. In the confined space, shooting was dangerous. Clawed hands gripped Marina's legs and something ripped the night vision goggles from her head. She swung her weapon about, trying to cut the dark with her TRU-UV everywhere at once, but the creatures moved so fast that it just glanced off them.

Marina opened her mouth to shout to the others, but as soon as she did a hand was jammed into it. She didn't dare bite down and risk breaking its skin. She tried to shove the bloodsucker away, but it was far stronger than she was. The vampire shoved another hand in there and started prying her jaws apart, pressing her against a wall at the same time. She tried to scream but could only make weak squeaking sounds, more than drowned out by the general commotion. A vampire still had her legs, pulling her off balance, and R.T., Spider John, and Tony H. were similarly overwhelmed. No help was coming from there.

The thing kept pushing her mouth open. Its head moved in close, in spite of her efforts to hold it at bay. A special Kevlar collar ringed her neck, so she wasn't worried about being bitten. But she sensed the creature right before her face. Then she felt saliva strike her cheeks, and she realized Jesus Christ it was trying to spit into her open mouth.

Marina kicked backward, at the bloodsucker behind her, then lashed out toward the one in front. She couldn't spit with those hands in her mouth, but she whipped her head from side to side, trying to break its grip. The gun was useless, trapped under her arm where she couldn't even get to the trigger. She closed her eyes. They weren't doing her much good anyway, and she didn't want to give it any additional ways to trade bodily fluids with her. She didn't know if vampire spit would harm her, but even Operation Red-Blooded's researchers admitted they didn't know everything about how vampirism was transmitted. She didn't want to be a test case.

Then she felt another bloodsucker grab her left arm and twist it toward her back. The pain was sudden, excruciating. She could smell the bloody stink of the first one's breath, closer than ever to her nose and mouth. Its upper lip made contact with hers in a horrible kiss, and she felt its tongue slide against hers. Even if she could bite it, she would get a mouthful of poison blood.

Instead, she snatched for the knife on her belt. Its blade was eight inches long, the top edge serrated. You couldn't kill a vampire with it unless you sawed its head off, separating it from its brain. But you could do some serious damage. She freed it from its scabbard with her right hand and stabbed up and forward.

The knife entered under the vampire's chin and drove up into its open mouth. It screeched in pain and bucked away. Somebody's TRU-UV light (maybe her own) flashed over them and in its glow Marina could see the steel blade, slick with blood, behind all those teeth.

She yanked it out and brought it in closer, slicing below one of the hands in her mouth. She cut wrist. Blood splattered her boots but the thing let go. Marina drove the knife to her left, stabbing the one holding her arm. It released her for an instant, long enough to drop the knife and bring up the gun. Tony, R.T., and John would have to fend for themselves. Marina opened fire, phosphorous rounds hitting vampires and exploding with bright white light and fizzing sounds and gagging smoke.

As she held the trigger down, she spat and spat, trying to clear any vampire saliva from her mouth. She prayed she hadn't swallowed.

Gradually her senses returned and the phosphorus lit the hallway well enough to see. Spider John was down, flesh peeled from his face in curling ribbons. A vampire was drinking from him. Marina swore and fired a quick burst into its head, spraying pieces of it the length of the hallway. R.T. was dazed, but appeared okay. Tony H. had fallen into a corner, where he sat on top of a pile of human corpses. He opened fire with his own gun, and in seconds the hall was clear.

"John?" he asked.

"He's done," Marina said.

"Shit."

"Yeah. You okay?" she asked. Meaning, did any of them bite you?

"I'm a little shaken up. Not bit." Tony put his hand against the corpses to push up off them, and it sank into a soup of decomposing flesh. "Oh, fuck me!"

"We've all got to sterilize ourselves."

"Yeah, but . . . shit, my pants are soaked from sitting on that crap."

Marina twitched her light at the pile. The bodies had started to melt into one another. A pool of fluid surrounded them. She tried to swallow a lump in her throat but it wouldn't go down, and then she remembered she never wanted to swallow anything again as long as she lived, and she spat onto the dead bodies.

Thunder on the stairs announced newcomers. "Marina! John!" The voice was Monte's.

"Clear down here!" Marina returned.

Monte, Kat, and Tony O. came off the stairs.

"Where's Jimbo?"

Kat tilted her chin up. "Watching the top of the stairs. We're fine. Couple hostiles on the upper floor, but they were easy." She looked at the mess surrounding Marina and Tony H., at Spider John's body. "You got the worst of it."

Marina nodded. "He's . . . John is . . ."

"Got you," R.T. said. He held the muzzle of his

weapon a foot from Spider John's head and squeezed off a burst. Spider John's head exploded and burned.

Marines brought back every man, but vampire hunters had to destroy any humans who were compromised. Marina had always understood that, but watching Spider John die was surprisingly hard. She had trained with these people, had hand-picked the team, and they were her charges. She'd had people under her before, but in her new position she felt a greater sense of responsibility for them, and the stress of balancing individual lives with the overall mission.

Compromised soldiers had to be killed, so that the mission itself wouldn't be compromised.

Marina hoped she didn't fall into that category.

"Let's clear the rest of this basement," she said. "Then get to sterilization, stat."

The Operation Red-Blooded bus had arrived by the time they got out of the building. They had found no more undeads, but a passage led into unused subway tunnels. They could mount a search operation, although from there the vampires could have gone anywhere. They had found more bodies and body parts, dozens of them in various states of decomp. Every time Marina closed her eyes in the sterilization shower, she saw pink organs and blackened skin, glistening muscle and patches of white bone, and the shower's spray felt like spit splashing her skin.

They all showered together, and she couldn't even

bring herself to check out the naked bodies of her co-workers. For a change she didn't want any hands or mouths on her, or her own on anyone else.

But the part where she had said fuck it and opened fire?

That had been fun.

That was worth repeating.

Marina almost couldn't wait for the next encounter.

10

"THAT ONE!" MITCH SAID. "She's good!"

They were crouched down in a weed-choked vacant lot, a few blocks off Chicago's Magnificent Mile. Tall buildings formed a wall between them and Lake Michigan, but behind them were nothing but two- and three-story structures, mostly residential. The scent of somebody's earlier barbecue lingered in the air like a memory. Mitch was pointing at a young woman carrying a cloth shopping bag that bulged with her purchases. She had on a red tank top and snug jeans and sneakers and short dark hair poked out from under a ball cap. White wires from an MP3 player in her pocket snaked up to her ears.

"Why her?" Walker asked.

"Why not? She's alone. She's close."

Both good reasons, but Walker didn't know if they were good enough. He wasn't feeling it the way he wanted to. "Shouldn't there be something more?"

"What do you want, someone wearing a sign that says 'Bite Me'?"

"That would be handy."

"Dude, she's gonna get away! Can we stop talking and go get her?"

They had taken their next two victims from the 'burbs of Park Forest and Oak Forest, then decided the pickings would be richer in the city itself. Walker was nervous about all the people surrounding them, but he couldn't argue with Mitch's reasoning, and their first Chicago victim, three nights earlier, had been easy to find and to take. Nothing about this woman suggested that she would be a problem—the lot was dark, and he couldn't see anyone else around, although he knew they were out there, in apartments and condos, driving past, maybe hunkered down in the shadows just like he and Mitch were.

"Okay, fine," Walker said. "Let's go." They cut across the lot, on an angle that would get them to the street corner before she reached it. When they were about ten feet away, Walker said, "Excuse me, miss?"

She stopped and looked at him, then pulled the ear-buds from her ears. She chewed gum with her mouth open. "Yeah?"

Walker's mind raced furiously. He felt dizzy. He had thought he would ask her to help him look for his dog, but then realized that line was so old it couldn't possibly work. Maybe if she was six. But she wasn't. She was a full-grown adult, a city dweller, no doubt wise to anything he could come up with.

"I thought I could get to Loomis this way," he said, reaching for the first halfway-convincing line he thought of. "Do you know where it is?"

"Sure," she said. She swung around and gestured

behind her. "Couple blocks that way, just keep going the way you are."

As she spoke, he kept closing the distance between them. "Okay, thanks," he said.

"No prob."

Walker was wearing a dark nylon Windbreaker, a T-shirt, and khaki pants, with a backpack strapped over the jacket. In the pocket of the Windbreaker he kept a straight razor. He whisked it out and open with a single smooth move, which he had been practicing almost nonstop for days. He took two more steps toward her, and as she returned the earbuds to her ears (he could hear, as if from a great distance, a Slipknot tune he recognized) his arm snaked toward her, blade out. She saw it at the last second and tried to block it, but too late, he was already there, and the blade was very sharp.

So sharp, in fact, that for a second he wasn't sure he had actually cut her. Then she opened her mouth and tried to scream, and that was all it took. The wound gaped open and blood jetted out. She clamped her hands over it, her shopping bag falling to the sidewalk. Blood flowed between her fingers like a creek running over rocks. As her knees buckled, Walker scooped her up in his arms.

She couldn't have weighed more than ninety-five pounds, but Walker grunted with the effort, breathing through his mouth, unable to form words. With Mitch guiding him, Walker carried her to the lot's lowest point. Precious blood trickled to the ground as they went; he felt it soaking his pants and was glad he'd brought a change of clothes in a backpack.

At the low point, he put her down on a broken concrete slab. He had given up trying to use a glass. She was still moving, squirming and twisting and pawing in vain at the sidewalk when he knelt beside her. He had rigged a suction device using a breast pump and some rubber tubing, and he had a collapsible two-gallon jug. He pressed the pump against the wound and started working it. Blood ran through the hose, expanding the sides of the plastic jug. It would take a few minutes, and during this part of the process he felt the most vulnerable to being seen and caught. But he and Mitch figured a real vampire wouldn't leave any blood in the body, or not much, at any rate, so they had to draw out as much as they could.

While the pump worked, he opened the backpack. He got out some individually wrapped towelettes to wipe their hands with, and their clean clothes. He shoved the bloody ones into zippered plastic bags and put them into the backpack. "Is it clear?" he asked.

"Looks like it," Mitch said.

"Let's get out of here, then." The blood in the tube had slowed to a trickle, so Walker disconnected the pump and sealed the big jug. He sucked out what was left in the tube, getting a good drink of salty-sweet blood. He was getting used to it.

More than that, he was starting to like it.

* * *

They were still a couple of blocks from the car when they saw someone walking toward them. He was a big guy, a block away and across the street, but nearing. He passed into the glow from a street lamp, but he was wearing a black hoodie, with hood up, and his face was lost in shadow. They couldn't tell if he was white or black, young or old.

"You think he saw what we did?" Walker asked. He was nervous, the jug suddenly almost too heavy to hang onto. He realized that cold sweat was running down his sides and into his jeans.

"I don't know. No way to tell from here."

The guy crossed the street. He kept coming their way, as if he had a destination firmly in mind and they were it. His hands were stuffed into the pockets of his hoodie. He was at least a head taller than either of them; and he moved with an athlete's sinewy grace.

"Let's just get to the car," Walker said. "Get out of here." Walker and Mitch tried to ignore the guy, but it was hard. He was headed toward them, as certainly as if he was locked on by some sort of targeting system. Walker thought he heard the guy whistling, but the wind was blowing and he couldn't tell for sure.

Then another idea struck him. "Dude, what if he's one of them?"

"One of who?"

"A vampire!"

"You think we're going to meet one so soon?"

"I don't know. They could be all over the place

around here. Maybe he's been following us for a while, and was just watching to see what we did."

"So what?" Mitch said. "You want to go introduce ourselves?"

"Not if he isn't one."

"You think there's a way to tell before he's close enough to shove a gun in your ribs?"

"A gun?" Walker repeated.

"What if he wants to rob us?"

"You're right," Walker said. "I guess we shouldn't take the chance."

"He's coming fast, man."

Walker looked back over his shoulder. The jug almost slipped from his sweaty hands. That would be just perfect, to dump all their blood on the street after what they had gone through to get it. But Mitch was right, the guy was gaining fast. Walker still couldn't see his face, but he was more sure than ever that he was whistling as he came.

Did vampires whistle? Could they, with all those teeth crowded into their mouths? He didn't know. "Come on," Mitch said. "Run!"

Walker tried to run himself. He was out of shape and he knew it, and the jug was so awkward and getting heavier by the second. His gait was somewhere between a trot and a fast waddle, he figured, and he was sure the guy in the hood was right behind him, maybe just inches away. He couldn't hear anything over the rasp of his own labored breathing. If the guy was a vampire then everything would be okay, Walker could explain what they were up to, offer up the blood as a gift, work things out. But if he wasn't, if he was some garden-variety Chicago street thug, then they were in trouble.

The car was right there, though, parked on a dark, still street, neighborhood businesses closed up tight. They had left it unlocked, in case a quick getaway was needed. But Walker had the keys in his pants pocket, and he had the blood in his hands. "Damn it!" he said. "Damn it, damn it!" He got to the car, afraid to look back again, to see how close the guy was. He pawed at the driver's door, got a finger under the handle, yanked it open, and tossed the jug into the backseat. It hit the seat with a heavy thump, but stayed there and didn't split open.

He shoved in behind the wheel and slammed his door. On his third try, he managed to get the key into the ignition. Silently pleading, he turned it. The car started. Walker shoved it into gear and it bucked away from the curb. His face was slick with sweat, his shirt plastered to him. He was breathing through his mouth, his lungs on fire, and he thought his heart was trying to break out through his ribs.

Walker yanked hard on the wheel, wanting to get turned around even though it meant going past the hooded man. As he did, he remembered Andy Gray's video from Barrow, Alaska, in which a vampire had jumped up onto a hovering helicopter and smashed through the windshield.

Maybe turning had been a stupid idea. He should have gone the long way, around the block. He should just get out of here any way he possibly could. He no longer cared if the guy was alive or undead—he was terrified and simply wanted to be gone, to get home to his comfortable little house in the suburbs as fast as the car would take him.

His headlights caught the guy, who stood on the opposite sidewalk. A white guy, in his early twenties maybe, with a scraggly red goatee and narrow slits for eyes. He grinned at them from under that hood, showing a gold tooth right in front—but they were normal teeth, human teeth, not vampire. Pulling his right hand from the pocket, he made it into the shape of a gun and snapped it at Walker, once, then pretended to blow smoke from the barrel.

The headlights moved off him, and he was lost in the shadows again. Walker floored the accelerator and the car raced down the street.

"That dude is no vampire," Mitch said.

"Don't you think I know that?"

"Why are you going so fast, then?"

"Mitch, if he was a vampire there wouldn't be a problem, right?"

"You think?"

"That's the whole reason we're doing this, isn't it? To meet vampires? I'm only afraid of people who aren't, at this point."

"You were running pretty hard there."

"Like you weren't?"

"I just want to know you're going to go through with this. You're not going to wimp out when things get too real."

"No way," Walker said. "I am in this, Mitch. All the way."

"Just making sure," Mitch said. "Maybe you should slow down, man. It'd suck to be stopped for speeding with a bottle full of blood in the seat."

"Yeah," Walker said. He eased off the gas. "You're right, dude, thanks."

As they made their way out of the city, he finally gave voice to a thought that had been nagging at him. "What if we catch something from these city chicks?" he asked. "I think in the suburbs there are fewer diseases."

"We talked about that," Mitch said. "It's easier to get caught there."

"Maybe so, but it seems like I'm always the one doing the dangerous work anyway."

"Man, if either of us is busted, we both go down. Even if you held the blade, I'm an accessory, right?"

"Yeah, I guess."

"For sure. I say we stick to the city. How many vampires you think hang out in the 'burbs? We want them to be able to find us, right? Isn't that the whole idea?"

"Yeah."

"Okay then."

But driving toward home, doubts surfaced again in Walker's consciousness. He feared that he was already becoming addicted to the hunt, to the kill, to the burning sensation of blood running down his throat. But if this plan was all wrong, if they weren't going to draw real vampires to them, then he didn't want to be hooked on that.

If there were no real vampires . . .

"What if Andy's wrong?" he asked.

"What do you mean?"

"You know, the government swears he's a nutbag. So what if they're right and he's wrong? There are no vampires and the whole deal was just some elaborate construction that he put together."

"Do you believe that?"

"I don't know what to believe. I'm just saying."

"If you think that, then I don't know what to say. I mean, we've been doing this because we thought they were real."

"Yeah," Walker said. He slammed his palm against the steering wheel. "Maybe they are! Probably. But what if they're not? What if Andy played us all for suckers?"

"Maybe we should pick up the pace," Mitch said. "Do one every night. Make sure we get noticed."

"Or caught."

"Chance we gotta take. You don't win if you don't play."

"I don't want to go to jail."

"Like you're not already in jail. Sitting in your little house selling other people's old shit on eBay."

"It's just—"

"Walker, you want to live, you have to take some chances. Maybe if you want to really live, you have to die first."

"I guess."

"Tell you what. When we get home, we'll check on some of those message boards and websites. We'll keep checking back there, looking for proof one way or the other. If something convinces us that they don't exist, then we'll quit what we're doing. Cold turkey. We'll go back to our old lives and forget we ever did this."

"Right, that'll be easy."

Mitch ignored his sarcasm. "But if we're convinced they're real, then we step it up a notch. Back to the city every night. Really try to draw one in."

Mitch could be convincing. He could be an asshole, too, punching Walker's buttons like nobody else. Walker gave up trying to argue. "Okay," he said. "It's a plan."

II

THE FIFTH PARTIALLY DRAINED female body turned up in an apartment four blocks from the University of Chicago campus on a morning in mid-May. By the time detectives Alex Ziccaria and Larissa Dixson got to the small apartment complex, the sun was shining and a warm breeze blew in off the lake, bringing with it a faintly briny scent and the squawking cries of gulls.

Patrol officers had taped off the parking lot and denied access to the building to anyone except residents. News crews and reporters worked the perimeter, vans with satellite uplinks jammed the block. One of the uniformed cops met Alex and Larissa at the yellow tape barrier. "Glad you're here," he said. "This is turning into a circus."

"Is there any reason to think the parking lot is part of the crime scene?" Larissa asked him.

"No, but blocking it off was the only way to keep the press out of the building. They're like sharks."

"It's that whole stupid vampire angle," Alex said.

Larissa shot him in the ribs with her elbow. "Don't say that word out loud."

"Yeah, I know, I'm sorry. It just has everybody so worked up."

Not only was the mass media obsessed with vampires these days, but when the first corpse had shown up, everybody in the squad room had started calling it the "vampire" case. Alex didn't believe in vampires or anything else that fell into the general category of the supernatural, hadn't since his seventh Christmas when he had found an Atari console in his parents' closet that had shown up beside the tree on the big morning unwrapped, a gift from "Santa." He was quickly finding that not everybody felt the same way he did. He had heard so-called experts on television talk shows discussing vampires with as much apparent certitude as if they had been talking about the latest economic issue or political maneuver. He glanced around, hoping no one from the press had heard his comment.

"Let's just get inside," Larissa said. She and Alex signed their names on the uniformed officer's scene log and ducked under the tape.

The building was a modern monstrosity of poured concrete, steel, and glass, constructed of interlocking rectangles that gave each two-story unit a sense of privacy. Doorways were staggered in different walls so they didn't face each other.

"How many units?" Larissa asked the cop.

"Eight."

"On-site manager?"

"No." The cop inclined his head toward a portly man

with a graying goatee, wearing a white shirt with sweat-ringed armpits and a cheap striped tie. He stood off to one side, mopping his face with a handkerchief. "That's the owner. He's thrown up three times already."

"He go inside?"

"No, he hasn't seen the DB. He's just a nervous type, I guess."

Alex let Larissa question the cop. She had a forthright style of speaking, without a lot of the wasted words that were often typical of cop talk. Alex supposed it came from a desire to be thoroughly understood, especially when writing reports or testifying in court, that led to the use of such redundant phrases as "subject was traveling in a westbound direction at a high rate of speed." Alex was more of a thinker than a talker, or he liked to fancy himself that way, at any rate. When he did speak it was judiciously, weighing his words, picking his phrases. If he let the moment carry him, it was too easy to make mistakes, as he had with the vampire comment.

"Don't let him leave, okay?" he told the cop. "We'll need to talk to him after we look around."

"Got it."

The cop led them around to the building's east side and pointed out an open doorway. The number 6 was tacked on the wall beside the door. "That's the one. She's inside."

"Thanks," Larissa said. The cop left them and disappeared around the corner. Larissa started for the door but Alex waited, turning in a slow circle, taking a look at what the apartment's resident would have seen outside her door. And who might have been looking back.

As he looked, he smeared Vicks VapoRub on his upper lip, to block the smells he would encounter inside. Larissa wouldn't use it, saying she wanted to experience the crime scene with every sense, but Alex figured trained crime scene investigators could go in with electronic sniffers if there were particular odors that needed to be isolated. He was all for crime scene preservation, but he wanted to preserve his own sanity as well.

There wasn't much to see outside. The complex's grounds were sparsely landscaped, pebbled walkways flanked here and there by low, carefully trimmed shrubbery. An eight-foot-high concrete wall interspersed with randomly placed frosted glass bricks surrounded the building. Alex tried to see out through one of the bricks but only vague patches of dark and light were visible on the other side, no detail. Over the top of the wall was the windowless brick facade of some other building. When the resident stepped out of her apartment, she would have seen stone and concrete and brick, plane upon plane, but unless a bird happened by she would have felt utterly cut off from sentient life. It seemed like a sterile existence, but then Alex preferred woods and leathers and fabrics, materials that created a sense of life.

Of course, the apartment's resident no longer fell into that category herself. Alex swung back around to the door. He couldn't delay going in any longer.

Larissa waited in the doorway, helping herself to some last breaths of fresh air. As soon as Alex joined her he caught a whiff of the sour/sweet smell of death and the sharper-edged tang of blood, in spite of the Vicks. "Let's have a look," he said.

The victim's name was Chantelle Durfey. A single woman, she worked in an administrative office at the university and had a weekend job at a bookstore nearby. From the looks of things, she spent most of her money on renting her nice apartment and not much on furnishing it. Alex would have been willing to accept that she just had a minimalist sense of style that went along with the sterile construction of her building, but the arms of her sofa were worn, the slipcover stained. She had an old TV and a boom box instead of a stereo system, both sitting on cheap composition-board cubes. Another cube, stacked high with hardcover books, served as a coffee table. Curtains blocked off a floor-to-ceiling window that would look out at the same wall he had seen from outside. A leather purse had been tossed to the floor, open, its contents scattered.

Across a serving bar was a modern kitchen, appliances chrome and black, floor tiled in black and white. Chantelle was crumpled on those tiles with drying blood pooled around her. Her skin was pale, her hair red and curly, her clothing intact but drenched in blood. Alex took latex gloves from his pocket and put them on with a snap. Larissa watched him, then sighed audibly and put on her own.

"We should make sure the CSIs look around outside," Alex said. "The way I see it going down, someone waited out there, where no neighbors could see. Maybe just around the corner from her doorway. She came home from a late shift and the perp came up behind her, forced her in, then opened her up in the kitchen. Right?"

"Maybe," Larissa said. "You read that new report the government put out? Forensic science has about as much validity as astrology, sounds like. Except for DNA, most new developments don't actually work, or at least not as advertised. And there's a huge discrepancy between one lab and another. Maybe if you look in her eyes you'll see the image of her killer captured there."

"I saw a story about the report," Alex said. He knew Larissa didn't put much stock in forensic science, and figured she would bring it up as soon as the opportunity arose. "Still, they've got those eagle eyes. If someone waited out there they'll be able to find traces."

"And then screw up the evidence before they get to court."

"They're not that bad."

"Individuals aren't that bad. As a class . . ."

Alex crouched beside Chantelle Durfey, wanting Larissa to drop the subject. He pressed two fingers against the woman's cool cheekbone and tilted her head. Like the other "vampire" victims, her throat had been slashed, a single strike with a sharp blade. The blood around her looked like a lot, but such a wound would have bled considerably more had someone not siphoned some of it away.

Or drank it, he thought. He didn't want to, but he couldn't help it. Every possible scenario had to be considered, even that. Teeth, however, had not made that wound. Teeth tore, and this was a clean slice.

He moved his fingers away carefully, lowering her head to its original position. She was a pretty woman in her midthirties, he guessed. She wasn't athletic; her body was curvy, even plump. But she was tall and healthy looking and had probably carried the weight well.

Alex preferred women like Larissa, who was blond and compact, five-six. She kept her hair short, curling in slightly toward a prominent jawline. In her work clothes, dark pants, light blue shirt open at the collar, with a dark jacket over it, she looked almost masculine, but Alex had seen her in other clothes, played tennis and run laps with her. When she put on a dress, she was as female as could be.

Screw it. He didn't just prefer women *like* Larissa, he preferred Larissa herself. His crush on her had been pronounced since her second day on the squad, and when they'd been assigned as partners, he had thought his dreams had all come true. He was physically attracted to her, he found her smart and interesting, and he liked her no-nonsense approach, even though it was so different from his. Because it was different, maybe—he thought their varied styles of policing made them complementary, so they would be less likely to miss anything.

But she, as it turned out, considered him overly cerebral. He had considered intentionally losing control once in a while, maybe clocking a suspect on a whim, spoiling evidence by clambering around a crime scene exclaiming over whatever he saw. That wasn't his way, though, and he didn't honestly think it would win her over even if she didn't see through it. Which, perceptive as she was, she probably would.

He wasn't her type of cop, and he wasn't her type of boyfriend.

So he suffered in silence, just glad to have the opportunity to work closely with her. *Maybe someday,* he told himself, *she'll see her mistake. Realize what she's been missing.*

Maybe she wouldn't, but Alex couldn't have continued to function as a homicide detective if he wasn't also an optimist, so he kept hoping.

If he couldn't close this case in a hurry, he might not continue functioning as a homicide detective anyway. The pressure from above was intense, and getting heavier with every passing hour. He turned back to the ravaged corpse, wishing a clue would fall into his waiting hands.

12

AFTER HIS SEMISUCCESSFUL rat experiment, Larry Greenbarger spent several more days inside the old man's house, re-creating his formula, with slight variations, for human use. Or *former* human use, anyway. He hardly slept, leaving his work only long enough to feed.

Now he believed he had it right. Had he been back at the Operation Red-Blooded facility, he could have had a selection of captive *nosferatu* on which to test his work. He hadn't run across any vampires since that April night, though. He had only one at hand.

He would have to try the stuff on himself.

He figured he didn't have much to lose. If it killed him—well, he was already dead. If he stopped walking around, that would just mean one less vampire in the world. No great loss. He liked being upright and sentient, if not alive, and he enjoyed his own company, but his guess was that if he finally died completely, he wouldn't be in any position to miss himself. He didn't have any faith in the idea of an afterlife. If heaven or hell did exist, their keepers wouldn't let vampires circumvent the system; therefore he didn't have to worry that by destroying himself he would subject himself to eternal torment. Still, as morning neared, he grew anxious, and when the sun crested the horizon his hands were trembling a little.

Larry had to reuse the syringe he had used on the rat, since he hadn't yet acquired a steady supply of those. He drew some of his formula up into the tube, pushed it down until it squirted, tapped the needle (which he had sterilized with flame). Then he tied off his bicep with a kitchen towel, squeezed his fist until the veins in his forearm popped, and stuck himself.

A moment's prick, and then a warm feeling spread through his arm. He began to sweat. The fire inside him heated up, turning his arm red and prickly. *Mistake? Maybe. Too soon to tell. Give it time.*

He felt his face flushing, and his chest. The fire moved through his body, but as it did it cooled off again. His arm started to go pale, and in another minute he was back to normal.

It hadn't killed him, at least not yet.

But he didn't know if it had done anything for him, either.

Only one way to find out. Larry yanked the back door open and stepped out into the yard, into the morning sunlight, before he could come up with some rationalization why he shouldn't. His steps were hesitant, faltering, but he was committed. He stood on the lawn, arms out, letting the sun take him.

He didn't remember it being so bright before. It hurt his eyes. He squinted, blinking back tears.

But his flesh didn't smolder, didn't smoke or burst into flames.

He touched his teeth, his face, to make sure he hadn't accidentally reverted to humanity. Nothing had changed.

He was *nosferatu*, but he could walk in the light of day.

And he hungered.

He had fed, just before sunrise, because he wanted to be at his strongest. It didn't matter. He was starving.

Nobody was outside, that he could see, but he knew there were houses not too very far away, and that they were occupied. People lived in them, bodies full of veins pulsing with rich, fresh blood. The blood that he needed, more than he had ever needed anything. He caught its scent on the air.

He ran toward the back fence, not bothering to open the gate. He jumped, and his leap carried him high over the fence, with feet to spare. He landed lightly on the other side and kept running. Across a stream, through a patch of forested land (he swatted at a small tree in his way; the trunk splintered and the treetop crashed down). Another fence, this one taller and wrought iron, stood in his way. He didn't know if he would be able to leap this one so he grabbed one of the iron bars in both hands and shoved it to the side, then did the same to the bar next to it, making a hole big enough to squeeze through. By the time he got to the house he heard people inside shrieking at him, or

at each other. He wasn't listening; the world was a ca-
cophony of sounds, bird noises, voices, distant cars, and
everywhere the constant liquid rush of blood moving
through veins and arteries.

Larry approached the back door and pounded on it
once with both fists. It was solid wood but it cracked
and groaned and the hinges snapped and the whole
thing fell inward with a deafening boom. He stepped
on the door and found himself inside. A white-haired
man faced him with a shotgun in his quaking hands;
behind him were a woman about his age, and a
younger woman, maybe just a teenager or not much
older. Tears glistened on their faces.

The man spoke, and Larry thought he said "Get
out!" But Larry hungered, and there were meals here
for the taking. He kept advancing. The man pulled
the trigger and the gun roared and Larry was knocked
almost off his feet by lead shot, his right arm, held out
in front of him, nearly torn off. He ignored the pain
and kept going. He noted, almost offhandedly, that
the wounds he had suffered were already beginning to
close, to heal.

Larry snatched the shotgun from the man's hands
and hurled it to one side. It smashed through plaster
and lodged in the wall, barrel first. The man screamed
something else and threw a punch. Larry caught
his wrist, yanked on it. The arm separated from the
shoulder, flesh tearing, muscle and tendon holding an
instant longer but then giving way. Blood showered the

floor, delicious blood. Larry didn't stop to feed, though. As the man fainted and collapsed, Larry brushed him aside and went for the women. They were screaming and battering him with small fists, their blows as meaningless to him as the footfalls of fruit flies. He backhanded the older one, nearly severing her head, then grabbed the younger one and pulled her to him and bit her neck where it met the curve of her shoulder, and he drank deep.

13

WHILE HE SAT INSIDE the neighboring home, filling himself and more on his three victims, the rage that had swept over Larry subsided. He realized he was eating himself sick, forcing more and more blood down his throat even though he was fully sated. He pushed the last body, that of the old man, aside, forced himself to his feet, and went to the window.

Broad daylight outside now, leaves and grass sparkling with dew that caught the morning sun. He had been in this house for most of an hour. The time had passed in a blur, not unlike the frenzy that had brought him here in the first place.

From the doorway, he surveyed the damage he had caused. The door was utterly destroyed; he was standing on it. The bars of the wrought iron fence bowed out like parentheses. He had cleared an eight-foot fence behind his borrowed house as easily as a track star taking a hurdle. The kitchen of this small house was covered in blood, ceiling, walls, and floor, from the unspeakable damage he had done to the people he'd encountered here.

Since becoming undead, his physical power had been remarkable. In life he had never been athletic or strong, so he had marveled at the things he could do after his transformation. But even then, he had never been this powerful. Not even close.

Larry took a couple steps out the doorway, into the sun. He felt its warmth on his bare arms, turned his blood-slicked face to it.

And he remembered the way his experimental rat had attacked and overpowered a much larger dog, before breaking its tether and racing away.

Even now, standing for just moments in direct sun, he felt a fury building up in him, a need to crush, to destroy, to maim and murder. Recognizing it, he darted back into the house. There he drove his fists through the wooden doors of a kitchen cabinet, grabbed the supporting posts, and ripped the whole thing from the wall. Dishes and glassware crashed to the bloody floor. He turned to the refrigerator, lifted it from its position next to another cabinet, and hurled it through the back wall and out into the yard.

His rage abated, Larry stayed in the house and out of the sun for another few minutes, trying to think.

The formula he had taken was a slightly altered version of what he had given the rat. Both had responded to sunlight with uncontrolled ferocity and impossible strength. But it hadn't incinerated either of them.

He knelt on the tacky floor next to the old man and was able to suck a little more blood from the corpse. Was everybody old in this neighborhood? He had thought Colorado full of young and vibrant people,

skiers and mountain climbers and bikers, but in this
area everyone he encountered had white hair and bodies that had long since given way to age and gravity.

The blood calmed him more, but he knew he had a
problem. He had to get back to the house he had borrowed, had to load up what stolen equipment he could
and get out of the area. He had thrown a refrigerator
through the wall of this house. If the authorities hadn't
been notified yet, they soon would be. Neighbors
didn't live right on top of each other here, but some
things wouldn't go unnoticed for long. His fit of demo-
lition would draw the police, and they would find the
bodies, and a massive hunt would ensue. He wanted to
be on his way before it started.

But if he went back out into the sun, he risked losing control again.

He went deeper into the house, tugged a bedspread
off a bed, and draped it over himself. So shielded, he
rushed out into the sun again, through the gap in the
fence (he could barely squeeze through it this time,
making him wonder how he had done it so easily before), and dashed back to the house he had occupied.

When the police found what was left of the bodies,
they would go over the house with the proverbial fine-
toothed comb. He would have to burn the place to the
ground to hide all traces of his occupation, and even
that would be no guarantee. So he would have to count
on the fact that he had left the old Larry Greenbarger
behind in Nevada, that even finding his fingerprints or

hair follicles or whatever else he might have left behind wouldn't point to where he was going. All those clues would point to was someone presumed to be dead, or at least missing.

Where he was going, even he didn't know yet. Away from Colorado, that was all he could say for certain.

He would need to find himself a new safe place, and soon. Someplace he could continue to study and experiment. He still had a lot of work to do, although he had made undeniable progress.

In all of history, as far as he knew, no one had come up with a means of enabling the undead to walk in the daylight. He now had done so, but his method was not yet perfect. There had to be a way to tamp down the sudden, out-of-control rage, while still accessing the incredible strength that came with it.

When he found the way and spread the word to the bloodsucker community, the nature of vampirism would be forever altered.

Larry had not become part of Operation Red-Blooded out of any special hatred of the undead. He had been skeptical well into the first year of his employment there, until he started interacting with vampires in person. Confronted with the undeniable evidence of their existence, he willingly altered his beliefs. He was a scientist, and Red-Blooded paid him— paid him well—to do science. They assigned a task and then got out of the way and let him work. Few professional scientists he'd known had a better situation.

So becoming one of them himself had not been as personally repugnant to him as it might have seemed. After all, even as *nosferatu,* he continued to do science, the kind he liked, with practical real-world applications. It was only the potential beneficiaries of his work who had changed.

Vampires had always been held back because the sun's rays could destroy them. That weakness kept them from ever making a real stand against humanity, from using their greater strength and ruthlessness to completely overwhelm their prey.

Without that limitation, though . . . anything was possible. Vampires who could survive the sun—who were, in fact, strengthened by its rays, who could tap into the ferocity it gave them without being so overwhelmed that they lost all control—would be unstoppable. Perfect killing machines.

Deep in their heart of hearts, every scientist wanted to make a difference.

Larry Greenbarger knew, finally, that he would.

In life, he had been one scientist among thousands, if not more. He would never have been an Albert Einstein, a Christiaan Barnard, a Marie Curie. In undeath, however, with his specific background in vampire physiology, he was unique, more significant than he ever had been in life. He would make a big difference indeed. The impact of his work would shake the world, and in very short order. He started loading up the car. As soon as darkness fell, he had to hit the road.

14

"YOU CAN'T GIVE THEM anything, Marina," Zachary Kleefeld said.

"I know that."

"I mean nothing at all. Volunteer nothing. If they ask you what day it is, you have to ask them to state what days it might be so you can choose one of theirs."

"Don't worry, Zach," Marina said. "I know the score."

"But you've never done it before. You don't know what it's like until you're sitting in that chair with all those old white men staring at you."

"Zach, a vampire tried to tongue-kiss me the other day. I'm just lucky it didn't actually drool in my mouth. I think I—"

He waved a hand dismissively. "That's nothing. Not compared to this. I've seen people—hard, experienced people who have been around the block—completely fall apart in that chair."

The Acting Director was trying to prepare her for testimony before a Senate subcommittee. The committee's focus was on homeland security, and they wanted to get to the bottom of the vampire story, once and for all, or so they said. Kleefeld had tried to get himself substituted as a witness, but they had insisted that they wanted to interview a field agent.

The problem was, Operation Red-Blooded's official line was that vampires didn't exist. The agency's main thrust in recent weeks had been pushing back against the media onslaught, trying to discredit Andy Gray and to drive stories about vampires off the front pages and back into the supermarket tabloids where they belonged.

If the public came to believe in vampires, not only would mass panic likely come about, but every law enforcement and intelligence operation in the country would want a piece of the battle. Maybe even the military. As long as no one knew they were a threat, Red-Blooded was free to function as it wished. Its funding was black bag, off the books, and they liked it that way. The agency's existence was so classified that there were people working in the Director of National Security's office who had never heard of it.

The subcommittee members were sworn to secrecy, of course. Senators sitting on that panel had security clearance to be there. Every senator could keep a secret, otherwise not one of them would ever be re-elected. But those secrets had a tendency to come out sooner or later, once an administration changed or a senator lost a seat or wrote a tell-all book.

Which left Marina with a precarious balancing act. She had to convince the subcommittee members that vampires weren't real but that Operation Red-Blooded needed to be left exactly as it was—or maybe funded a little more heavily—in order to keep them that way.

When Kleefeld had first described the problem, she openly wondered if there was someone she could kill to make the whole subcommittee disappear.

Kleefeld had buried his ruddy face in his hands. "Oh my God . . . you . . . you can't kill a senator, Marina," he had said. "You just have to lie under oath. And you have to do it convincingly, because these people see liars every time they look in the mirror, so they know all the signs."

"Lying won't be a problem," Marina had said. "I'm good at that."

But that hadn't been reassurance enough for Kleefeld. He had insisted on going over every aspect of her testimony with her, trying to anticipate every question that might conceivably be asked. It always came back around to the tightrope. *If vampires are not a problem, why do we need Operation Red-Blooded?*

Because you want to make sure they don't *become a problem* was the preferred response. Not quite the same as admitting that they existed—but not so far off, either.

She got to the Capitol an hour and a half before her testimony was to begin. There were security checkpoints she had to go through. Even though she was licensed to—*expected* to—carry firearms anywhere, she had left hers locked up in her car. Then she had a private meeting scheduled with Georgia senator Bobby

Harlowe, chairman of the subcommittee, to discuss the
rules of her appearance. Kleefeld had offered to have an
agency attorney with her for that meeting, but she had
declined. The lawyer would be at her side during her
testimony, and that was good enough for her.

Marina was not easily impressed, but the vast ro-
tunda of the Capitol always did the trick. She walked
slowly through the building, listening to the click of
her heels on marble floors, watching people she usually saw only on the evening news. The sense of history
was palpable, weighing as delightfully heavily on her
as a truffle on her tongue. She was a killer, a brawler, a
woman who loved violence and sex with a ferocity that
more intellectual pursuits could never inspire. But she
had a powerful appreciation for history, too. Although
her father had been Japanese and she was raised in both
countries, she had grown up thinking of herself as an
American, and being in this place forced her to take
that citizenship seriously.

She loved her job because she got paid to kill bloodsuckers. But she loved killing bloodsuckers, in part,
because every one she killed meant some number of
Americans would not be murdered in the night.

An aide showed her into Senator Harlowe's inner
office. It was vast, paneled in dark wood, anchored by
a desk that must have weighed as much as one of the
faces on Mount Rushmore. Fighter planes could have
landed on its surface. The senator had animal heads
and skins on one wall, four TVs—two of which were

tuned to Fox News and CNN even though the sound was muted—a sitting area with rich, comfortable leather furniture, and a full bar.

"Can I offer you anything to drink, Ms. Tanaka-Dunn?" he asked.

"Some water would be nice." No way she was going to drink before giving congressional testimony. She needed to stay sharp, to keep the lies straight.

"Fine, fine. Have a seat." He waved toward the sitting area. In a corner formed by a sofa and an over-stuffed chair was one of those giant antique globes, the kind on which you expect sea monsters to be painted in the oceans. She sat on the couch and he brought her a glass of water and himself something that looked like bourbon over very few rocks. "We appreciate you coming by today."

"I didn't think I had a choice."

"Well, you didn't. But we appreciate it, just the same."

"Anything I can do for my country," she said.

Senator Harlowe sat down in the chair. He had difficulty, Marina noticed, tearing his gaze away from her legs. She crossed them one way, then uncrossed them, then crossed them the other. The whole time, he stared, absently licking his lips. *Maybe they don't get a lot of women testifying,* she thought.

Then she thought something else, and uncrossed them again, tilting slightly more toward the good senator.

* * *

Marina wondered if he could have been more obvious. He called to an aide to make sure they weren't
disturbed. He locked the door with a loud click. He
grunted and groaned out loud, especially when he
took her up against the wall, her back pressed into
the musty pelt of some ancient, half-lame creature he
had shot. She believed that she had become some sort
of trophy, just like the dead animals. After she was
gone, he would laugh with his male aides. "See what I
bagged today?" he would ask. Hysterical.

But after his pants were fastened and her clothes
were returned to something resembling the state they
had been in originally, he sat down at his huge desk
and made a couple of phone calls, while Marina waited
in a visitor's chair. "I don't think we actually need to
have that meeting today," he had told her. "Operation
Red-Blooded is too important to be compromised, and
to tell you the truth I don't entirely trust some of my,
ah . . . colleagues on that panel. Let's just put through
the funding for the next fiscal year and call it a day."

Marina had stretched, then made a little wincing
noise. "I think I'm just a little bit sore," she said.

"Maybe with a five percent increase," he added with
a smile.

"Thank you, Senator."

"And I'm sure we can keep the funding spigot flowing . . . as long as you stop by for a visit every now and
again." He gave her a smile that was more of a leer,

and Marina wondered if there had ever been a woman who thought that was sexy. She supposed a man with his power didn't need to be genuinely attractive in any other way. "To keep me updated, of course, on all of Red-Blooded's vital activities in the national interest."

"Of course."

"Fine," he said, and started making the calls.

On her way out of the office he pinched her ass hard enough to leave a mark.

She didn't realize it was something men still did in this day and age, but it was fine with her. It would give her something to focus on next time she needed to summon her inner vengeance demon, to beat the life from a bloodsucker.

And it would make her yet more indispensable to Operation Red-Blooded, and to Zachary Kleefeld, or whoever ended up becoming the organization's new director once it chewed up and spat out the "Acting Director."

She had taken one for the team, and she would no doubt take more. If it would allow her to keep killing bloodsuckers, she was glad to do it.

15

MARINA LEFT SENATOR HARLOWE'S office and headed down the broad Capitol corridor with a half-smile on her face. Despite her initial reservations, she had just been getting worked up when the senator finished, so she was far from satisfied. But she knew that sometimes retreat was the most diplomatic option. It wasn't like she had gone there looking for sex, after all, and now she didn't have to worry about testifying. The sex had only been okay but the bargain was more payoff than she had hoped for, and all in all she thought it was an hour well spent.

She was less than halfway to the exit when she heard hurried footsteps behind her. The building was a busy one, so the footsteps could have belonged to any of thousands of people. Just in case, she glanced back over her shoulder and saw one of Harlowe's aides rushing toward her. He was young and earnest, with short spiked dark hair and splotchy red cheeks. He wore a light blue shirt with the sleeves rolled up over nice forearms, a striped tie, and dress pants. She stopped and let him catch up.

"Ms. Dunn!" he said as he neared her.

"Tanaka-Dunn," she corrected.

"I'm sorry. Ms. Tanaka-Dunn. Can I talk to you for a second?"

"It seems as if you already are."

"Yeah." He chuckled, catching his breath from his short dash. "Right, sorry. Maybe outside, though?"

She had no reason to deny him that. She had expected to be in the building for hours yet, suffering through a grilling from Harlowe's committee. Since the senator had spared her that, she could spare a few minutes for his aide. Anyway, the day was warm, with the humidity that would set in later in the summer nowhere in evidence yet, so spending the time outside would be no hardship. "Sure, no problem."

"Great, that's great."

He didn't say anything more until they had passed through security and started down the big flight of stairs outside. She didn't prod. This was his game, whatever it was; she would let him reveal the rules.

Halfway down the stairs, he touched her arm. "I know what you do," he said.

"What do you mean by that?"

"My name is Barry Wolnitz, since we didn't actually meet. I know all about Operation Red-Blooded. I'm a policy aide for Senator Harlowe. To tell you the truth, if it wasn't for me, he wouldn't know if he was a Republican or a Democrat."

"I thought he was an Independent."

"See how bad it is?"

Marina laughed, and they went the rest of the way down.

On the street outside the building, they walked close together. "So what are you talking about?" she asked.

"I advise the senator on all kinds of policy matters. That means I have to know what's going on. That means I have security clearances out my ass."

"Nice image," she said.

"I didn't figure you for a dainty flower."

She guessed if he knew that much about Harlowe's business he probably also knew what it meant when the senator locked his door with an attractive woman inside. "You were right. Dainty I'm not."

"Point is, I know you're like this big-shot vampire hunter or something, so let's not kid ourselves. I know they're real, and I know that you guys need every dime of your budget to deal with them."

Marina didn't know how to answer him. He might have been fishing, might have put two and two together but be looking for confirmation. She couldn't give him anything until she knew what he already knew. "And?"

"And I want to see."

She stopped walking, turned to face him. "Excuse me? See what?"

"I want to go out with you sometime. I want to see them for myself. Vampires."

"Why?"

"Ms. Tanaka-Dunn, really. Maybe you're used to

the existence of the undead, but for the rest of us? It's a pretty big deal. It blows away just about everything we've ever been taught about how the world works, about life and death, religion, God, everything."

"You might be giving a little too much importance to something that's basically a scientific anomaly."

"I think it's more than that. *The dead walk*. That's a major thing."

"Okay. . . ."

"And I want to see it for myself."

"That's impossible, Barry."

"Why? I've gone on ride-alongs with the DC gang unit and a stakeout with the FBI. I sat in on a hostage negotiation that took fourteen hours. I flew into Baghdad on the fifteenth day of the war. I've done all kinds of dangerous things."

"So you're some kind of thrill seeker?"

He shook his head. "It's not the danger. It's more . . . I don't know, a compulsion. I want to know, to understand what goes on in the world."

"I wish I could help," Marina said. "Really, I do. But—"

"I can make things a lot easier for you."

"Easier how?"

"I know the senator very well, I can assure you. I'm sure he had a great time today, and I know he made certain promises to you. I notice the committee meeting is canceled, and you're off the hook."

"So?"

"So those promises he made can be easy to keep, or they can be hard. I'd like to make them easy."

"Are you blackmailing me?"

"Not at all. I really want to help. I think what you're doing is valuable work. I just want to see it for myself once. After that, *anything* Senator Harlowe wants to do for you, I can make it happen."

Marina didn't have to consider the idea for long. He was no doubt right. Senator Harlowe probably didn't write his own legislation, much less handle the day-to-day affairs of his office. He would be too busy raising money and appearing on talk shows. Having someone else on the inside to keep things running smoothly would certainly help.

"Okay," she said.

"Okay?"

"I just said yes. Can you be ready at ten o'clock?"

"What, tonight? You're saying they're right here in Washington?"

"I'm not saying anything. Just be ready to go at ten. Don't say a word to anyone, not even Harlowe. Especially Harlowe. Wear dark clothes, and shoes you can run in."

"Okay, but . . ."

"Are you in or not?"

"I'm in. Trust me, I am so in." He started to reach for his wallet. "Here, I'll give you my address."

"Don't bother," Marina said. "Barry Wolnitz. Works for Senator Harlowe. I'll see you at ten."

16

THE JET LANDED IN Philadelphia shortly before midnight. Barry Wolnitz hadn't been told where they were going, and shades had been pulled over the windows. He had known better than to try raising them. The flight hadn't been long, and if he knew Philadelphia, he might be able to recognize it once they were on the ground. Marina didn't care if he did or not; she just didn't want to make it too easy on him. If something went wrong tonight, she didn't want him coming back here on his own, launching some sort of personal crusade. She didn't necessarily think that he was the sort who would, but she had only just met him and didn't like taking unnecessary chances. People could be every bit as unpredictable as bloodsuckers. More so, because all a vampire wanted in the end was to feed. Humans would forgo nourishment for the stupidest of reasons.

He was nervous, jittery, tapping his fingers nonstop against his legs, as if on a meth rush. He had done what she'd instructed, worn a black turtleneck under a black leather jacket and brand new black jeans, still creased from the store shelves, and black sneakers. He had even colored over the white parts of his shoes with black marker. She was a little surprised he hadn't put on black greasepaint. On the plane he drank two cups of coffee, which Marina didn't think would help with the nervous energy. But better that than booze.

There was a car waiting for them on the Tarmac. The keys were inside. No driver, no one visible in any direction. From here, it was just the two of them. She had arranged the flight and the car through Red-Blooded, but without filing any paperwork or telling anyone what she was up to—one of the perks of her new position. Marina didn't think she would ever advance higher in the agency; she just wasn't a team player and she was impulsive, and although it was an unusual bureaucracy, all bureaucracies shared certain characteristics in the end. This kind of thing would drive Zachary Kleefeld nuts.

So no one she worked with or for would probably understand why she had granted Barry's request. Or having done so, why she didn't take him out on a pre-arranged show-and-tell mission with the full team. She thought if he really wanted to see what life was like on the front lines, she would let him. Show him something that resembled the real thing. If they found bloodsuckers, fine, and if they didn't, well, that was reality. More nights than not, they went home empty handed. Barry might be disappointed, but he wouldn't be able to claim that she hadn't taken him seriously.

What she wouldn't tell him was that the site they would visit had been swept just over a week ago. A den had been taken out. Chances that any others would have moved in were slim, but he would still see evidence that they had been there. He would come away with a sense of what they were like, without having to face any himself.

She drove into the city. Barry was quiet most of the way, twitchy but nonverbal; he had figured out by now that although she was taking him along, she didn't intend to answer a million questions about her work. She didn't go into Philadelphia's historic district, which he certainly would have recognized, but into a run-down neighborhood south of downtown, near the Schuylkill River.

"Crappy neighborhood," Barry said.

"Maybe it needs some federal dollars."

"Don't they all?"

"You tell me." Marina brought the car to a stop in the parking lot of an abandoned supermarket.

"We there?" Barry asked.

"We're there." She got out, went around back and opened the trunk. Barry joined her there. "I'm telling you now, it's going to be dangerous," Marina said. "You sure you're up for this?"

"You sure you're up for this?"

Barry Wolnitz looked at Marina. Small, dark haired, sexy. She looked strong and capable, but she didn't

look like his idea of a warrior. Certainly not like the
Marines he knew from around the Capitol. Barry was
no warrior, either, but he had played baseball in college, boxed a little. He worked out three times a week
at a gym near his house in Arlington. He ran most
mornings before work. He had been raised in a hunting
family, in the hills of western Pennsylvania. He knew
his way around firearms.

He was pretty sure they were back in his state now,
had recognized some of the buildings around the airport. The air smelled right, not like the air of home but
like that near the river in Philly, that particular eastern
corridor mix of industry and never-quite-clean river
water.

Anyway, maybe he had never killed a vampire, but
that didn't mean he couldn't—only that he had never
had the opportunity. "I'm pumped," he said.

Marina opened a locked case in the trunk and took
out a big automatic rifle with a flashlight clipped on
top. There was another waiting in the case, he noted.
"This is loaded with special phosphorous rounds," she
said. "You don't want to fire them into anything that's
not a vampire, because they'll burn hot and they're
hard to put out. Get one in yourself and you'll be re-
gretting it for a long time, if you live. Get one into the
building and you just might burn it down around us."

Barry fought back the impulse to swallow. It would
look like weakness, and she would certainly notice it.
But there was a lump in his throat like a tennis ball,

and he had no spit. "Okay," he said, ashamed of the way his voice croaked.

She handed him a couple of clips. "Extra ammo," she said. "Put them in your pockets. You know how to use this thing?"

Before he could even answer, she ran through the basics: aiming, firing, recoil, reloading. He nodded along the whole time.

When she finished she took the other one out for herself and loaded spare clips into her pockets. "The flashlight at the top is called TRU-UV," she said. "Sunlight kills vampires, and this replicates the specific properties of sunlight that do the same thing. Just try to hold the light on one as long as you can and it'll burst into flames."

"Okay," he said again.

She handed him big goggles. Night vision, he had seen those before. "Put these on so you can see in there," she said. "The power's out. We wouldn't want the lights on anyway, because they'd be able to see us that much better. Their night vision is more efficient than the goggles, but we go for every slight advantage we can get."

"Of course," he said, slipping the goggles on over his head and cinching up the straps. Everything had a greenish glow, but they cut through the darkness even better than he had expected.

Marina closed the trunk and started walking toward the empty market. It had the usual huge front windows, a flat plane above them where a sign had once been, a pitched roof on top. It was dark and still; hard to believe looking at it now that once families had spilled out pushing carts laden with their weekly groceries and the blank expanse of parking lot had been filled with colorful vehicles.

"Did you bring a crucifix?" she asked as they crossed the lot.

Barry touched his chest anxiously. "No, should I have?"

"Vampires don't care if you go to church every Sunday. All they're interested in is killing you and drinking your blood. There's a lot of crap you might have heard about them from movies and books. Forget all of it. They don't have to sleep in coffins, they don't avoid crosses, garlic doesn't bother them in the least. They're strong, they're vicious, and I can assure you there is nothing sexy or romantic about them, unless having your throat ripped open or being torn to pieces turns you on."

The info dump made Barry's head swim. To be entirely accurate, it was already swimming, the reality of what he had asked for and how quickly it had happened setting in. He hadn't really thought she would go along with it, had expected her to refuse his request flat out. Then he would have felt good about having asked, would have felt courageous and strong.

But now that he was here, he realized what an idiot he had been. This sort of thing was way out of his

league. And just two of them? What was up with that?
He'd thought at the very least he would go in with a
squad, everybody watching out to make sure he wasn't
hurt. He worked on a United States senator's staff, for
God's sake!

There was no backing out now, though. He would
have to tough it out and stick close to Marina. "Fine,"
he said. "Let's do it."

They approached the front of the store and Marina
gave the glass doors a gentle push. They swung open,
unlocked. "Play time," she said quietly. "I'll go around
back. Give me ninety seconds to get to the back door,
then we'll go in at the same time."

Sudden panic clenched icy fingers around Barry's
throat. "You're leaving me here?"

"We'll meet up in the middle," she said, flashing him
a quick smile. Then she dashed off, and in a couple of
seconds he couldn't even hear her footfalls anymore.
He checked his watch, wondering if he should run after
her or stick to her plan.

If he chased her, though, she might be inside before
he caught up anyway. And she would be pissed. Better
to just go in. She wouldn't really have left him on his
own if there was a chance they'd encounter vampires,
would she?

On the other hand, he was the one who had pushed
for this. Maybe this was her way of teaching him a lesson. Maybe even a lesson he wasn't expected to survive.
Marina had insisted that he not tell anyone what he

was up to, and stupidly he had obeyed. If he disappeared tonight, no one would know where to look. He should just go back to her car and sit inside until she returned.

Time was up.

Fuck it, Barry thought. He took a deep breath and pushed through the front doors. *I'm going in.*

17

MARINA KICKED IN THE rear door. It had been rammed in during the recent raid, and not repaired, but she wanted to make a lot of noise. Even if vampires hadn't taken the place over again, homeless squatters might have moved in. Either way she wanted anyone inside to hear her entry, and she wanted Barry Wolnitz to know where she was. The most dangerous part of this whole thing was the possibility that he would shoot her with some of those phosphorous rounds. She had considered leaving his gun unloaded, but then if he did run into trouble before she reached him, he would be out of luck.

For the same reason, she stomped through the back room, the concrete-floored loading and storage areas, past the big walk-in freezer units, and slammed into the swinging double doors that opened into the main store. Anyone inside who posed a threat would be heading her way. She was sure Barry could survive if a few homeless people passed by him.

She could smell bloodsuckers as soon as she got inside. Operation Red-Blooded agents would have come through after the raid and cleaned out the bodies, but they wouldn't have bothered scouring the place clean, and a den developed a particular stink of rotting flesh, spilled blood, and the rats and insects attracted to both.

The smell was tart, sickly sweet, and fresher than it should have been.

From the front of the store she heard the sound of Barry's entrance, a couple of seconds behind schedule but not too bad. The store's largest fixtures remained in place, shelving units standing in empty rows, big freezer sections between her and the doorway, so she couldn't see him yet.

"Barry!" she called out. "It's—"

And then she stopped because a flurry of motion caught her attention, the brisk flap of fabric and limbs darting toward her from the blackness of the girders overhead. She snapped her weapon up, clicking on the UV and squeezing the trigger at the same time. Phosphorous rounds stitched across the roof, but two of them hit the falling figure. The bloodsucker—if that's what it was—screeched in pain and plummeted down. Marina dodged its fall. It landed with a heavy thud next to her, then tried to crawl toward her, hissing and scratching at the floor. She fixed it with the beam and it flinched away. A final short burst blew its head apart.

Phosphorous rounds in the ceiling were still glowing, starting to burn.

Exactly what she had told Barry to avoid. They'd have to get out of here fast.

Speaking of Barry . . . She called out his name again.

Then she heard his gun.

*   *   *

The store reeked.

He didn't know if it was spilled, rotting food, rodent droppings, or what—some combination of those and more, probably. He felt a big sticky patch underfoot right after he walked in. He got the feeling that the owners had emptied out the shelves and then just walked away, making no effort to clean the place. Probably driven out of business by the economic downturn, and they couldn't wait to be free of the supermarket's debt.

Banging noises from the back had to come from Marina, or so he desperately wanted to believe. Then she called him. Then she started shooting. Barry freaked, his hand almost reflexively yanking the trigger before he stopped it. Her bullets glowed with an intense white heat, burning into his retinas. The goggles only made it worse. When he heard something else, something closer, he swung around to try to see it but ghost images from her bright rounds in his eyes half-blinded him. And it was dark against dark, just a rustle of motion passing from one shelving unit to another. Could have been a big rat.

Or something else.

He blinked, afraid to leave his eyes closed longer than a fraction of a second. While they were closed he heard something else, louder and closer. Marina's voice sounded very far away. He opened his eyes again. The ghost images had faded a little, allowing him to see better through the goggles.

He wished he couldn't, wished he was blind.

Instead, he saw a horrible thing charging him. Its forehead was swept back, tiny eyes bright, nose jutting forward. Below that a gaping mouth held jagged teeth, way more teeth than anything needed. A wave of fetid air reached him before the creature did. Barry fell back, slipped to one knee, and tried to swing the gun around with its light and its brilliant ammo. As he did his finger clamped down on the trigger and the gun started firing. Barry, startled, not expecting the recoil to be so powerful (*but she warned me, Marina told me it'd punch my shoulder like a heavyweight fighter if I wasn't careful*), was knocked off balance. His left knee, the one in contact with the floor, skidded sideways. He landed on his ass, rolling backward just as the thing reached him.

He kept firing, kept trying to bring the light up, to drive the bloodsucker off him with the UV rays. But it was on him already, the smell gagging him, claws jabbing into him, tearing through the leather jacket like it was paper, slicing skin. Barry kicked and bucked and tried to hit it with the gun, but the strength was flowing out of him so fast now that he couldn't even lift the thing.

Finally the thing, the vampire, he knew now—*real after all, and ain't that a bitch? Because really, who would have figured it?*—reared back, and he saw that huge mouth open wide, all those teeth pointing every which way, lines of saliva dangling off them like waterfalls after a storm, and he wished he had never put on the goggles at all, wished he had just poked his eyes out with his fingers, because the only thing worse than dying this way was seeing it happen. . . .

Marina blasted the undead sonofabitch drinking from Barry's throat. It fought for a moment but the combination of phosphorus cooking it from inside and UV burning it from outside was too much for it and it tried to scramble into one of the shelving units, then just lay there on the bottom shelf, curling like a bug under a magnifying glass on a sunny summer day.

A third one tried to get the drop on her from behind, but she heard it despite the ringing in her ears from her own gunfire and she blew its head to pieces before it got close. She swept the place quickly. The roof was on fire, bits of flaming debris falling like space capsules on reentry, and she had to get out of there.

It was too late for Barry Wolnitz. She picked up his gun, took the goggles off his head, and scanned him quickly to see if there was anything else that could point back to her. The extra clips in his pockets. She plucked those out and dropped them in with hers. He was still alive, but barely, his feet tapping softly on the floor and blood still gurgling from his ruined throat. He wouldn't last long enough for medical help to get there.

Good thing she had instructed him not to tell anyone where he was going. She didn't want him coming back, so she swallowed hard, held the barrel of his own gun against his head, and squeezed the trigger.

The gun roared and kicked and pieces of his skull and brains skidded across the floor like a disintegrating hockey puck on fresh ice.

Marina went out the front door, ran to her car. Neighborhood like this, she had maybe three or four more minutes before first responders made the scene.

Plenty of time.

She put the guns in their lockbox, dropped the goggles in the trunk, slid behind the wheel and drove away.

Three bloodsuckers down. If there were more, the fire would drive them out, and they would have to find new digs. Not a bad night's work for a solo mission. Effectively solo, anyway.

It was too bad about Barry Wolnitz, though. Whoever Senator Harlowe hired to be his next policy aide might be less enthusiastic about her cause. And she had sort of liked him, had been looking forward to his company on the flight home. All that nervous energy would have had to go somewhere. Worse, she felt the same way killing him that she had when Spider John died. He hadn't done anything to deserve such a horrible death.

But he had pestered to go. And, who was she to turn down a senator's senior policy advisor?

Three for one wasn't the greatest score, but for tonight, it would just have to do.

18

LARISSA DIXSON WAS THE daughter of cops—her mother had been one of the first female homicide detectives in the history of the Chicago Police Department, and her father made it to Captain before he retired—and her grandfather and great-grandfather had been cops as well. Police work ran in her veins instead of blood, she often said.

But her brand of police work, learned as a child when her parents told her war stories at bedtime instead of nursery rhymes or fairy tales, didn't leave room for modern ways. So when Felipe Ruiz of the crime lab brought Alex Ziccaria and Larissa the results of Chantelle Durfey's autopsy, Larissa sighed and rolled her eyes and fiddled with a pen on her desk the whole time Felipe spoke. Alex was used to it, but that didn't mean he wasn't a little embarrassed. Felipe didn't seem to let it faze him, but he was a guy who let things roll off him pretty easily. Alex figured that was a healthy trait in someone who spent most of his time talking to corpses.

Alex kept his seat when Felipe approached; at a skinny six-four he towered over Felipe and Larissa, but his height wasn't so noticeable when he was sitting down. He had never been undercover, because although his face wasn't particularly noteworthy—just a face, he liked to say—people noticed his build and remembered him. He wore his hair on the long side, for a cop, lying over his ears and curling in at the neck. He was forty-three, the hair showing silver here and there, and he wore glasses to read. He had never married and always figured if he did settle down it would be with someone like Larissa who understood the demands of the job.

Felipe was holding an orange paper folder, glancing down at it as he spoke. "COD was blood loss due to the neck wound."

"No shit, Sherlock," Larissa said.

"Yeah, that part's no surprise. What *is* a surprise is that there was some weird perimortem bruising around the wound."

"What kind of bruising?" Alex asked quickly, before Larissa could say anything. He liked letting the experts do their work, even enjoyed doing the paperwork that most cops despised. It let him organize his thoughts, which was key to figuring out the puzzles confronting him. In the field, there was always the possibility that someone would point a gun at him. That had happened twice, and both times he had frozen, once even pissing himself a little, although since it had been during one of those punishing summer thunderstorms Chicago enjoyed, no one had really noticed but him. He wasn't a physically courageous man, that was the point, but he was a smart detective with a good conviction record.

"A circular pattern of some kind," Felipe said. "As if something was pressed up against the wound."

"Something round?" Alex asked. "Like an impact bruise?"

Felipe consulted the orange folder and shook his head. "ME thinks it was some sort of suction device."

"Somebody cut her throat and then pumped her out?" Larissa asked. She was interested in spite of herself, Alex noted.

"There were less than two quarts of blood left in her body when we got her," Felipe said.

"So somebody took about four quarts out," Alex said.

"That's the general rule," Felipe said. "Six quarts is the norm."

"See?" Larissa said. "Vampires." She was smiling— she might not have believed in forensic science, but she sure as hell didn't believe in vampires.

"No tooth marks on the victim," Felipe reported. "But if vampires use blades and pumps, then maybe."

"Why take that much blood out of someone?" Alex wondered. "What's the point?"

"Killer has pet vampires at home," Larissa said. "Make the kill, take the blood, feed the pets."

"That still requires believing in vampires, doesn't it?" Alex said. "I don't buy it."

Newt Lofgren came out of the break room stirring a paper coffee cup with a plastic stick. "Say, Ziccaria," he said.

"Yeah?"

Newt gave him a worried look. "My daughter's dating a pale kid with stupid hair and sparkly skin. Maybe you should check him out." He broke into a wicked laugh.

"I would, Newt, but the way I figure it, all she wants is a way to move out of the house so she doesn't have to look at you every morning."

Newt kept chuckling as he walked away. "Better requisition some wooden stakes," he said. "I think you're gonna need 'em!"

Felipe watched him go, then continued as if they hadn't been interrupted. "One more thing working against the vampire hypothesis. If anyone had taken a drink directly from the wound, they would most likely have left trace evidence around it. DNA, skin cells, or something. We got none of that, just the bruising from the pump or whatever."

"So our 'vampire' doesn't drink from the victim, just takes the blood away from the scene?" Alex asked.

"Right."

"You get anything else helpful?" Larissa asked. She spun the pen around on the desktop.

Felipe looked down at the open folder. "I guess that depends on your definition of 'helpful.' There probably was someone hanging around outside the apartment for a while before the vic got home, like Alex thought. We found scuff marks in the dirt, a partial footprint that didn't tell us much—Nike athletic shoe, very common, size nine and a half, also common. Nothing really useful inside the place. I don't think the killer stuck around there for long. Got what he wanted and took off."

"That's the impression we got," Alex said. "Nothing was taken, closets and drawers weren't disturbed as far as we could tell."

"Just makes it worse," Larissa said. "Killing for the sake of killing. Not stealing anything—"

"Except blood," Felipe interrupted.

"There any value on the open market for blood?"

"Plasma banks pay for it. Not a lot, though. And they prefer to extract it from the donors themselves."

"So we're looking for a dirty plasma bank?" Alex asked. "One that buys through the back door?"

Felipe shrugged. "That's one possibility."

"And the other one possibility is vampires?"

Larissa tossed the pen onto the desk with a clatter. "Some days, I wonder why I bother to get out of bed."

That night, Alex sat in his leather easy chair, feet up on an ottoman that sagged in the middle like a broken-down plow horse's spine, watching Cecil B. DeMille's silent epic *The King of Kings*. He watched not for the religious aspects, although those didn't bother him, but for the spectacle. And he liked silent movies when he was embroiled in a homicide case. He had to pay attention to the exaggerated facial expressions, to gestures, had to try to interpret the layers of meaning on the

title cards. A movie like this, with a sweeping narrative
to it, took close study to really appreciate.

That study drew his mind away from his immediate problems. The flickering black-and-white images
were like ghosts stalking through his living room, but
watching them was easier than closing his eyes and
seeing the ghosts that haunted him then: the faces of
Chantelle Durfey and Gina Hooper, the first victims of
the "vampire" killer.

It was always this way for him. If he could close a
case within the first day or two, then the ghosts didn't
stay with him. But if someone's killer—particularly
the murderer of a child or a young woman—stayed
on the loose, killed again—then they came more frequently. His sleep was affected, his appetite. Every
time he looked out a dark window he saw a victim, not
his own reflection, staring back. The same for pools of
water. It got so he was afraid to look into a mirror. He
heard their voices, too, even when he never had during
their lives, speaking snatches of imagined dialogue that
almost seemed to make sense, pretended to drive him
toward solutions that weren't really there at all.

Modern movies, the kind with color and sound,
didn't involve Alex enough, didn't take his mind any-
place new. They were facile, too easily understood. He
needed the challenge of the silents, or foreign films at
the very least, with subtitles and some emotional com-
plexity to them.

Only those could put the ghosts to rest. And then

only for a short while, the duration of the film or maybe a little longer.

Of course, even when he didn't have murder victims haunting him, he saw a woman's face in his sleep and during most of his waking hours, heard her voice through the long hours of dark morning before the sun came up. That face, that voice, belonged to Larissa. Obsessed? He supposed he was. That knowledge didn't help him, though, didn't do anything to break the cycle. He worked beside her during the day and at night hungered to feel her lying next to him.

Some nights he almost welcomed the murdered ones, because as much as they tore at what remained of his heart, he didn't have to face them the next day, didn't have to listen to them talking about lives that only contained him during a working shift.

He realized his attention had strayed. He picked up his glass—one Glenlivet, neat, each night, any more than that would make him a cliché that he didn't want to be—and returned his focus to the screen, where the ghostly figures in shades of gray postured for him and him alone.

19

WALKER HAD BOUGHT A cargo van, a white beast with no windows on the sides or rear. He and Mitch tacked up a curtain behind the front seats and covered the rear walls and floor with thick shag carpeting from a remnant store. They also rigged up a huge roll of plastic sheeting with a rope running through the middle, lashed around the seats, so they could easily unspool enough to stretch over the cargo area, front to back. He got the thing from a used-car lot in Gary, Indiana, hoping that the out-of-state sale would make it harder to trace if it was somehow tied to their murders. Of course, he didn't have any fake ID, so even though he paid cash—a *Man from U.N.C.L.E.* attaché case auction had heated up at the end and paid off nicely—he had to use his real name for the purchase, and the Illinois registration and license plates.

He liked the anonymity it gave them when they drove around, and the space to toss a body if they didn't have the privacy, wherever they happened to take her, to finish the job. His old car was too well known in Harvey and some of the other local suburbs around there, and they had decided they were better off back in the 'burbs. In the city there were plenty of pro-spective victims, but the easiest ones to find and take, the hookers and drug addicts and homeless people, were also the ones likeliest to be carrying blood-borne diseases. So it was the suburbs for them, only Walker was worried about being recognized in his usual ride, and nothing Mitch could say made him feel more at ease about it.

It was a trade-off, but the van helped make the deci-sion palatable.

Now they were sitting in the parking lot of a mall in North Riverside. It was nine o'clock, and the stores were closing, lights shutting off inside the Old Navy and Carson Pirie Scott, final shoppers trickling out to their cars. Mitch indicated a woman loading four bags into a Toyota Camry. She was African-American, maybe thirty, with a body that would have caught Walker's attention under any circumstances. "How about her?"

"She's got too much stuff," Walker said. He read the store names off her bags. "Gap, FYE, Sears, Athlete's Foot . . . She's not just buying for herself, she's shop-ping for a family."

"She's kinda hot though."

"She is. That's not our main consideration though."

"No reason it doesn't have to be a side consider-ation."

"Dude, I don't want to add necrophilia to our list of crimes. Or sexual abuse of any kind."

"Like they wouldn't throw the book at us if we get caught."

"There are levels of badness. If we go to prison I don't mind being known as a stone killer. You get a lot of respect for that. But I don't want to be known as a pervert."

"*They'd* get to know you soon enough," Mitch said.

"Look who's talking."

"How'd you get to be so expert on the prison system, anyway? You been watching those *Lockup* shows again?"

"You'd be surprised. There's a lot of good information on those."

"You just keep telling yourself that, Walker."

Walker drummed his fingers on the steering wheel, watching a woman heading into the lot with a single bag in her hands, from Forever 21. She was past twenty-one by a couple of decades, Walker guessed, but she was trim and well put together, a white woman with short blond hair, wearing a red top and white pants. He grabbed binoculars from the floor between the seats, focused in on her. "No wedding ring," he said.

"She's sort of MILFy."

"That a problem?"

"Not for me."

Walker started the van's engine, clicked on the lights. "Remember, no funny stuff with her."

Mitch chuckled. "Gotta love your moral sense, man. Killing's fine, but touching is out."

"It is what it is. Anyway, there's a reason for the killing."

"I know, I'm just giving you shit."

During the days, when they weren't sleeping or working their online auctions, they had been spending most of their time at the various vampire sites they knew. The pushback against Andy's revelations—plenty of people had posted Andy's information, although Walker had refused to—had been hard, and still continued. But since then there had been pushback against the pushback. There were people online claiming to be vampires, and others claiming that vampires had never existed and all those who said they were *nosferatu* were liars. It was impossible to tell who was telling the truth. Some accounts, though, by "vampires" and by people who swore they had encountered them in one place or another, seemed more heavily weighted with convincing detail. Walker and Mitch chose to believe those.

If vampires were out there, Walker and Mitch wanted to make contact. They couldn't exactly post about what they were doing—Mitch pointed out that law enforcement was almost certainly watching the same websites, and however anonymous you thought you were online, someone could always track you down—so they stuck with their original plan. Make the vamps think there were more of their kind in the area, and draw them in. That was the other best reason for sticking to the suburbs—if the real vampires went looking for them in Chicago, they might never know it.

The plan wasn't without its flaws, but for now it was the best one they had.

The woman had climbed into a red VW Beetle, one of the new ones. That was a good sign, too—people with kids drove sedans or SUVs or minivans. It was hard to shove a whole brood of no-neck monsters into a Bug.

Her lights came on and she pulled out of her parking spot. Halfway across the lot, Walker did the same.

He batted his thumbs against the wheel, nervous now. Nervous and excited.

The killing got easier, the more they did it. The drinking he had kind of come to enjoy. But the part before all that, the hunt, the taking . . . that was still scary, still tense.

Stiff-armed, he maneuvered the van through the parking lot so that as the woman in the VW made the turn onto Cermak Road, the van was two cars behind.

The blonde lived in La Grange, in a little blue ranch house with a postage stamp yard. She was a patriotic sort, which Walker had started to suspect when he noted the red and white clothes and the red car. The curtains in the front window of her house had red and blue stars on a white background. She had a flag decal on the front door, and a sign declaring I SUPPORT OUR TROOPS stuck into her front yard. Walker didn't know anyone who didn't support the troops, but support them or not, it didn't change the plan.

The house next door had gone into foreclosure, according to a FOR SALE sign on the unkempt lawn, and there were no lights on inside. The neighbors on the right were home, but a bluish glow seeping through curtains suggested that at least some of the house's occupants were under television hypnosis. Across the street was a house with a double lot, the extra space taken up by grass and trees, and the house next to that had a picket fence around it, as if in defense against having its space swallowed up as well. No lights burned in the front of either of those. The only living person Walker noted was someone inside a garage a couple of houses down. He worked on a car and blared rock music with the big door wide open. That might even be helpful—the guy probably wouldn't hear anything or come out from under his car, and his noise would help drown out any the blonde might make.

She pulled into a carport beside the house and got out, her Forever 21 bag in one hand. With the other she locked the car doors and shook her keys, isolating the one that would open the house. Walker waited until she had the door open, then pulled into the driveway, behind the Bug, blocking it in. The woman stopped, pinned in the headlights and staring at the van's windshield. Walker doubted she could see much detail through the high beams.

He got out. "I'm glad we caught you!" he said.

"What do you mean?"

"Your taillight cover fell off back there a few blocks," he said. "I guess it came loose, but it didn't break so I picked it up. Then I was afraid we would lose you."

"It did?" Keys in one hand, bag held loosely in the other, she stepped back out, leaving the house door open, to check the VW's rear end.

That gave Walker the time he needed to close the distance. He started toward the car, but then shifted at the last moment, as she was approaching. On a collision course, her eyes widened and her jaw set. "What are you—?"

Walker kept up his fast, steady advance. He brought up his left hand, catching her at the top of the neck and the bottom edge of her jaw, effectively choking off any verbal response. She made a soft, strangled noise and her eyes went even bigger, bulging out as he propelled her backward into her house. He waited just inside for Mitch to catch up, then kicked the door shut. He already had the blade in his right hand, and he flicked it open.

During the instants between when he released her with his left hand and when he slashed across her throat with his right, she found her voice and her defiance. She let out a shrill screech and started punching him with small, bony but surprisingly solid fists. That only lasted a second, though, and then her hands were clasping at her neck, as if she was trying to hold back the flood with her fingers, and blood gurgled up into her mouth, and splashed on her clean entry tiles, and then she was down, on her stomach on the floor, wasted blood flowing from her throat.

Going back to the van for the pump-and-jug assembly, Walker was surprised to find one of the neighbors from next door, the TV house, standing in the front yard. He was a big guy, about thirty-five, a Bulls T-shirt and khaki shorts barely containing an expansive gut, and he had a Budweiser can in his hairy paw. His sudden appearance startled Walker. "Everything okay over there?" he asked. "I thought I heard Maddie scream."

"Fine, yeah," Walker said. He and Mitch had already cooked up a cover story for this sort of encounter, and although it nearly fled his thoughts, he managed to hang onto it and to deliver it in a voice tight with fear. "We're just . . . uh, delivering some new electronics and getting them installed for her. I dropped a box and it startled her, but it was just cables and junk, nothing fragile."

"Cool," the guy said. "What'd she get?"

"I can't tell you what a customer bought, sir, that's confidential. Since you know her, if you come over after we're done with the install, I'm sure she'd be glad to show off. We're just a little busy right now."

The man took a swig of beer, belched, and crushed the can in his fist. "I'll do that," he said. "Maddie's good people."

"I'm sure she is, sir," Walker said, agreeing even though he hadn't had a taste yet. He figured Mitch was getting his fill, though, and he needed to get inside and make sure he kept focused on what was important. "I should get back to it."

"Okay," the guy said. "Take it easy."

He started toward his own house. Walker opened the van, got out his pumping equipment, and hurried back in.

The pool on the floor had spread, and Walker hoped they could get anything at all out of her.

As he set up the pump, he explained about the neighbor to Mitch.

"Close call, man," Mitch said.

"Too close." Walker held out a quaking hand. "I'm still freaked."

"The story worked, that's the main thing. The dude left, right?"

"The dude left. The story worked." Walker had the pump in place and going. After a few moments, maroon liquid lined the sides of the rubber tube. "The story worked. But if we don't have any more near misses like that, I'll be a happy guy. Let's hurry up and get the fuck out of here."

20

A SERIES OF CONFIRMED vampire attacks around Nags Head, North Carolina, was close enough to home that Marina's team was able to drive down in their van instead of flying. The bloodsuckers had been preying on wealthy families with beachfront homes, leaving parents and children alike drained in their homes, beached in rolling surf, or floating out with the tides. When Marina and the others came to town, they fanned out to the other homes nestled amidst the dunes, telling the locals they were part of a federal task force aimed at stopping the serial killer who had been terrorizing the neighborhood. They warned off the local media, assuring them that any media presence would inhibit the investigation, but promising exclusive access later—a promise they had no intention of keeping.

The bloodsuckers might have moved on already, of course. But Marina had a gut feeling that they hadn't. The houses they had hit so far were far enough from their neighbors that vampires could invade one without alerting the rest. The residents were prosperous and healthy, for the most part. The nights here were dark, the sky dotted with stars. It was good hunting territory, and Marina's hunch told her the vamps would stick around a while longer.

Some of the residents balked, but enough of them didn't that when night fell, Marina's team members were spread throughout houses along the coast. Marina sat on a screened porch listening to the rush and rumble of the surf. Behind her, the lower floor of the house was mostly open, with windows all around, kitchen separated from the living/dining area only by a chest-high counter. You could stand on the porch and look through to the backyard, where a volleyball net wavered in the breeze.

The cries of gulls had tapered off after the sun had fallen, and the occasional vehicles passing on the road came far apart, almost an adjunct to the ocean noises instead of a distraction from them. The Rouleau family, who owned the house, had had seafood for dinner, and the fishy smell lingering in the air mixed with the salt and seaside grasses and ocean smell. The effect was almost artificial, like something pumped into the air at Sea World.

The Rouleaus had gone to a motel for the night. Marina had a radio plugged into her ear, and she could hear the other people on the team talking softly to each other.

She didn't feel much like slinging the shit, so she kept quiet, responding only when directly addressed. She strained to hear anything out of the ordinary. She had no guarantees that the vampire or vampires would strike tonight, and no promises that any attack would be at this house instead of one of the others. Her prey might as easily pick one of the houses where the owners had declined the team's assistance. All she could do was wait and hope.

Midnight came and went. She took off the night vision goggles to give her eyes a rest, rubbed them with the meaty part of her palms. Most of another hour ticked by. Alone with her thoughts, she was haunted by Barry Wolnitz, who had put his trust in her only to end up as a bloodsucker's lunch. She had known plenty of people who had died, and had killed her fair share, but this one kept coming back to visit. She was disturbed by how much his death affected her. Was it because he was just an innocent victim—the kind of person she should have been trying to save? She killed people like Andy Gray because she had to, because they were interfering with the mission in some way. Barry, on the other hand, could have been helpful, and instead she had led him right into the grave.

She walked around the porch, avoiding the spot where the floorboards creaked. She stretched, going up on tiptoes and reaching for the rafters, then bent at the waist and pressed her fingertips to the floor. She sipped from a bottle of water. The radio chatter had mostly died off. She hoped no one had fallen asleep.

She was about to start checking in with them one by one when a strange noise alerted her. She was sure it was the sound of a shoe scuffing sand. She dropped to a crouch and scooped up her weapon. She was starting to whisper an alarm when Jimbo's voice came into her ear.

"My twenty," he said.

"I got bogies here," Monte said.

"Same here," Kat whispered. "Multiples."

"I've got company too," Marina said. "Is there anyone who doesn't hear any?"

"Nada here," Tony H. said.

"I ain't sure," R.T. said.

"Hold on," Tony O. said. "I think there's something out there."

Marina yanked the plug from her ear for a moment and listened. There it was again, closer this time. She thought she heard something else that might have been hushed voices. She shoved the earplug back in.

"Multiples here," she said. "If your station isn't compromised, head on over to one that is."

"Roger that," someone said. Marina barely heard. The scuffing sounds were coming more frequently now, from various points around the house. The porch faced rolling dunes and then the Atlantic Ocean, but she was certain that the house was surrounded, with bloodsuckers coming from every side.

The idea had been that with someone stationed in each of several different houses, when the call came that the bloodsuckers had targeted one house, the other members of the team could swarm that house and catch the vampires in the crossfire.

It didn't appear to be working out that way, and

suddenly the porch didn't seem like the best place to be. Bloodsuckers could already be inside the house, working toward her, trapping her instead of the other way around.

As Marina snatched up the night vision goggles and pushed through the front door, she caught a flash of movement between her and the ocean, briefly blotting out the strip of moonlight frothing in the surf. She whirled around, raking her gaze across the inside of the house. Shadows darted this way and that, just beyond the rear windows.

No time to put on the goggles. Marina dropped them and clicked on the TRU-UV light clipped to her gun.

From down the beach she heard the stutter of automatic weapons.

Her heart hammered in her chest. She loved action, so why was she so afraid? What had changed?

Her UV light bounced off the windows at the back of the house, blinding her to anyone outside. Bad idea. She lowered the light, blinking to clear her vision.

And something crashed through one of the windows.

21

MARINA SWUNG HER WEAPON up again, UV light lancing through the room. She squeezed the trigger as she did and phosphorous rounds burst from the barrel, tearing through the toothy face before her. The Rouleaus would regret turning their house over to the Feds, although not spending the night in a hotel.

The roar from her gun drowned out any sounds of battle from other homes, and a ragged cloud of smoke bit at her nostrils. Behind her, footsteps pounded up the front stairs and the porch door banged open. She spun, holding down the trigger, laying down a line of fire that would destroy yet more of the house. Some of the rounds plowed into a bloodsucker charging through the front door, driving it backward.

At the crashing of another window, Marina twitched the gun that way and fired another burst. A bloodsucker hissed and snarled as the rounds chewed into him. Forward momentum carried him into Marina. She bashed the weapon's stock into his face, knocking him away.

And then the house was quiet.

Up and down the beach, though, firing continued. Flashes ignited the dark sky. Marina found the goggles and pulled them on, scanning the room for any vampires she might have missed. Phosphorous rounds sizzled in some of the walls. She should call the fire department, but not yet, not until the area was secured.

She raced from the house, vaulting the front steps and landing in sand. A brisk breeze blew off the water, rustling the tall grasses. Marina threaded between dunes heading for the nearest house. Jimbo was there, but now she couldn't remember if he had reported vampires or not.

The burst of action had distracted her, but on foot, running across glowing green sand, the fear was coming back. She had brought these people here, had developed the plan. If it backfired, that would be more lives on her conscience.

A stretch of fence stood before her, half-buried by a drifting dune. She jumped over it, but something slammed into her at the peak of her jump. They both went down, Marina on the bottom. She landed on her back with her left arm flung out, and something else latched onto it, encircling her wrist with a clawed hand. The goggles had shifted in the fall; instead of helping her see they blocked her field of view and she couldn't get a hand up to move them.

She still had the weapon in her right hand, finger inside the trigger guard. She squeezed and the gun barked and bucked into the sand. Marina writhed in the grip of two bloodsuckers, trying to twist away. She kicked out, felt the satisfying give of flesh and bone beneath her booted foot. Teeth gnashed at her shoulder but she was able to draw back her arm and smash her elbow into the thing's face. It gave a pained grunt. Suddenly she was free. She adjusted the goggles and rolled to her feet, grabbing the weapon as she did. She pinned the nearest vampire with the TRU-UV beam and watched it try to curl away, its flesh beginning to smoke.

When it fell, she put a couple of rounds into it and continued toward the nearest house. The second vampire that had attacked her was out of sight, but she didn't think it had gone far.

Marina reached the house, where the front room blazed with light. Jimbo stood inside blasting away at his attackers. Marina could see them around him, moving fast. One had picked up a floor lamp and swung it like a club, but Jimbo sensed it coming and dodged the blow. Another took advantage of his being momentarily off balance. Marina aimed through the window and unleashed a burst into the house. The wailing of dying bloodsuckers was like sweet music, helping elevate her mood.

She and Jimbo cleared that house and moved on to the next one. By this point, people were on the radio again and she had a better sense of who was where. She couldn't raise R.T., but there were two more houses before they reached his.

The original plan started coming together. At the next house, they caught the bloodsuckers between Marina and Jimbo outside and Kat inside. Once that was cleared they shifted up the beach to the next, taking out a handful of vampires on the way. This must have been a big den, Marina thought, before a more disturbing idea came to her—what if it wasn't a single den, but multiple ones joining forces? Since Andy Gray's manifesto had made the news, vampires across the country seemed intent on making sure people knew they were real, and a major assault on a well-to-do area could only help their cause. The attack on the Red-Blooded facility in Nevada had been easy to hush up, because of its remote location, but one on a prosperous beach community on the East Coast would be noticed.

By the time all the members of the team had been accounted for, she figured there had been more than twenty vampires destroyed. A good night's work.

But R.T. and Tony H. had been bitten.

Marina took the responsibility onto her own shoulders for ending them, blowing their brains to bits with phosphorous rounds. When she did it, tears stung her eyes; an unfamiliar sensation, and one she didn't like. On top of the strange sadness over Barry Wolnitz that she couldn't seem to shake, she wondered if she was going soft. Did everyone have a boundary of some sort, a number of killings beyond which it was impossible to function? Marina had never expected to reach any such line. She had never thought of herself as a murderer, because her killings were always done in the service of the greater good.

Keeping R.T. and Tony H. from coming back as

vampires was also in the greater good, she knew. And they had been valuable members of the team, when they lived, each one putting down numerous bloodsuckers. So their lives hadn't been wasted.

Somehow, at the moment, that knowledge didn't help much.

Operation Red-Blooded's budget would cover the damage to the houses, and the residents, law enforcement, and the media would all be pressured to tell the story as one of a serial murderer targeting local families, killed by the task force as he tried to gain entry to one of the homes. Evidence supporting this tale was already being manufactured—Operation Red-Blooded had a special "community relations" unit dedicated to misinformation of just that sort.

Marina knew the truth, though. She knew that she had cost two good agents their lives, that her plan had been flawed, that she never should have stationed any of her people alone. She had underestimated the enemy. She had wanted too much to destroy bloodsuckers, above and beyond any other considerations.

Was it maturity? Or just the recognition of loss, the understanding that she couldn't win every battle? She wasn't sure, but there was an aching in her gut that was as new to her as the tears she had shed.

War was hard, with a cost almost too high to bear. It had never hit her before, not in quite the way it recently had. She wasn't simply a soldier anymore; she was calling the shots.

Now the weight of lost lives pressed down on her, a responsibility she hadn't known would be so hard to handle. She could only hope it didn't slow her down, because the war was far from over. More lives would be lost, she was certain.

And for the first time in her professional life, she wondered if she would be able to see it through to the end.

22

Without a vampire mentor, Larry Greenbarger had to rely on bits and pieces of data he had picked up as an Operation Red-Blooded researcher to know what his limits and capabilities were. It had taken hours of practice before a mirror to perfect the ability to appear human, even though he had known for some time that vampires could do so. Now that he'd been at it for a while, he could do it more quickly, but holding it for very long was still a strain, and he wondered if there was some trick to it he didn't know.

But he needed access to a library, to read some journals that hadn't yet been posted online. So he wore his human disguise as best he could and went into the night, to the McGoogan Library at the University of Nebraska at Omaha, where he was able to find what he was looking for. It was hard to concentrate, surrounded by humans. He tried to shut out the sound of the blood coursing through them, the smell of it tempting him, and he had to keep dabbing saliva from the corners of his mouth as he read.

What he learned encouraged him. Vitamin D had been thought of for ages as crucial to bone growth and development, but new research showed that it worked throughout the entire body, not just on bones. It played an active role in preventing cancers and certain infectious diseases, in regulating autoimmune systems, and in strengthening cell defenses. At one time, it had been the only known therapy for tuberculosis, and was also effective against rickets. The more scientists studied it, though, the farther reaching its effects were found to be.

The thing about vitamin D was that it wasn't an actual vitamin at all. Although it could be obtained by eating fish, it could also be manufactured by the body through exposure to ultraviolet B light.

Sunlight.

This was the link Larry needed. He read feverishly, jotting notes on scraps of paper. Since becoming undead, some changes were completely unexpected—his fine motor skills, for instance, had diminished slightly, so his handwriting had become scrawled and scratchy, even though his strength was much greater.

Through the action of vitamin D, in ways expected and not, sunlight influenced the development and defense of cells throughout the body. Larry had to believe that the vampiric response to sunlight had to do with the effects of vitamin D, and if he knew that then he could figure out how to finesse that response to get the reaction he wanted.

Larry tapped his chin absently as he read, and at one point noticed that his facade had fallen. He summoned the will to reclaim his human appearance, but he had to get out of there. It was too hard to keep it up so long, and in a place like this, full of people and security cameras, being observed could cause unwanted problems.

On his way out the door, he passed two young women with their arms full of checked-out books. One didn't become a scientist without passing plenty of time on university campuses, and while he had never been to this one before, it shared certain familiar characteristics with others. Spirited conversation, lithe young bodies, trees and walls plastered with flyers and signs promoting an incredible variety of causes and events, and people with a thirst for knowledge were everywhere. So were people just looking for a good time, and others intent on career preparation, thinking only about earning those paychecks once they graduated, hungering for the cash.

Larry Greenbarger's hunger these days was of an entirely different sort. He sought knowledge, albeit of a very specific type. But looking at women he once would have wanted to date—although he doubted he'd have had a chance, not with these beauties—all he wanted now was to bend over them and tear through flesh and expose arteries.

He hurried from the library, back to a truck he had stolen in North Platte, on the way out from Colorado. By the time he reached it, his vampire countenance had returned, and he ducked his head and avoided people until he was driving away through the night.

* * *

Since his stint at the old man's house outside Denver, Larry had taken to moving around a lot. He changed cars more often, and he stayed in motels when he couldn't find victims who lived alone and in sufficiently private surroundings. The hard part was carrying out his scientific research while changing residences frequently, but something he could only classify as a finely tuned survival instinct had kicked in, telling him never to rest for long.

When he came to a new town, in addition to hunting for food, he hunted for vampires. He guessed that they would be drawn to the same quarters he was: places where people were out late, where streets weren't crowded but not sleepy, as the farming communities and suburbs were. People leaving bars were good options, or prostitutes working lonely street corners, or their customers. Sometimes he came across an insomniac walking around a suburban block late at night, but he couldn't count on that. Most of the lost souls who inhabited the night lived in the cities.

Larry became increasingly anxious to meet others like him. He needed to know more, to have questions answered that never would have occurred to him as a human researcher. And he needed subjects for his own researches. If he was successful, he would need ways to communicate that success to others.

So during the days, when he couldn't travel or hunt, he divided his time between research and continuing his quest online. He haunted websites and message boards he had heard about during his days at Red-Blooded, and he discovered new ones. He read post after post from people who either claimed to be vampires or who idolized them.

Finally, he decided to take a more proactive approach. He spent an hour composing a post, and then more hours spreading it to every vampire-related site he could think of. *"Do you yearn to walk in the Light of Day? To feel the sun without peril? It can happen. I can help you come out of the night."*

He had made it to Joplin, Missouri, before he got a response that seemed legitimate. Most of the responses were clearly from wannabes, and a few from vampires—or poseurs—who thought he was laying some sort of trap.

Which he was, but his bait was the truth.

In a seedy motel on the edge of Joplin, a place where the smell of smoke had soaked into the walls and beds and carpet, and burn marks cut brown divots in the plastic bathroom counter, he checked his in-box and found a response he could barely believe.

"I've seen your message," it said. "And I believe you. I long for daylight, long to no longer feel hemmed in by the dark hours. Hunting during the day . . . if you can do this, you're the savior our kind needs. I'm in Louisiana but can travel to you."

Larry wrote back immediately, informing his correspondent that he was in Missouri but they could meet in Little Rock, splitting the difference. When he got an affirmative reply, he could barely contain his excitement.

Another vampire, at long last!

And someone upon whom he could test his revised formula.

It was all he could do to wait until dark to hit the road.

23

THE MEET WAS SET for 2:00 AM, at Twelfth and Woodrow in downtown Little Rock, not far from the State Capitol. Larry got there a little early and cruised around the neighborhood. There were still a few people out, liquor stores open, bars just shutting down. He saw one police car drive slowly past a clutch of scantily dressed women who scattered at its approach. The car moved away.

Larry drove around for another few minutes, then parked and hiked back to the intersection. He picked a shadowed doorway, a couple of buildings down from the corner, and waited there.

A copper SUV chugged slowly around the corner. Larry stepped from the shadows, just enough so a vampire would know he was there. The darkness wouldn't interfere with a vampire's vision, but he wanted the one he'd been corresponding with, who said his name was Cecil, to know where to look.

The SUV had two people in it, white suburban kids from the looks of them, probably looking to score dope. They took one look at Larry and the driver stepped on the gas, leaving rubber on the asphalt as he peeled out. Larry was heading back into the shadows when a big dark blue Dodge sedan rumbled up to the curb. There were six people inside, three up front and three in back. The one behind the wheel, a wiry, muscular guy with short dark hair, leaned out through his open window.

"You Larry?"

Larry hadn't been expecting to meet an entire den, just the one named Cecil. The whole thing felt wrong to him. The driver appeared human, as did the car's other occupants. Larry could appear human, too, but wouldn't in this sort of situation. This was supposed to be a vampire-to-vampire meeting.

"No," he said quickly.

"That's him," someone in the back said. "Look at him!"

"Get him!"

The doors flew open and all six of them flooded out. They were between nineteen and thirty, Larry guessed. Good old boys, or they would be when they got older. White T-shirts, Western-style snap-button shirts with the sleeves torn off, jeans, heavy boots. Most of them carried wooden stakes, but one had a revolver and one a crossbow. *Too much Buffy,* Larry supposed.

They weren't *nosferatu,* though. Larry had walked right into a trap, set by what appeared to be half-stupid, redneck vampire hunters. They might have been spurred by the media blitz about vampires, or by the explosion of online discussion about them, or perhaps something more personal. He wasn't inclined to sit and chat with them, though. At the moment, he felt pretty stupid himself.

"Freeze, bloodsucker!" one of them called.

Larry smiled. For a moment he had thought they might be a genuine threat. Until he heard that. Then he had to revisit his half-stupid description, rounding up. Two-thirds stupid, maybe. "You're not serious," he said.

"As a fuckin' heart attack."

"God, you're like a bad country song. Do you know how to say anything that's not a hopeless cliché?"

The guy with the revolver aimed it at him. The crossbow was pointed in his general direction, too, but it looked like something from the toy department at an outlet store and he doubted it would do any damage. The four stake-wielders had fanned out around him. No one wanted to close in on him, either afraid of him, their friend's bullets, or both. "Fuck you," the gunman said. "Now you die, bloodsucker."

"Too late," Larry said. He didn't wait for the first bullet, but lurched to his right and grabbed the closest guy. He swatted the man's wrist, snapping it, and the stake flew out of his hand. The guy screamed. Larry lifted him by collar and crotch and threw him into the Dodge hard enough to cave in the roof.

The gunman squeezed his trigger and chips flew from the brick wall behind Larry. Bullets wouldn't kill him, unless the man was lucky enough to destroy his brain—his encounter with the university guard had proven that—but that didn't mean he wanted to deal with the pain should one accidentally strike him. He darted forward, grabbing the throat of another stake-wielder with his left hand and ripping through it, pulling out the man's Adam's apple and throwing it, along with gobs of blood and tissue, to the ground. The gunman stared in horror and revulsion, rooted in place, and Larry tackled him next. He broke the man's arm, jammed his own finger inside the trigger guard, bent the man's shattered arm up so the gun barrel was inside the man's mouth. Tears ran from the man's eyes and he made pathetic whimpering sounds until Larry pulled the trigger.

A crossbow bolt finally sailed from that weapon. It glanced off one of the remaining stake-wielders, who was spinning around to take off at a sprint. He screamed and the crossbow guy started to reload, to what end Larry couldn't fathom. Did the man imagine that a projectile that couldn't pass through a T-shirt and a few layers of human skin would hurt him? Larry jumped onto the hood of the Dodge, sprang off it again, and landed on the crossbow guy, knocking him to the ground. Larry tore his throat open with the claws of one hand while shredding his face with the other.

Two remained, and they were running in opposite directions. Larry picked the one who had been hit by the crossbow bolt. He didn't have much time until people started coming out to see what all the commotion was, he believed, even in this neighborhood. The guy had covered most of a block at a dead run, and was just starting to glance back over his shoulder, probably thinking he had a good head start, when Larry caught up to him. He slammed his fist into the guy's back, dropping him onto the sidewalk where he tried to curl into a ball. Larry stepped on his hand.

"Have you found any others?" Larry asked him. "Like me? Any leads?"

The guy was sobbing, almost hysterical. Larry got off his hand, crouched beside him. "Just tell me and I'll make the pain go away."

"There's . . . m-maybe one . . . in . . . Port Gibson. . . . We're supposed . . . to meet him . . . after you. Tomorrow."

"Is there anything in the car? A meeting place, a schedule?"

"R-Ronnie has it all . . . written down. In . . . the g-g-glove."

"You mean Cecil?"

"Y-yeah. R-really Ronnie."

"Thanks." True to his word, Larry made the pain go away.

Leaving the bloody corpse where it was, he hurried back to the car, yanked open the glove box, found a piece of paper and a map. He pocketed both and ran. Sirens were closing in on the neighborhood, but Larry was far away before they got there.

24

USING THE ARRANGEMENTS MADE by a half-assed group of vampire hunters against one of his own felt like a kind of betrayal, but Larry told himself that the whole species would benefit from his researches. Risking one to help many was a time-honored tradition in the world of applied biomedical sciences. Anyway, continuing to experiment only on himself could be disastrous, because if he failed to survive any of the tests, then his whole line of research would end with him.

Jesse, the vampire with whom "Cecil" had made arrangements in Port Gibson, Mississippi, was apparently far more trusting than Larry was. He had given an address at which to meet, instead of a street corner. When Larry got there, he found that the address belonged to an abandoned juke joint outside of town, a place with a tin roof and a collapsing screened-in porch and faded signs painted on the outside walls. A dirt road, hemmed in by overhanging trees, led to where it stood by the Bayou Pierre, surrounded by a patchy gravel parking lot. The rusted red-and-white door of a pickup truck leaned against one of the walls. The night was alive with insects—crickets, or cicadas buzzing incessantly, mosquitoes droning all around. The bass notes of croaking frogs came from the bayou, along with occasional, unidentified splashing sounds. Larry's sensitive nose caught traces of blood nearly submerged beneath the heavy, fertile scents of bayou water and night-blooming flowers.

Getting out of his truck, he realized how isolated it was here. Was this another trap? Maybe he was just a born sucker. There was no way to approach the place surreptitiously, as he had hoped—either one came down the road or up the bayou. With no other choice, since he was already here, he walked up to the door. "Hello? Anyone here?" He didn't even know if he was looking for a male or female Jesse.

Male, as it turned out. Jesse was a tall African-American, late twenties in apparent age, with short hair and a long beard. He had been in far better shape than Larry during life, and looked like he would be hard to take in a fight. Maybe this would turn out to have been a really bad idea. But an undercurrent of excitement made Larry's nerve endings tingle—this was the first real vampire he had met since becoming one himself.

"You Jesse?" Larry asked.

"Yeah . . . ?" His voice was almost as deep as those bullfrogs out on the bayou.

"Well, I'm not Cecil. My name's Larry. I just wanted to tell you, Cecil was a fake. He and some friends were just trying to meet our kind so they could get their kicks killing us."

"That right?"

"Yeah. You . . . you have internet in here?"

"Got power, internet, whole deal."

Jesse made no move to invite Larry in. "Look, I'm, uhh . . . I'm new at this. I mean, I was turned a while ago, but by a vampire who didn't stick around. I haven't met any others. So I thought I would keep the appointment that Cecil made, just so I could meet you. But now . . . well, I don't know what to do."

Jesse moved slowly, with what seemed like great deliberation. Larry supposed he had to speed up when he hunted, but so far he didn't look like a guy to whom fast action was familiar. He shifted his shoulders, raised his head slightly, and extended his right hand.

Larry was surprised. Vampires shook hands? Then again, Jesse had been on the internet, had done something to attract Cecil's attention, or responded to some outreach by Cecil. Maybe he wasn't very experienced, either.

He put his hand in Jesse's, cold skin around his, and they shook. "Have you met many others? Did you have anyone to show you the ropes?"

Jesse shrugged again, a motion that took a while. "Couple."

Larry needed to find a way to overpower the larger vampire. In the truck he had heavy ropes and thick chains, padlocks, a leather face mask with built-in ball gag from a bondage shop that wouldn't come close to fitting over Jesse's huge head. He had prepared for the transport and storage, but figured he would have to come up with the capture on the fly, once he found out what the lay of the land was. Now that he was here, he was fresh out of ideas.

At Operation Red-Blooded they'd had ways of rendering vampires unconscious, souped-up forms of anesthesia. Larry hadn't taken any of those with him when he left, and had been too busy working on his sunlight research to try to invent one. Anyway, without vampires to test it on, he wouldn't know what would knock out and what wouldn't. He had come to Jesse because he needed a test subject, so he was stuck in a vicious circle.

Jesse watched him with a thoughtful expression. *Probably wondering why I'm here,* Larry thought, *why I don't say anything.* His mind rushed in every direction at once, never settling on anything helpful. He felt the same way he had in life on those rare occasions when he found himself trying to get acquainted with an attractive woman.

"Listen, Jesse," he said at last. "This will sound kind of weird, but when I was alive, I was a scientist. Now I'm still doing science, trying to work out a formula that will let us go out in the daylight without being destroyed. I need someone to test it on. Would you be willing to do that?"

Jesse shrugged again, a little more animatedly this time. "Here?"

"I have my equipment set up in a place in Arkansas.

Little Rock. We'd have to go there. And we should leave tonight, while it's dark."

Jesse looked at the run-down juke joint. "I got some stuff."

"We can take it."

"Okay," Jesse said.

And just like that, Larry had his guinea pig.

25

THEY DROVE THROUGH THE night and made it back to the house Larry had found near downtown Little Rock just before dawn. The house's original owner, a woman in her early fifties with lustrous black hair and skin like café au lait and blood as sweet as any he had ever tasted, was still in her bedroom, starting to go a little sour now. The house was on a corner, with two floors and a side yard surrounded by a high stone wall, which was what had attracted Larry to it in the first place. The indescribable flavor of its owner was merely a fringe benefit.

"This your place?" Jesse asked as they pulled into a garage with an automatic door opener. He hadn't said much on the way up, just asked a couple of questions and answered Larry's with single-syllable responses.

"It is now," Larry said. "For a while. How long have you been in your place?"

This was answered, naturally, with a shrug. "Some while," Jesse added.

Larry closed the garage door, then took Jesse into the house. He had learned that in life Jesse had been a fry cook, had been out of Mississippi only a couple of times, to neighboring states, and had been turned more than ten years ago but less than twenty—he couldn't narrow it down any further. He was, Larry decided, on the slow side, but agreeable. And Larry was glad he hadn't had to chain him up.

Over the next few days, they hunted together at night and Jesse sat in the house's living room, mostly watching TV, by day. He had brought his computer with him, an ancient Gateway that Larry was surprised could still connect to the net, and he spent a little time on that each day. Jesse proved that he did have hunting skills and the ability to move quickly when necessary, and seeing his strength, Larry felt relief that he hadn't tried to take the bigger man. Having him here voluntarily was much easier.

During the days, Larry worked harder than ever, trying to apply what he had learned about how human cells transformed sunlight into vitamin D, and then made use of it throughout the body. He believed he had come across the right answer, and he thought he knew how to modify it, along the same lines he had already tested, to work in concert with the Immortal Cell instead of causing the destructive reaction it did now.

On the fourth day he was finished.

He felt elated. In spite of his nearly constant hunger, he could still do science. He could still develop a theory and then find his way toward a definitive test of that theory. He knew how to combine chemicals to achieve a desired result.

All that was missing now was that definitive test.

That's what Jesse was here for.

He should have waited until morning, let Jesse get a good meal in his belly before injecting him. But there were a couple hours of sunlight left, and Larry was anxious. He went into the living room, where Jesse was sitting in front of the TV, rubbing his stomach with his right hand.

"We're ready, Jesse."

"For what?"

"For the test I told you about. For you to go out in the sun?"

"Now?"

"In a minute. After I give you the . . . the medicine."

"Don't like needles."

"You'll hardly feel it, Jesse. You're strong."

"Yeah."

"You'll love this. Not only will you be stronger than ever, but sunlight won't hurt you. In fact, the sunlight will make you stronger still. You want that, right?"

"Yeah."

"Come with me, then."

Jesse clicked off the TV, rose from the chair, and followed Larry into the dining room he had turned into a lab. Larry had already filled a syringe with the formula. "Give me your arm, Jesse."

Jesse held his arm out. The veins in his forearm were prominent, so Larry didn't even bother tying him off. "Look up at the ceiling."

Jesse obeyed, and Larry stuck the needle in his vein. Jesse barely flinched. Larry pushed down on the plunger, emptied the cylinder into the bigger vampire. Jesse shuddered as the liquid began to circulate.

"That's it," Larry said. "Now let's see how it works."

"How?"

"You go outside. Out into the side yard."

"Outside? It's daytime."

"That's the point," Larry said. "The sunlight won't hurt you now. It'll make you feel better than ever."

"You sure?"

"Absolutely." Larry led Jesse back through the living room. Heavy drapes kept the sunlight from pouring in through a sliding glass door. "You'll go out here, in the yard. I'll be watching from upstairs."

"You sure?" Jesse asked. Larry couldn't tell if he was just repeating himself, or if he meant was Larry sure he would be watching. In fact, it would be difficult, but he could stand to the side of the window. At this time of day, direct sunlight wouldn't land on him there, and he could still see the whole yard. There wasn't much direct sun left in the yard, but there was enough for a test run.

"When I'm ready I'll shout to you. Then you go out through the drapes and the glass door, and just stand in the yard. Nobody will see you because of that wall. When you're there for a few minutes, the sun will start working on you, making you stronger than you've ever been. When I yell down to you through the window, then you can come back in, and I'll look you over, check what happened to you."

Jesse just looked at him.

"Okay, Jesse?"

"Okay."

On the other side of the side yard wall was a fairly busy main street. Traffic flowed along it most of the day and late at night. But the wall was eight feet high and topped with broken glass, so no one was likely to look over it. The house's owner had liked her security, but she hadn't reckoned on a vampire coming along.

Her mistake.

"I'm going upstairs now, Jesse." Larry had learned to be very clear when talking to Jesse, and it didn't hurt to repeat himself. "I'll let you know when to go out."

"Okay."

Larry left Jesse and hurried upstairs. It was probably fine that Jesse wasn't visibly excited, because Larry was excited enough for both of them. When he got to the window, double-checked to ascertain that he could stand out of direct sun, with the curtain closed except for an inch or so at the side, and see the entire yard, he called down. "Go on outside, Jesse! Just stop when you get into the sun and wait to feel it on you!"

Jesse didn't answer, but Larry heard the rustle of the drapes and the rush of the sliding door. He held his breath. Jesse, wearing a sleeveless white T, stepped out into the afternoon sun.

As Larry had instructed, Jesse stood there. Every few

moments he twitched his uncovered shoulders or shook out his arms. Larry knew what he was experiencing. The warmth of the sun on his flesh was no longer a familiar sensation, and it had been far longer for Jesse. He was no doubt nervous, dread of the sun having become second nature. But he was a trouper.

Most important, he didn't catch on fire.

This would only be the first test, of course. Larry would have to devise ways of measuring Jesse's strength, indoors and away from the sun as well as out in it. But this was the critical one, because if he had not survived—or if he had gone mad, as Larry had the time he had tested on himself—then the others would be moot.

He let Jesse stand out there for five minutes. He was about to call him back in, but decided to let it go a couple more. Jesse was mostly still, as usual, twitching and scratching a little but otherwise showing no reaction.

Eight minutes passed. Jesse showed no visible effects. Time to bring him in. Larry slammed his palm against the window, protected by the curtain, to get his attention. "Jesse!"

Jesse jerked, startled. Then, as if the fright had flipped a switch, his face changed, the usual disinterested expression turning into a furious scowl. He dropped to a crouch, hands out at his sides, as if threatened by something. Saliva flecked the corners of his mouth.

Larry backed away from the window's edge. He recognized the symptoms of uncontrolled rage, and didn't want it directed his way. But Jesse didn't look up toward him. He spun around in the yard, as if he felt trapped, surrounded by enemies. That glass door wouldn't hold him for an instant if he wanted to come back inside.

But he didn't. Maybe he felt that the inside of the house was the source of the suddenly chaotic fever gripping him, and he didn't want to return to it. At any rate, he did as Larry had done before, leaping over the high wall.

Larry, however, had done it in a quiet exurban neighborhood. Jesse landed in a street, with cars coming toward him from both directions. Drawn back to the window, Larry watched as Jesse, panicked, ran from one vehicle and slammed into the hood of another. Horns blared. Jesse rolled off the hood, having left a deep dent in it, broken part of the grille, and dislocated the front bumper, and smashed his fists through the driver's window. The driver screamed and tried to move away, but was constrained by his seat belt. Jesse dragged him through the shattered window, glass slicing furrows into him, and tore his head most of the way off. Jesse helped himself to a few swallows from the gushing neck, then seemed to notice that the street had come to a standstill, everyone staring at him.

His reaction was fierce. He ran from person to person, car to car, sowing devastation at every step.

Jesse flipped a compact car with just the strength in his hands and shoulders, killed three more people, bathing in blood. Larry could smell the sharp, sweet scent, and for an instant he wished he was out there in the street, taking part in the carnage.

By the time seven people had died, the others seemed to understand that they would be next. Cars reversed, or swung around and raced away. One pickup truck hit a woman whose car was trapped and who was trying to escape on foot. She landed on the sidewalk, head first, and Larry watched blood spread on the pavement.

Then he heard sirens and saw the flash of lights closing in fast. Jesse didn't seem to register the danger. He was too busy throwing car parts through the windows of nearby houses and dismembering his victims. Squad cars braked at all angles and the cops poured out, hemming him in from both sides. Even then he paid them little mind, just glanced at them as if noting new prey.

Larry watched them aim pistols and shotguns at Jesse. They couldn't know he was a vampire, and if that concept even crossed their minds, they wouldn't believe he would be out in daylight. All they saw was an incredibly strong madman, some guy cranked up on PCP and drenched in blood, and a slew of victims. Their voices were muffled by distance and glass but Larry knew they were ordering him to freeze, to lie down with his hands behind his head. Jesse ignored their commands.

Finally, as if perturbed by their interruption of his spree, Jesse started toward them. That move was met by a hail of bullets and lead shot. Jesse's body jerked as each one hit him, but he kept going until a desperate officer's shotgun blast pulverized his head.

Kill the brain and you kill the vampire. That had been drummed into everyone at Operation Red-Blooded. The last-ditch survival tactic.

Jesse's body finally stopped, swayed, and fell. Even then the frightened cops put more bullets into him, until they were absolutely certain.

The sun was almost gone. Night would fall soon, and Larry would need to get out of the area. The police would certainly go door-to-door, interrogating neighbors, trying to figure out who the hell Jesse was and where he had come from. Larry had no right to be in this house, and that would be obvious quickly enough.

He packed fast. As soon as it was dark enough, he had to go. The driveway was on the far side of the house from the side yard and the street, so maybe he would have a chance to get away before they caught him. He carried equipment and supplies out to the truck, stowed safely in the garage for now. When the bed was loaded he covered it with tarps and tied it all down. Then he got a jug of blood from the refrigerator—traveling food—and sat in the truck, behind the wheel, thinking over what had gone wrong.

Jesse had lasted longer in the sun than Larry had, but finally the rage had overtaken him, too. Jesse had become much stronger than Larry in the sunlight—both were strengthened by it, but Larry wouldn't have been able to flip cars. In the end, though, any survival instincts Jesse should have possessed had been subsumed by the madness. He might have been lacking in that area in the first place, since he had so willingly left his safe place behind at a stranger's request. But Larry thought some of it had to be attributable to the formula, to the sun-rage.

He had more work to do. And he had to do it away from here.

He was still sitting in the truck when he heard the cops ring the front doorbell. They hammered on the door for a while, announced themselves, but didn't enter the house or look in the garage. Larry waited another half hour, until they had moved well away, and then opened the garage, backed out, and drove like hell away from the neighborhood.

Time to find a new temporary home, a new test subject. Ultimate success had been forestalled. But it would be his.

Of that, he was more certain than ever.

26

EVERYTHING COULD BE SNATCHED away in an instant.

That was a lesson Rocco had learned many times over. The lesson, though, couldn't be applied in any practical way. Knowing the shit could hit the blades at any time didn't mean that you knew when that time would come. He had learned it first as an eleven-year-old, on the streets of Brooklyn when it had been a much different place than it was now. He had been out playing stickball on the street when his father came striding up the sidewalk in that way he had, like he hadn't a care in the world, like it was the world that should be checking over its shoulder in case Sal DelVecchio was coming up behind it. He had a paper bag in his arms, bottles clinking together inside it, and a cigarette clamped between his lips. When he saw Rocco in the street, he sucked in a big drag and blew the smoke out his nostrils in twin streams, like a dragon. The stunt never failed to bring a smile to Rocco's face.

This time, though, he had just finished with his dragon smoke when he saw a couple of bruisers heading toward him from the corner. They both wore long black coats and fedoras, in spite of the day's warmth. Their hands were tucked in their coat pockets. They walked with stiff-legged determination, like they knew where they were going and what they'd do once they got there.

"Those are some of Caputo's men," one of Rocco's buddies said. "I've seen them before."

"Are not!" Rocco said.

"They are."

He might have said more, but Rocco wasn't listening. His father had stopped on the sidewalk and the men had reached him. The clink of the bottles in the bag became louder, more insistent. Rocco had never seen his father afraid before, and now that he did, he liked it not one bit.

His father tried to put up a brave front. He argued with the men, and then he spat the cigarette out, tip glowing in the dusk, and it bounced off the crisp pants leg of one of the men, sparks flying, and landed in the gutter.

The man brought up a shotgun, looking, in Rocco's memory, like a giant steel phallus rising suddenly from underneath the raincoat. Rocco's father dropped the paper bag. Bottles smashed on the sidewalk and booze burbled over the curb. Sal DelVecchio started to turn, to run away for what must have been the first time in his life, but the shotgun, held waist-high, ejaculated flame and smoke and Rocco's father was cut almost in half, blood and flesh pelting the brownstone behind him like a heavy spring rain.

Rocco had not known that his father was involved with gangsters, or that the man knew the meaning of fear. He had not known, either, until weeks later that his mother had been seeing Mr. Canilo from two blocks over, even during the time that his father was alive. But he learned fast.

The next time that everything he knew and believed was snatched away from Rocco was thirteen years later. He had worked for Mr. Caputo for a couple of years by then. Caputo was getting old, but he still ran the neighborhood, and he pretended he didn't know what had happened to Rocco's father, so Rocco pretended the same thing. He was working his way up in the organization, biding his time, waiting for a chance to remind Caputo of what he had seen.

Then one night Rocco was out with friends, other guys on the come, and they had a few drinks in a bar and then a couple more. While they were sitting at a table, laughing and telling dirty stories, a couple of women in a booth, who were nursing Bloody Marys like they had cost a hundred bucks each, started giving Rocco and Benjy the eye. Rocco sent over another pair of Marys, although they still hadn't finished the first two, and when they acknowledged the gift, he touched his fingertip to his brow in a casual salute. One of the women, the one with straight black hair and a red satin blouse, touched her fingers to her lips. Rocco knew which one he was going home with.

Outside, they started to get acquainted. Her name

was Maria and she lived with her roommate, but they
had separate bedrooms. She didn't follow baseball but
thought the Yankees were all right, and she liked to
go to the races. She liked everything fast, she said, the
faster the better. Rocco laughed and took her in his
arms and squeezed her, and she let one of her hands
slide down and cup his ass. "There's an alley right over
there," she whispered, her voice pleasantly husky.

He led the way, not about to let a woman make all
the moves. When they got into the alley he kissed her,
forcing his tongue between her lips. It met her tongue,
and there seemed to be a lot of it, swirling against his,
and then she held his arms in her hands, her grip impossibly strong, and then took her mouth away from
his and kissed his cheek and then his neck and then she
tore into him like a starving dog that had happened
across a roadkill squirrel.

And so Rocco learned his lesson again. At any time,
it can all go away.

The Feds had taught him the same thing again most
recently. He had known it could happen, of course. The
whole point of a safe house was that it was safe, but
also that it could be walked away from with no notice
whatsoever. You didn't keep anything in it you didn't
mind losing, because if you came back and found it
compromised, you weren't even going inside. He had
thought it was secure, though, had been using it for a
couple of years now without any problems. Even other
vampires, in the United States from overseas to try to

reduce the sheer number of *nosferatu*, hadn't managed to find them there. It was on the kind of block where people kept to themselves, where no one wanted to ask questions because they wouldn't want to answer any that were asked of them.

Probably, in retrospect, they had stayed too long, let it become too comfortable. Because somehow the Feds figured out where they were and they rushed the place with their guns and their UV lights. Rocco and the others had various escape plans in place, of course, each of which involved the willing sacrifice of certain members of the den. Still, they had lost Valentine and Lothar, Ivy and Caleb and Moe. That left only Rocco, Shiloh, Goldie, Winston, and Brick. The whole thing had been a disaster. Half the den, gone.

In an instant. Fuck.

They had spent that day in the basement of a building in New York's midtown, tucked in cages along with the personal possessions of the tenants, the rolled-up carpets and old TVs and boxes of baby photos that didn't fit in the apartments but that the owners couldn't bear to part with. When night came they moved on, but it took four more nights before they found a suitable haven. Barely suitable, at that. The building had been a market, so close to the East River they could smell it. A supermarket had come into the neighborhood and the market had died a slow but certain death, and since then no one had leased the space. The outside was covered with graffiti now, overlapping so thickly that almost nothing could be read, including the real estate broker's sign. The fact that the broker hadn't bothered replacing the sign was testament to the hopelessness of the place.

A few bums had been squatting there, but the *nosferatu* made a meal of them, and even turned one, a strapping Puerto Rican guy named Angel. They needed to start reconstituting the den, and it wouldn't hurt to include someone who knew the ins and outs of the neighborhood. Besides, his name made Rocco laugh.

They were sitting in the new place, in the back where there had been storage shelves and a couple of wooden desks, enjoying the last of Angel's former friends. Rocco had been deep in thought, but Shiloh leaned her head against his leg. A trail of drying blood ran down her chin and the curve of her left breast, disappearing beneath her loose blouse. "Everything okay, babe?" she asked.

He almost gave the glib answer, but he stopped himself. "No," he said. "Everything is far from okay."

"What's the matter?" she asked.

He shook long dark hair off his face. "What we have here . . . we could lose it again. We exist from day to day, from minute to minute, always at their mercy. They're cattle, but they're cattle with claws and they want our utter extinction, nothing less. Not coexistence, not truce, but extinction."

"Tell us something we don't know," Goldie said. "Always been that way, always will."

"No!" Rocco burned with a righteous wrath. He had to let it out or it would burn him from the inside out. "No, it will *not* always be that way. We can't go on like this, surviving at the whim of a society that despises us when it even acknowledges our existence. More than ever, I know we're on the right path. They can operate freely, by night or day, while we've stayed hidden away so they wouldn't know we're here. We've already taken the first steps toward changing that—targeting public figures and making it clear who did it. Some in the press try to claim that we're only pretend vampires, brain-damaged humans who want to make it seem like we're *nosferatu,* but the word is getting through that filter, little by little."

"That's because you're a genius, babe," Shiloh said.

"Possibly," Rocco said. "Anyway, we're on the right track. And we've been badly damaged, lost some good friends. We can't let that slow us or dissuade us, though. We need to keep up the pressure, strike whenever we can, leave bodies in the streets empty of blood so everyone will know that we're out here. We need a way to make an even bigger splash next time."

"Isn't that how they found us before?" Winston asked. "Because we didn't try to hide our meals?"

"Possibly. That doesn't matter. Our individual existences don't matter. What matters is the statement. I almost feel like I'm being self-aggrandizing here, but what matters to me isn't my undeath, it's what we're fighting for. That's bigger than any of us. It's more important than survival. We're talking about an entire species, a superior species. We can't let them rule our world any longer. The time has come to take it back, and I for one won't rest until we do."

The *nosferatu* murmured assent, and Shiloh clapped her hands together, palms flat and fingers splayed out, like a four-year-old.

Rocco wished there had been more of them around to hear his speech. A dozen, a hundred, even a thousand. One night, there would be. One night, he would stand before legions, and he would whip them to a frenzy, and they would go forth and conquer the bloodbags.

It would take a while to reach that stage, though, and in the meantime he was hungry. "Angel?" he asked, "is there anything left in that woman you're sitting on?"

27

WALKER SAT IN FRONT of the computer with a tall glass of blood close at hand. He had developed a real taste for the stuff. It was the right combination of salty and sweet, like popping a potato chip and a Hershey Kiss in his mouth at the same time. It was rich and thick, not quite milkshake consistency but more substantial than water or soda. He could taste slight variations from one person to another, which he guessed had to do with diet more than anything else. So far he hadn't been able to predict whether or not one person's would taste better than another's, but he figured that would come when he had more data.

He had finished checking his auctions for the day. An original 1950s Roy Rogers kids' guitar looked like it would bring a couple grand. There were lots of replicas on the market, but the real thing didn't come along very often.

As always in the early evenings, before it was dark enough to go hunting, Walker spent some time skipping around the profusion of vampire sites. He had correspondences going with various people on them, some he had known when he was doing Andy Gray's bidding, others he had met since Andy's disappearance. Most of them claimed to be vampires, but he didn't believe any of them. Sleeping during the day, wearing black, and drinking a lot of tomato juice didn't make someone a vampire. He and Mitch weren't even vampires, and they were killing real people and drinking real blood.

But he was starting to wonder if there was something about vampirism that made them fear the internet, or interfered with their ability to use a keyboard. Sure, the net had always been about nine-tenths fakes and poseurs anyway. But that percentage got even worse when it came to the undead. Vampire fans talking about being vampires with other vampire fans seemed like a particularly strange means of masturbation, and it wasn't getting him anywhere.

He took a swig while yet another message board was loading. He set the glass down with a clunk and watched the topics appear on the screen. Same old, same old . . . wait a second. This one was new. He clicked on the subject and went to the message.

"Listen to this, Mitch," he said.

"What?" Mitch was across the room, lying on a couch. He had a glass of good old type AB nearby too, along with a bag of Cheetos.

" 'Do you yearn to walk in the Light of Day?' " Walker read. " 'To feel the sun without peril? It can happen. I can help you come out of the night.' "

"Sounds like some sort of feminine hygiene product."

"Bullshit," Walker said. "It's a post on here."

"On a vampire site?"

"Yes, on a vampire site, what do you think? Dude, sometimes you're just thick."

Mitch rustled the bag. "I keep eating these, I will be."

In truth, they were both in somewhat better shape than they had been in years. The nights of hunting, the physical exertion they put into the task, had been good for them. "So what do you think?"

"Of what?"

"Of the post I just read you, duh. Sounds interesting to me."

"I guess."

"I mean . . . all the fakes and wannabes on here don't have to really worry about sunlight, do they? Only the real deal has that concern."

"I don't know," Mitch said. "Some of those pale Gothy types might stroke pretty bad if they went in the sun."

"That's not the same thing. It won't kill them."

"True."

"You think it's legit?"

"I have no idea, man."

"I mean, it sounds like kind of a come-on. Like this person is selling something. It's like those 'make your dick bigger' ads or something. But there's no mention of money. And even if it is . . . nobody's going to buy unless they're for real, right?"

"I wouldn't think so."

"I'm going to answer it," Walker said. "Let's see what this is all about."

"Knock yourself out, Walker."

"Bite me. Okay, here goes."

Walker drained his glass, then began typing, reading aloud to Mitch as he did so. "'I'm intrigued by your post, to say the least. Can you really help with the sunlight concern? I'm so tired of giving daylight to the cattle. I would like more information, please.'"

"Fine, whatever," Mitch said.

"Or, wait . . . it's not just me, it's *us*. And if they think we're a whole group of vampires, we'll probably get a quicker reply." He corrected the email, using the plural, and adding, "'We're all very excited by the prospect of hearing from you.'" Once again, he read it to Mitch.

"That's better," Mitch said.

"Yeah. That ought to make us sound interesting. If this was posted by a vampire, maybe we can set up a meeting."

"That's what this has all been about, right? I'm tired of waiting. I want to be undead, and the sooner the better."

"Working on it, dude," Walker said. "Working on it."

28

THERE WAS A SAMENESS to the crime scenes that Alex Ziccarria found depressing.

It had been more than a week since there was a new one in the city. But some had cropped up in the suburbs, out of the Chicago PD's jurisdiction. The MO had sounded so similar, however, that he and Larissa Dixson had appealed to the Clark County sheriffs for help tracking any possibly related cases throughout the county, and when the most recent body was found, they got the word almost as quickly as the locals did.

This one was in Tinley Park. Like most of the others, this victim was an unmarried woman. One victim had been married, but her husband was on his third deployment in Iraq, so she lived essentially alone. Their ages varied, but they were usually between their mid-twenties to midfifties, and most in their thirties. The majority were firmly middle class, although a couple in the city had been poor, one a prostitute and one working full-time but below the poverty level. None had been wealthy. With wealth came bigger houses, better security, more people around. Whoever was preying on these women liked to target those who didn't have a lot of people in their lives, who were lonely, who worked late hours and came home well after dark. The usual routine seemed to be to follow them home, or possibly to choose them and then wait near their homes, to force their way inside when the victim arrived, to cut the throat and drain the body.

The perpetrator (or perpetrators) had so far managed to avoid leaving much behind in the way of trace evidence. What there was, occasionally a hair or fiber or bit of soil or skin cells, was stacked up in the crime lab behind a lot of similar evidence from other crimes. That didn't bother Larissa in the least, but Alex found himself grinding his teeth in his sleep, thinking that something was getting past them that might lead them to the killer.

They had arranged to meet a local detective at the Tinley Park location, and he was waiting in his Crown Vic when they pulled up. He made them for cops, got out, showed his badge. He was young, thirty tops, with thick blond hair and an open face. To Alex he didn't look like he'd been on homicides long, because that job put lines in your face that he didn't have. The detective's arms and shoulders strained the seams of his navy blazer.

"Wow," Larissa said.

"What?"

"He's hot."

"I guess," Alex said. *If you go for tall, handsome, and muscular.*

"Just saying." She opened her door and strode briskly toward the local. Alex had to hurry to keep up.

"You the Chicago detectives?" the man asked, putting away his badge.

"That's right. Alex Ziccaria, Larissa Dixson."

"Pleased to meet you." He shook Larissa's hand first, then Alex's. "I'm Greg Fielding. I've been inside already. It's a mess, I'm afraid."

He said it like he was personally responsible, like he had invited them to his house and failed to clean up for company.

"We've seen others," Larissa said.

"Yeah, I heard there were some in the city. I guess someone's branching out."

"Chances are," Alex said. "The only way to find out is to have a look, isn't it?"

"What happens if they are related?" Greg asked. "We form some kind of interdepartmental task force?"

"Something like that," Alex said. "You, us, sheriff's detectives."

"Cool. I mean . . . it's not cool that some skeeve is icing people, here or in the city. But I haven't been out of uniform that long, and I haven't had any task force experience yet. Kind of looking forward to it."

"Can we see inside?" Alex asked.

"Oh, sorry, sure. Come on."

The yellow tape blocked off a yard that needed weeding and a house that could stand a paint job. The peeling wood siding was a reddish brown that bordered on rust. Or dried blood, Alex noted. The windows were dirty, the curtains moth eaten and sun bleached.

"Who's the victim?" he asked as they went up the walk.

"Rosana Orozco," Greg said. "Legal immigrant, trying to get citizenship, but this kind of puts a crimp in her plans. She worked swing shift at a dry cleaner's and cleaned houses for a few families in Oak Park."

"Any drug connections?" Larissa asked. "Or smugglers?"

"Not that we know of. Seems like she was a pretty straight arrow."

"Witnesses?"

"We canvassed the block. Nobody saw or heard anything. Here we go." Greg opened the front door. Alex took a deep breath, filling his lungs with the last fresh air they would get for a while. Then he followed Larissa and Greg into the house.

Apparently cleaning other people's homes didn't leave Rosana Orozco a lot of time to deal with her own. It was neat, but not spotless, with a layer of grime on the kitchen cabinets and an overflowing wastebasket in the corner. The smell of her last meal hung heavy in the air. Budget store furniture and appliances, cheap dinnerware, some candles with saints on them. The pantry was sparse, the refrigerator bare. She had a stack of Spanish-language magazines; *telenovelas,* they were called. She had DVDs of American and Mexican movies, mostly romances. A shelf was filled with Happy Meal toys.

"She have a kid?" Larissa asked.

"No. Neighbor said she had a cousin somewhere in the area who came by sometimes with her two toddlers, but Rosana lived alone."

"No roommate?"

"It's a two-bedroom house," Greg said. "But the second one is tiny. She has an ironing board in there, and a mending basket. She wasn't making piles, but her landlord says she was never behind on the rent. And we found a bankbook. Twelve hundred bucks in a savings account."

"Hardworking woman," Larissa said. "Putting money away. Came to a new country, alone, to try to make something different of her life. It's a damn shame."

"And she did it the right way," Greg said. "Followed the rules."

"Where is she?" Alex asked.

"In her bedroom."

"Show us."

"You got it. Coroner's people will be glad to get the okay to come and get her."

"Was there any sexual assault?" Larissa asked.

"Doesn't appear to be." Greg opened the bedroom door. The stench came out in a rush. Rosana's bladder and bowels had evacuated at death, and those smells overwhelmed those of blood and mortality. For now, anyway, although Alex knew that the smell of death was one that could conquer almost anything, given a little time.

Her body was on the floor, at the foot of an unmade bed. Like the others, her throat had been sliced open. The olive skin was pale underneath the pigment, with little blood in the veins to darken it up. Rosana was short, probably just topping five feet, if that, and on the stocky side.

"Has there been a crime scene team in here?" Alex asked.

Greg laughed. "That would be me," he said. "We're a small-town force, don't have much in the budget for that sort of thing. Way I see it, good police work is all you need."

Larissa looked at Greg and smiled. She had already been checking out the swell of his arms against that blazer.

Just what I need, Alex thought. *For her to have a crush on some local yahoo.*

Not that she was interested in him. That, he could live with. But if she started dating someone like Greg, and he had to hear about it every day?

That was the kind of thing that drove a man to the bottle, or worse. As far as Alex was concerned, it wouldn't be a very long trip.

He just hoped he could stay sober long enough to find out who was killing women in his town, because drunk he wouldn't be worth a damn.

29

ZACHARY KLEEFELD'S DESK WAS like something from another era, a massive construction of wood with slabs of what looked like marble inlaid into it and ornate gold filigree accenting that. He kept its surface free of anything but a couple of telephones and whatever paperwork he was looking at. When he needed to use a computer, he had a separate workstation for that, in another part of an office nearly large enough for a formal ball. Where much of the black-bag budget went, Marina supposed. As long as she got hers, she wasn't about to pass judgment.

Zachary Kleefeld labored under no such restrictions. He was a master at passing judgment and not shy about letting people know it. Just now he was looking at Marina with his head tilted slightly back, brows raised, wrinkles cresting across his bald head like waves moving toward shore. His nostrils were flared and she half-expected him to snort. "What do you know about someone named Barry Wolnitz?" he asked.

"Is he a vampire?" Playing innocent, not that he was likely to buy the act.

"No, but he was the *victim* of a vampire."

"Then nothing, I guess."

"You didn't meet him when you went to Senator Harlowe's office?"

"I met a lot of people, but the senator made the biggest impression."

"Marina, we've shown Wolnitz's photograph to the crew on the airplane you took that night. We know it flew the two of you to Philadelphia. Where Wolnitz died. His body was mostly consumed by a building fire, but not entirely, and the Philadelphia police department was very disturbed by what they found in the ruins."

Marina shrugged. The truth was that she had been more shaken than she wanted to admit about Barry's death. She kept picturing his face when she closed her eyes. She hated it when her people died, but at least they knew the risks going in. They were trained to be able to handle themselves. Barry's life had been in her hands and she had screwed up. She couldn't afford such mistakes, especially not when the lives of her own people were at stake, too.

If this was conscience, maybe she could find a way to have hers surgically removed, because she didn't like it one bit.

"Okay, maybe I knew him a little. He blackmailed me into taking him along. But he made a mistake and let himself get eaten, so I left him there."

Zachary shook his head slowly. "My God. What are we supposed to do with you?"

"Well, I don't know. Do you have anyone else who's as good at finding and killing bloodsuckers?"

"You know we don't."

"How about anyone else who has an understanding with Senator Harlowe, guaranteeing continued funding with no questions asked?"

"Not that either."

"Then I guess you leave me alone and let me do my job. You could give me a raise if you wanted."

He smiled, which made his jowls jiggle like semi-inflated balloons. "Let's just leave things as is for now."

Marina started to get out of the visitor's chair. "If that's all—"

"It isn't," Zachary said. "You'll want to see this." He shoved a photograph across his desk. Marina reached for it, perused it briefly.

"That's the missing scientist," she said. "Greenbarger." He had been photographed from above, pumping gas into a pickup truck. Insects buzzing around overhead lights showed up in the picture as glowing spots.

"Larry Greenbarger, yes."

"When was this taken?"

"Two nights ago, in Little Rock, Arkansas."

Little Rock, Marina thought. The agency had been buzzing about Little Rock. "So he's alive."

"Not necessarily," Zachary corrected. "You heard about the little difficulty there the other day."

"Of course. A vampire causing havoc in the daytime. I was planning to head out there this week."

"We've determined that a household on the corner, right where the vampire went berserk, was used as a base of operations. The house's resident was found inside, dead and drained. Her credit card was used at a gas station the night before the event, but after she apparently died. When it was determined that the card had been used fraudulently, we looked at the gas station's surveillance video. He turned up, and facial-recognition software identified the presumably late Dr. Lawrence Greenbarger."

"So you think he's one of them?"

"We *know* he is. Once we had that, we went back over the victim in the house. Greenbarger's DNA, not the berserk vampire's, was found on her wounds. He sucked her dry."

"Fascinating."

"Troubling, I'd say."

"Well, that, too."

"Obviously someone's been in the house. Any sign of where he might be now?"

"Not that we've found," Zachary said. "But you might want to get out there. I don't know what the good doctor is up to, but we need him stopped."

Marina smiled. This was the kind of challenge she enjoyed.

Especially when "stopped" was a euphemism for "killed."

"I'm on it, Zach. Send me everything you've got. I'll be on the road."

"That's just where we want you, Marina," he said, dismissing her with a wave of his hand. "On the road. Please."

30

LARRY FELT LIKE HE had pushed his luck far enough in the South, for now. Little Rock was a fair-sized city, but he would feel more comfortable losing himself in the more populous northern states. He started working his way up Interstate 55, not worrying about covering much distance and leaving plenty of time to hunt, to find safe haven, and to continue his research as he went.

He had spent a couple of days at a motel in Overland Park, on the edge of Kansas City. Deeply immersed in some difficult calculations, he paid little attention when the sun went down. Hours passed, and Larry worked.

Then he achieved a satisfactory result. The answer he was looking for, or so he believed. He smiled and pushed away from the little motel desk.

He was starving.

He had been working so hard, he'd paid little attention to the demands of his body. He still had more calculations to go, to apply the answer he had just found more specifically to the problem at hand. But he needed to feed; now that he had noticed, he wouldn't be able to concentrate until he'd had his fill.

He slipped from his motel room, shutting the door quietly behind him. The motel had two buildings, at right angles, with parking in the middle. Each building had two floors.

Larry walked quietly to the other building, found the staircase next to a humming soda machine and a grinding ice machine. Condensation from window air conditioners pooled on the sidewalk. He climbed the stairs and strolled along the upper walkway, glancing at each curtained window he passed. Finally, three rooms from the end, he saw a light burning and heard the faint mutter of a television tuned to a porn channel.

Stopping in front of the door, he tapped lightly. Immediately, the rustle of sheets sounded, then feet brushing across the carpet. A man opened the door wide, wearing only red bikini briefs, gold chains around his neck and wrist, and so much cologne that Larry almost choked. He had a bottle of cheap champagne and two glasses on the nightstand. "Really?" Larry said. "I don't know who you're expecting, but wearing that?"

"Hey, fuck you, who are you?" the guy demanded. He had a deep chest but a bigger gut, arms that showed the results of occasional exercise or manual labor, and skinny legs that seemed inadequate to support his weight. His hair was curly, his face florid. He started to swing the door shut, but Larry moved into it, shoving it open again, barreling into the man at the same time and driving him back into the room.

"Look, you gotta get out of here," the guy began. "I got company coming."

Larry cut his complaint off with a hand around the man's throat. The guy made gagging sounds. His ruddy face started turning purple, his eyes bulging. Larry kept up the pressure, intensified it. The man went limp, his red briefs soaking through at the same time.

Not Larry's ideal situation, but a meal was a meal. He dragged the guy into the bathroom, put him in the tub, sliced him open and drank deep.

Partially sated, he went back into the bedroom and turned off the porn. He left the light on and sat on the edge of the bed, thinking about daylight and the Immortal Cell, trying to work out some last details while he waited for the guy's hooker to show up.

In the morning, the police knocked on his door, as they had on every other door in the motel, asking questions about the dead pair upstairs. Larry let them in and answered their questions, showing them notebooks full of complex calculations they couldn't begin to understand so they would think him an innocent, nerdy scientist. He feigned a cold, which they bought completely, remaining bundled in a blanket and holding a tissue over his nose and mouth, insisting that the curtains stay drawn. They didn't stay long. When they had left, he got online to see if he had any new correspondence. As usual, there were a few emails from people he could tell at once were phonies. A couple of them might have been from real vampires; at least, the writers seemed to understand the problems and frustrations of the night dwellers.

But one message, from someone tagged as Walkin_ Dude, struck Larry more than the rest. It was simple, straightforward, to the point. And it indicated that a group of vampires were interested in what he had to offer.

That was better than one vampire at a time. When he rolled this out, he wanted the biggest possible audience. This discovery would revolutionize the vampire world, and as a result the entire world. One vampire protected here or there from the sun was almost meaningless in the greater scheme of things—he needed to get it out to thousands. Millions, if there were that many.

Larry replied at once to Walkin_Dude. *I can help with the daylight situation. My method is new, still somewhat experimental, but will be perfected shortly. It needs to be administered face-to-face though—is that a problem?*

Through the walls, he listened to the police for a few minutes, questioning other guests, milling around the parking lot. The prevailing assumption was that the killer had followed the prostitute in, or had known somehow that she was coming. Chances that it was someone staying in the motel were remote, detectives theorized, because who would be stupid enough to do that?

Soon his computer chimed, letting him know that a message had arrived. He rushed to look. It was from Walkin_Dude. *Not a problem. I don't know where you are, but some neutral ground would be good. How about Chicago?*

Chicago would be fine, Larry wrote back. *I can be there in four nights.*

Four nights would be pushing it, but he had made a breakthrough. He thought he could synthesize the new formula over the next day or two, and then spend the next couple nights traveling. He was nearly certain he had eliminated the problem he had come to think of as sun-rage. The vampire species should be able to get the benefit of the increased strength and ferocity that sunlight could give them, but without the accompanying total loss of mental control.

If he still needed to make alterations to the formula, he could do that during the days, when he couldn't drive.

And when he got to Chicago, he would have test subjects ready and waiting.

All his efforts would soon pay off. And the things that science had not delivered to him as a human—appreciation, recognition, reward—would finally be his at last.

All he'd had to do to earn it was to die.

31

WANDA CASE HAD BEEN rude to Walker, last time he'd been to Cap'n Bligh's Fish 'n Fries. She had shafted him on onion rings, leaving the bag at least two short, a hollow shell of what it should have been. When Walker complained, she had made a fuss, sighing audibly and rolling her eyes at the people behind him in line, as if he hadn't been standing right in front of her. The moment he left the counter, he heard her bitching to her co-workers.

Mitch thought he should have said something to the manager the next day. But Walker hadn't. Instead he had let it simmer and stew, and now, four nights later, he was finally going to do something about it.

Wanda Case was going to get hers.

She worked swing shift, which was perfect. He knew her last name even though her nametag just said "Wanda," because he had asked her once, hoping it was something he could turn into a suggestive joke. Something that would rhyme with "screw," maybe. He hadn't been able to do anything with Case, but he had remembered it. Looking her up on the internet was easy—if you knew the right sites you could find ridiculous amounts of information about people, and he was able to find her address and phone number in a heartbeat. Then he searched for the restaurant, obtained its number, and called it. He asked for Wanda and was asked to wait a moment. The person answering shouted her name, hand held loosely over the receiver, so he took that as confirmation that she was working tonight and quickly hung up.

Walker and Mitch headed over to her place a little before ten. She lived fifteen minutes from the restaurant, so they had time to scope out the neighborhood. Wanda's house was small, the yard surrounded by a chain-link fence that a half-decent wind could have blown over. There was a light on over the door, but the windows were dark. Walker cruised past, went around the corner, and parked under a willow that blocked the light from the street lamps.

An unpaved alley bisected the block. The homes had gates onto the alley, and garbage cans lined it for pickup in the morning. Walker and Mitch went up the alley until they reached Wanda's place. Same pointless fence, three feet high. The backyard was in worse shape than the front; weeds had overpowered the grass and traffic had worn footpaths along the most traveled stretches, from the house to the garbage cans and there to the gate. A rusted swing set with only one swing stood on another bare patch, looking more like a historical relic than anything people still used. The lights on this side were dark, too.

The house didn't have a garage. Walker and Mitch decided to hang in back until Wanda came home, wait for her to get inside, then knock on the door while she was still getting settled. Chances were that she would open the door immediately and they could go in and take care of business. They huddled in the yard, close to the corner so neighbors wouldn't be likely to spot them. If there *were* neighbors. Except for the barking of a dog a couple of blocks away and the lingering smell of some late night smoker's cigarette, the whole area might have been deserted, the site of some sort of holocaust.

Wanda shoved through her front door and dropped her purse on the table. Her uniform was stiff and grease spattered, and she needed a shower. She came home every night smelling like grease, her fingers burned half the time, her feet aching, and she was tired of it. But it was a job, and if it didn't pay a lot, it was at least something. A lot of folks didn't even have that.

"Momma?" she called into the quiet.

A door down the hall creaked and her mother emerged, wearing a threadbare robe and old yellow slippers. Her hair had gone gray and thin, her once rich brown skin ashen. She looked old in a way that she hadn't, even five years before. "How was work?" she asked wearily.

"Fine," Wanda said. Wanda's father had been white, and her skin was lighter than her mother's. Her hair was straightened, dyed yellow. She was taller than her mother, and heavier, and she couldn't quite imagine herself ever shrinking down and graying to that extent. But she was only twenty-three. Her mother had put off having children until she was in her midthirties, and Wanda had been the fourth and last. Those four kids, she thought, were the reason for her mother's dramatic aging. Not a problem she ever wanted to have. "You know, it was work."

Wanda was about to say something else when there was an insistent knock at the door. This late? Sometimes Suzette from next door came over after work with a bit of neighborhood gossip she couldn't wait to share.

"I'm going back to bed," Momma said.

"Goodnight, Momma." Wanda went to get the door. She glanced through the peephole, sleepy and expecting Suzette, but it was some white man she didn't know. She tensed and took another look, and then she knew who it was. Onion Ring Boy?! He had come to the restaurant off and on for months, and he always stared at her boobs and tried to act cool. What the fuck was this?

She yanked the door open. "What the hell you doin' here?" she asked him. "Don't you—"

And then she saw the razor.

"Shut up, Wanda," Walker said, already pushing in against her, raising the blade toward her throat.

"Just shut up and get inside. We won't take long, I promise."

Wanda took a couple of steps back, a reflex action, but that was enough. Walker and Mitch drove forward, using her own momentum to propel her back. Her mouth was working but no sound came out, which was just fine. Once the door was closed, Walker hooked a leg behind hers and swept it forward, pushing her chest at the same time. Already scared, she went down on the floor. He followed, putting enough weight on her to keep her off balance while he raked the razor across her throat. She managed one strangled cry before he slammed his hand against her chin, pushing her head back.

And for the first time—it had been coming for a while but he hadn't made the leap, not until he was here with Wanda, Wanda who he was angry with, Wanda who still smelled like the kitchen of Cap'n Bligh's—he lowered his mouth to the gash he had made, where blood bubbled up like water from a natural spring, and he closed his mouth on it and he drank, right from the source.

Someone screamed.

"She saw you, man!" Mitch said.

Walker looked up from Wanda (blood spilling from his open mouth, coating his chin, spattering his shirt) and saw an old black woman in a tattered robe glaring at him, eyes wide, fists clasped in front of her chest.

"I'm calling the police!" she cried.

"Walker, you gotta do her, too!"

"Shut up, dude! No names!" The name didn't matter, though; Mitch was right. She had witnessed him slicing Wanda open and feasting on her blood.

He had never killed an old lady, and he hadn't planned to start. The point of the killing he had done was to become a vampire, and he had mostly killed women he found somewhat attractive, figuring there was something intimate about drinking their blood. With his mouth on Wanda's neck, one arm pressed against her pillowy breasts, her body still warm and writhing in his grasp, he had been growing aroused.

But the old lady was backing toward an open doorway, and if there was a phone in there, then he and Mitch were only a 911 call away from serious trouble.

"What do we do, Mitch?" he asked/

"You know, Walker."

"No, what? What? It's an old lady."

"So what?"

"I can't do an old lady, man. I can't."

"Walker, she can ID us."

"I don't care!"

"You have to!"

"Why me? Why is it always me?" Walker cried.

"You have the razor, your prints are all over it, and you're soaked in blood. What's the difference between one and two?"

Walker heaved a sigh, extricated himself from

Wanda, and covered the space between them in three big steps. The lady had turned away, shuffling as fast as she could and spewing an obscenity-laden tirade at them as she did. Walker caught her bony shoulder in one hand and spun her around. He pressed her up against the wall, leaning into her with a forearm. She rained ineffectual blows down on him with her thin fists.

"I'm really sorry," he mumbled.

She spat in his face.

He shifted his forearm so it was against her larynx, crushing it. He didn't want to open her, to bleed her. That was special.

He closed his eyes so he didn't have to see the hate in hers, and he held her there until her hands fell to her sides and her feet stopped stamping and kicking, and then he held her a little longer just to be sure. When he looked again, her eyes were wide open, her face purplish, mouth sagging, bloody flecks at its sides. He let her flop to the floor, but he didn't drink, not this time, not from her.

He did, it seemed, have his limits after all.

32

WALKER COULD BARELY SEE to drive home, his eyes burning with grief and rage, his grip weak on the wheel. They made it somehow, parked the van inside the garage, and then he sat there for a couple of minutes before he had the strength to open his door and walk into the house.

"What have we done?" he asked Mitch when they were inside. "An old lady! That's not what we talked about."

"I know," Mitch said. "But we didn't have a choice, did we?"

Walker collapsed onto his old butt-sprung sofa and buried his face in his hands. He hated being like this in front of Mitch, whining like some kind of pussy, but he couldn't make himself stop. It was as if all the murders had been building up inside him like stomach bile, and now they were spewing uncontrollably out of him.

The whole idea might have been stupid from the start. If vampires were looking for them, they didn't know it. And they had covered their tracks well enough that he didn't know how a vampire was actually supposed to find them. The cops were definitely looking for them, though—the news was eating up their murders with a spoon, a rich, juicy story the likes of which usually involved Chicago politicians.

Mitch put a hand on his shoulder, squeezing hard. "It's gonna be okay, man. We'll meet that guy with the 'Light of Day' ad and he'll turn us, and then we'll leave this fucked-up life behind for good."

Walker sniffed and swallowed, rubbed his eyes and looked over at Mitch. "But . . . what if he's pissed off when he finds out we're not really undead? What if he just decides to kill us instead of turning us?"

"One way or another," Mitch said with a shrug.

"He'll see we're sincere, right? That we really want this?"

"Couldn't say. I hope so. But who knows how a vampire's mind works?"

"But . . . if we did all this for nothing . . . I don't think I could live with that."

"All we can do is try, Walker. Like I said, one way or another it'll be settled when we meet the guy. If he kills us or turns us. Out is out, right? Done is done."

"I guess so."

"I'm telling you. Done is done."

Marina and her team landed in Little Rock, where the local cops showed them what they had on the broad-daylight vampire incident. Some citizens had captured bits and pieces of it on mobile phone cameras, and of course when the police arrived their cameras captured the end of it. They had managed to convince the press to call it a case of a drug-maddened murderer, without releasing the more inexplicable elements of it.

When she saw the footage, though, both from the police and the confiscated phones, she knew that the initial reports had been correct. The guy had been a vampire, no doubt about it, and he had been out in daylight without experiencing the traditional spontaneous combustion.

She was sitting in the police captain's office. He had all the furniture in the room shoved up against the walls, as if he needed the space in the middle clear as a dance floor. He was sitting at his desk, while Marina had a stiff-backed chair next to it instead of facing it. Tony O. leaned against the wall in a vacant spot, as silent and blank as an empty file cabinet. The others waited in a sitting area in front.

The police captain wore an old-fashioned aftershave that reminded Marina of her maternal grandfather, who had worked for most of his life in a Georgia train station. The captain was a lean, sad-faced man with thick gray hair and slumping shoulders. Every time she looked at him she expected him to burst out in tears. Then again, considering what he'd had to witness, he might have been entitled to.

"You've got to bury this footage," she said. "Bury it deep."

"So you do think it's really a—"

"I couldn't say."

"I read the news, of course. Like everyone else. The controversy—"

"Look," Marina said. "Vampires aren't real. You saw what you saw, but there's a perfectly legitimate explanation for it. You saw the guy's tox screen, right?" Red-Blooded's "community relations" people had made sure it showed ridiculous amounts of drugs in the man's system.

"Yes. But I saw the house, too. That poor woman . . ."

"I know. People can be sickos, no doubt about it. Especially hard-core drug users." Marina shook her head sadly, a sorrow not entirely faked. Marina had seen that too—the woman whose house had been used as a base, and whose stolen credit card had triggered the search that had revealed Larry Greenbarger as the thief.

Greenbarger had been inside the house. He had some connection, then, with the bloodsucker who had run amuck in the street.

What that connection was, she couldn't be sure. The house didn't look like it had been occupied by a whole den. Maybe the two of them had just met somehow and stuck together. That is, until one of them had figured out that he could go out in the sun.

That explanation would have been more convincing if Marina didn't know that Larry had been an Operation Red-Blooded scientist, a researcher whose field of study was vampire physiology.

Evolution could, she supposed, account for the unknown bloodsucker's newfound talent. But she didn't believe that for a minute. No, Larry Greenbarger had definitely been turned, and he was up to something.

Whatever it was, Marina was determined to stop him. She had never liked the guy anyway, and the whole being undead thing just aggravated the hell out of her.

33

"ROCCO, BABY," SHILOH SAID.

Rocco glanced over and saw her sitting cross-legged on the floor with a laptop braced on her thighs. "Yeah?"

"Look at this here."

Rocco eased down off a display case and went to her side. "What?"

"This website posting."

He suppressed a sigh. Shiloh loved hanging out in vampire chat rooms, and he had drummed into her over and over, like she was some fourth-grader, how important it was not to give away any information that the authorities could use to find them. He believed she was being careful, but so far she had never reported learning anything useful, just a lot of stupid arguments, flame wars, and soap opera–worthy nonsense that he couldn't imagine helped anyone.

"What?" he asked again. Love was a human emotion, not something to which he was susceptible, but he couldn't deny a certain fondness toward Shiloh. She could get away with just about anything around him, and he always forgave her.

"Just look."

He read the text above her finger. "Do you yearn to walk in the Light of Day? To feel the sun without peril? It can happen. I can help you come out of the night."

"What about it?" he asked.

"Don't you think it's, I don't know, interesting?"

"I think it's bogus."

"Why, babe?"

"It's a crock. We can't go out in the sun. It's someone trying to get us to fry ourselves."

"But what if it's not?" She gazed at him with puppy dog eyes, like she could will him into believing just because she did.

"If it's not, if it's for real, then . . ." Rocco paused to give himself a few seconds to think it over. "Then it changes everything."

"You really think so?"

"Absolutely. Without the sun holding us back, we win. The end. We're stronger than the meat, smarter, faster. Without the sun keeping us at bay, then human dominion is at an end."

"That's kinda what I was thinking. Pretty sweet, huh?"

"*If* it's real, Shiloh."

"I think it is."

"Why?"

"I don't know. Just a feeling. Intuition, whatever. But I believe it."

Rocco folded his arms and leaned back against the wall. Other members of the den were watching them now. Probably waiting to see what he would say. He was the undisputed leader, and they all looked to him for guidance on issues large and small, even the new members they had taken on: Chip, Ciara, Kenton, Nightmare, and Angel and Dragon Lady, who was physically stuck at twelve years old, but had been for most of the century. This was probably one of those small issues, but if it was real—and he could barely wrap his mind around that possibility—if it *was,* then it wasn't even large, it was huge. As big as they came.

And yet, why would someone post that just for a goof? It wasn't like he or she was asking vampires to hold their hands to the computer screen to be blessed, and then run outside.

"Write back," he said after a while. "See what it's all about."

"Seriously?"

"Sure, why not. If it's some sort of scam, we'll know when we get an answer. If it's for real . . . then like I said, it changes the whole game."

Shiloh graced him with her happiest smile, showing plenty of bloodstained teeth.

A reply came within the hour. Shiloh squealed, waking Rocco, who had drifted off with his head against her hip. "What is it?"

"It's from Light of Day," she said.

"Who?"

"That's what he calls himself. Or his email address, whatever. Light of Day."

Rocco realized what she meant. "Oh, okay. What's it say?"

"He says he's meeting a den in Chicago in a couple of days. It's kind of a test, he says, and he's willing to meet with more while he's there."

Rocco knew a den in Chicago, one that had been formed by a onetime friend called Lucky Strike. As far as he knew, it was the only active den in that city, or at least the biggest, with seventeen members, last he'd heard.

But those in Chicago were on the opposite side of the philosophical divide. They believed vampires were best off staying in the shadows, remaining feared creatures of legend, rather than declaring all-out war against humanity. Maybe they would see the value of what seemed to be on offer, but Rocco didn't think so. Coming into the light was the antithesis of what they wanted—the ability to do so would naturally lead to the desire. That would blow the mythological quality they were after.

"I don't know who he's talking about," Rocco said. "But get back to him and see if you can find out when and where they're meeting. Tell him we'd love to be test subjects, too, only we're going to have to leave tonight to get there in time."

"I'll let him know, Rocco."

"Good." He figured Shiloh would get the information he wanted—he knew from experience that it could be hard to resist a full-on Shiloh charm offensive. He very much wanted to learn what this Light of Day business was all about. If it was real, he wanted to be in on the ground floor. When the ultimate war with the humans finally began, the struggle for *nosferatu* supremacy would be right on its heels, and something like this could provide an important edge.

And he *really* wanted to know who this Chicago den was.

34

Larry Greenbarger's trail led to Kansas City, east to St. Louis, and then northward, through Springfield and Bloomington. He had eluded everyone for longer than expected, but once they knew his pattern he was as easy to track as if he had been tagging his name on walls with pink Day-Glo spray paint. He took a victim, fed, stole whatever cash he could get. Sometimes he spent a day in that victim's home, other times he used the cash or a stolen credit card to pay for motel rooms and gas. By following the credit cards taken from drained victims, Marina and her team stayed just a step behind him.

A glance at the map showed a possible destination of Chicago. A phone call from Zachary Kleefeld confirmed it.

They were in a van with Jimbo at the wheel, having just left a scene near Decatur. Marina rode in back, between Tony O. and Kat. The landscape was flat, with trees cutting the sunlight into jagged slices that flashed across the windshield. Quarters were cramped, especially with all the gear they carried, but she wanted to be on the ground and ready for action. The air conditioner blew hard but couldn't erase the male sweat and testosterone as thick as smoke inside the vehicle. The group was smaller than it had been before the massacre at Nags Head, but no less determined.

Marina was more resolute than ever. She had put Barry Wolnitz in danger and had lost him. Then she'd made bad decisions about how to handle the North Carolina situation, and had lost two more of her own. From now on she would carry the memories of all those lost with her, and every vampire she met would have to answer for them.

"Fuckin' bankers, man," Monte was saying. "Oughta cut us loose from chasin' bloodsuckers for a couple days, let us go to town upside some bankers' heads for the shit they pulled. Only difference is the bankers and shit are suckin' everybody's blood at once, not just one at a time."

"I'd do that job for free," Tony O. said. "Marina, you think we could get unpaid leave for that?"

"Hard to say. Maybe. I don't think anybody much loves those guys right now."

"Shit, one of their annual bonuses would set me up for life," Monte went on. "Taxpayers have to pay those motherfuckers that kind of bonus, they could just pay me one and I wouldn't trouble 'em no more."

"The taxpayers are paying you, Monte," Kat said. "Anyway, you're just pissed because it turns out bankers and stockbrokers are better thieves than you ever were."

Everybody laughed at that. The financial sector had come under a lot of verbal fire from Marina's team lately. Considering their own greatest contribution to society came in the form of pulling triggers and kicking in doors, Marina didn't think they had a lot of room to complain, notwithstanding the fact that she was just as angry at the ones who had thrown a giant boulder through the economy's fragile plate glass walls as they were.

She was about to say something to that effect when her phone rang. She looked at it and saw Kleefeld's name on the screen. "Shut up, everyone," she said. Then she flipped it open. "What's up, Zach?"

"We've been intercepting some interesting email traffic lately," he said.

"What have you heard?"

"I think our boy Greenbarger has something going on."

"Seems that way from here. Do you have anything specific?"

"He's been posting ads online offering vampires the ability to go out in the sunlight."

"Like that one in Little Rock?"

"Exactly."

"He getting any takers?"

The van made a tight corner and Marina slid over so her thighs brushed against Kat's. She gave the other woman a smile, then scooted away.

"Yes. He's got a meet set for tomorrow night in Chicago."

"I figured that's where he was headed. Who's he meeting?"

"Looks like some bloodsuckers near the area, and then another set coming in from New York."

"Sounds big."

"It could be."

"Is there any progress on figuring out what was done to the one from Little Rock?"

"They're still studying him," Zachary said. "But given the fact that we've placed Greenbarger at the scene, I think it's safe to say that he was involved. Maybe that one was a test subject, someone he found in person instead of online."

"Makes sense. Do you have a location yet for the Chicago meet?"

"Not yet, but we will soon."

"We're not too far away, so we can definitely be on the scene."

"I'm counting on it, Marina."

After she ended the call, she briefed the others in the van about what Zachary had told her. "So head for Chicago, Jimbo," she said. "That's where Larry's going, or maybe he's already there."

"Chicago it is, boss."

"There's a good steakhouse there," Monte said.

"You like your meat bloody?" Jimbo asked.

"I don't like it attached to a man," Monte said.

"Maybe you just haven't tried the right cut."

The others laughed, and Monte turned red around

the neck and ears. Talk turned to what they would do once they found Greenbarger and the other vampires. Bullshitting about physical violence against white-collar finance types was over for the moment, and Marina was glad. She didn't like bankers any more than the others did, but she wanted her people to focus on the undead. Personally, she wanted to focus on the business at hand—Larry's actions felt like a betrayal, and one she wanted to avenge. For all the unexpected qualms of conscience she'd been having lately, one thing hadn't changed—bloodsuckers and those who supported them had to die, and she felt fine about that end of it.

She hoped she could make her vengeance drawn-out and painful, so Larry would really have time to under-stand that you don't fuck with Marina Tanaka-Dunn. Not unless you're invited to.

35

BEING INSIDE THE CASE HOUSE made Alex physically ill. His stomach churned and complained, and once he had to step outside and spit hot bile into the yard. He hoped he wasn't contaminating any evidence.

Greg Fielding and Larissa were still inside, walking through the scene again and again, trying on different scenarios for how it might have all gone down.

Alex spat once more, took some gum from his pocket, unwrapped a stick and shoved it into his mouth. He didn't like gum, but he kept some on hand for just such occasions, and because it was sometimes a handy icebreaker to offer to a witness or a suspect. Chewing hard, tasting a blast of spearmint, he took a last breath of fresh air and went back in.

They were still at it, rehashing events with all the enthusiasm of football fans running down the winning plays of the big game. ". . . did the mother last," Greg was saying. "Because she wouldn't have been able to put up much of a fight."

"Yeah, I'm sure the killer took out Wanda first, then her mom," Larissa said. "Boom boom."

"Are we sure it's the same guy?" Alex asked. "He's

always picked single victims before, never a household."

"Serials can escalate, right?" Greg replied. "Anyway, Wanda's been drained. That's a pretty good sign that it's our so-called vampire."

"She fits the profile in every other way, and so does the approach," Larissa said. "Maybe he didn't know there would be anyone else here. Or maybe like Greg said, he's escalating. Just taking one life isn't good enough anymore. It's become old hat, not the thrill it once was."

"Could be," Alex admitted. "I'll feel better if we can find some fingerprints or DNA matching the earlier crime scenes, though."

Larissa met Greg's gaze and did an eye roll. She didn't think Alex could see, but he did. "I know," Alex said. "I know how you feel about DNA, but hell, fingerprints? That's old-time police work, isn't it? The kind you're okay with?"

"I'm okay with anything that scrapes the scum off the street, Alex," Larissa said. "But you know we haven't found anything useful at those earlier scenes. Plenty of prints and DNA, but no match to anybody we've been able to find."

"That doesn't mean we can't match one scene to another," Alex said. "Then at least we'd know if we're looking for the same guy here, or someone else altogether."

"Same guy," Greg said. "I can feel it."

"You've . . ." Alex let the sentence trail off, unfinished. Greg had only been to one of the other scenes, the one in Tinley Park. He hadn't seen the ones in the city, or the other suburban ones. Any gut instincts he had on this one were based on almost zero evidence.

But Larissa regarded him like he was some sort of cop genius, a badged Da Vinci.

As if her worshipful gaze wasn't enough, she said, "I think you're right, Greg." She might as well have been shucking her top and sliding down her pants.

"I'm going to talk to the neighbors," Alex said. "See if maybe somebody saw something."

"Okay," Greg said. "Good idea."

Obvious idea, anyway. But Alex wanted to be out of the house, and away from Larissa and Greg before they started holding hands or something.

He went to the house directly across the street first. Lights burned inside and he had seen someone at a window looking out at the emergency vehicles when he had arrived. Those had mostly gone away now; a coroner's bus waited to take the bodies away, and there were a couple of squad cars parked outside, along with the unmarked he and Larissa had driven down from Chicago.

He rang the doorbell, waited a minute, punched it again. Moths whirled around a light fixture above the button. A man pulled open the inner door and stared at him through the screen. He was African-American, maybe fifty, stocky with short gray hair and an expression of distrust. "Yeah?"

Alex showed him a badge and jerked a thumb toward the Case home. "You know what happened over there tonight?"

"Someone killed 'em?"

"That's right. You know them?"

The man shrugged. "Some. Not well. We stick to ourselves mostly, they did the same."

"Still," Alex said. "You're neighbors. What happened over there . . . could just as easily have been here, right?"

"I guess. Maybe."

"So let me ask . . . did you see anything tonight? Anything at all unusual, out of the ordinary?"

"I . . . don't know."

"Well, did you or didn't you? It's a pretty simple question, isn't it?"

"Well, some people think the visitors are unusual, but you know, if you know how to watch for 'em you see 'em all the time."

"The visitors?"

"From the Pleiades."

"Like, UFOs?"

"Only that assumes they're unidentified. It's more like they're illegal aliens—they got no papers but it's no big secret where they come from."

"And you saw these . . . aliens from the Pleiades across the street tonight."

The man nodded, and even through the screen door Alex could see the liquid glint of madness in his eyes. "They hover over that house all the time. That's why I keep my family away from there."

"I see."

"You think I'm nuts."

"Did I say that?"

"Any time someone like you says 'I see,' that's what they mean."

The man was right, and there was no way Alex could see to extricate himself with any grace. "I'm sorry if I gave you that impression," Alex said. "But the fact is, I don't have jurisdiction over residents of the Pleiades, so I may have to put this down as unsolved."

"Wish I could help you more," the man said.

"Yeah, me too." Alex started backing away from the door. "Thanks for your time, though."

"Glad to," the man said, beginning to push the inner door closed. "Watch out on the next new moon— that's going to be a very active time for them!"

"Thank you, sir. I'll keep that in mind."

After the door had closed, Alex walked back across the street to try the houses on either side of Wanda Case's. This was the kind of cop work Larissa loved: canvassing the neighborhood, wearing out shoe leather, going one on one with the citizenry. So why was she inside the house, presumably examining forensic evidence, while he was out here?

Because he was weak, that was the only answer

he could come up with. Because he couldn't tell Larissa how he felt about her—he'd hinted at it, tried to
demonstrate it, but he couldn't just come out and say
it. And since she had developed her instant crush on
Greg Fielding, he had hardly been able to talk to her
at all. He ought to be brave enough to either say what
he thought or turn his back and let her find happiness
with Greg or someone else, if she could. Instead, he
swallowed his pain and tried to hide.

He went to the next house, blinked, and rang the
doorbell.

"I might have something," Alex announced when he
walked back through Wanda Case's front door. The
coroner's people had been taking a body out, and he
had to wait outside while their gurney passed through.
He swallowed, tasting bile again. He was going to have
to see a doctor one of these days, see if the burning in
his gut meant ulcers.

"What?" Larissa asked. She came down the hallway,
from the direction where the mother's body had been.
Greg followed. Alex couldn't help looking for signs
that they had been fooling around—makeup smeared,
clothing out of place. He didn't see anything.

"Well, discounting invaders from the Pleiades,
someone around the corner . . ." He checked his notepad. ". . . Mrs. Williams, saw a white van parked there
during the evening. For a couple of hours, she said. She
noticed it because her husband drives the same kind of

van, for his locksmithing business, and at first glance she thought it was his and wondered why it would be parked where it was. Then she realized it wasn't his, but it also wasn't a vehicle she had ever seen in the neighborhood. The longer it sat there, the more notice she took."

"She get a plate?" Greg asked.

"Just a partial. She only remembers the letters DMP because her daughter is Darla MeShelle." He had to check the notes again to confirm the spelling. "I've already called it in, waiting on a call back."

"Do vampires travel in vans?" Greg asked.

"I guess they'd have to get around somehow," Alex said. "If they were real."

"All I'm saying is, I've been thinking. I mean, we all heard about that Bureau guy, and what he said about them. That they're real and all."

"And the Bureau said he went nuts and murdered his own family, then became some sort of loner wack job living off in the Alaskan wilderness. I don't put much stock in what he said." He glanced at Larissa, as if for confirmation. Greg was sounding as nuts as the Pleiades guy. "*We* don't."

"Alex is right," she said, backing him up. "We've basically discounted that theory. But Greg's right, too, Alex . . . we keep finding bodies that have been partially or largely drained of blood. That's not natural. What if we're ignoring an important possibility because we don't believe in it?"

"I suppose that's possible," Alex said. "But then, what if it's the Wolf Man? Or a ghost? If we start down that road, where do we draw the line?"

Greg's jaw was tight as piano wire and his hands were curling into fists. Alex didn't want to let him push Larissa into accepting impossibilities, since it would only make everyone's work harder. He had to keep up the pressure, and just hoped it wouldn't make Greg attack him.

"It's not like you haven't heard other rumors," Greg said. "I mean, you're a big-city detective and all. You've heard about those attacks in Barrow. That woman sheriff from there who wrote a book about it and was the center of some big crisis in L.A. There've been plenty of stories."

"I've heard them," Alex countered. "And the same names keep coming up, when you get any actual details at all. Andy Gray is one of them. The Olemaun woman who wrote that book, and wanted to sell copies, is another. I've heard a lot of stories about Bigfoot and the Loch Ness Monster, too, but people have been trying to find them for years without any luck. That's because there's real life, and science, and there's storybook nonsense, and I'm not going to go into an investigation looking for the storybook crap because that's the best way to make sure you never get anywhere. We need to stick with the *real* leads. We have a vehicle description and a partial plate, and that's what I plan to focus on."

"Well, I think Greg might be on to something," Larissa said. She had read the situation, kept her distance from the two men equal, made sure her hands were raised toward both. Playing peacemaker, even as she took Greg's side. "Discounting any possibility is dangerous. Bodies keep piling up, and we've got to keep our minds open."

Alex was about to answer when his phone rang. He flipped open his notepad to an empty page, clicked his ballpoint pen, and tucked the phone between cheek and shoulder. "Ziccaria," he said. "You got the scoop on that plate?"

As he listened, he wrote down the information, pressing hard on the paper as if he could force the other two cops to trust him through sheer will.

He doubted it would work. But with them or without, he would follow through on this, their first real potential lead, and he would bring an end to all this vampire nonsense. Maybe this was even the edge he needed—if he could prove to Larissa that Greg Fielding was a nut case, he could shake Larissa's crush on him.

He wasn't sure which would give him more satisfaction, that, or cracking this case at last. Doing both at once, though, would be good. And doing it before another half-dozen blood-drained corpses showed up? That would be the best of all.

36

THEY MADE YOUNGSTOWN THE first night, most of the den sloshing around in the back of an RV, Rocco, Shiloh, and Angel in the cab. They all holed up inside that day, curtains drawn against the offending sun. But when night fell again, they were hungry and cooped up and had to run and stretch before the next leg of the trip.

Rocco made everyone stay put while he drove around looking for a good spot to play. He settled on a sad little enclosed mall on the city's fringe. Blank spots on the walls showed where signs had once been, but few remained, and some of those were unlit, indicating that they'd be coming down soon. Clusters of vehicles huddled near the entrances, though, so the place wasn't entirely deserted.

Rocco parked the RV near the food court entrance. "Okay, folks," he said. "There are multiple exits, and people in stores with land lines and cell phones. We're not going to be able to stay for long. But after we're gone, they'll be talking about us for a long time."

"Let's do it!" Goldie called from in back. "I'm starvin'!"

"What are you waiting for?" Rocco replied. "Get in there and make a mess!"

The back door opened and *nosferatu* poured out, screeching and howling and hollering. They dashed across the parking lot and through the double glass doors. Shiloh grabbed Rocco's hand and held it all the way in, laughing and letting out an occasional whoop. They were the last ones inside, Rocco watching all the way in to make sure no one observed them until they made it in. The mall's air-conditioning wrapped them in a chill as soon as they cleared the doorway.

Panic had already started. The food court wasn't crowded, but there were a few diners there, and people staffing seven of the eleven restaurant spaces. The vampires had charged into the court and spread out quickly. Over the aroma of greasy food and the screams of the humans, Rocco smelled spilled blood and heard the satisfied gnawing of his kind. Pride filled him, the pride of a father watching his kid graduate from college or of a business owner seeing his enterprise succeed. He looked upon the carnage, and he smiled.

Maryann Choi didn't *love* her job—she didn't know how one could love working at a struggling shoe store in a failing mall—but she didn't hate it, either. Yes, people's feet sometimes stank, and some of them didn't want to accept their real sizes, or wanted to wear shoes because of the style regardless of whether or not they fit correctly. Customers could be brusque, rude, even downright nasty. But sometimes they were pleasant, nice, appreciative of Maryann's efforts, and those were the ones who made the job more than simply bearable.

The past six months had been the worst she had ever seen at Shuckey's Shoes. People had been let go one at a time, to the point that for the last half of her shift, after five, she worked alone. That meant if she wanted anything to eat after that she had to have it in the store with her and wolf it down during slow periods—which, unfortunately, were all too common—or she had to lock the store while she went to the food court. Even there, the options were getting more limited all the time. Just last week the A&W had closed, and she heard the Subway might be next.

She had just been turning the corner, past the jewelry store that had been there forever until two months ago, when she heard the raucous crowd rushing toward the food court door. For an instant, it sounded like a bunch of kids from the high school she had graduated from two years earlier. But school was out for the summer, so it wouldn't be the football team or anything like that. Maybe summer school kids?

Whatever it was, she wanted no part of it. High school had been a bad time for her—so bad that she had decided to take a couple of years off before starting community college or a trade school, in hopes that nobody she had known would be in attendance. Her parents had hated that; they believed in education, the more of it the better, and still harbored hopes that

Maryann would become a doctor, or at the very least would marry one. She still knew people at the school, and she hated when they happened into the shoe store; if they were part of this crowd she didn't want to be seen.

She froze there at the corner and watched them come in.

They didn't look like high school students. Nor did they act like them—not even at their worst. They charged into the food court, slamming back the doors so hard Maryann was surprised they didn't shatter. Some of them wore rags, others black leathers, others jeans and T-shirts and heavy boots. They were varying ages, which was strange—usually one didn't see old people screaming and laughing along with kids, and certainly not in such an aggressive manner.

Maryann took a step back, then another, watching through the corner store's double layers of window. When one of the newcomers jumped onto the counter at Sbarro, she was shocked. When that newcomer, a middle-aged blond woman, reached out and tore off most of the face of Janis, the Sbarro cashier who gave Maryann her mall discount without ever having to be reminded, she was terrified.

Fighting back the urge to vomit, Maryann ran back to Shuckey's. Her hands were quaking so much she could barely get the keys from her pocket, and then she dropped them on the floor. They fell with a loud clatter, but no one at the food court would have been able to hear it because there was too much screaming going on there now.

The people—the gang, Maryann thought, that's what this had to be, some sort of gang deal—who had attacked must have been killing everyone there, showing no mercy, no humanity, really.

Maryann scraped up the keys and found the right one, shoved it into the lock, and turned it. The bolt slid back with a click. She pushed on the glass door, accordioning it back just far enough to slip inside. The store was brightly lit, with everything in its place—she'd had plenty of time that evening to straighten up, and few customers to hamper her efforts. Shoes on podiums, shoes on shelves, boxes stacked beneath display counters . . . it was lovely, but it felt very open, very exposed. She hurried in, closed the door behind her and locked it again, leaving the keys hanging in the lock.

She ran through the store to the back room, where the light switches were, hoping that whatever was going on in the food court was keeping the gang occupied so they wouldn't notice a brightly lit shop suddenly going dark. She swiped her open palm down over the switches and the lights went off, except for the emergency light mounted high on one wall that always came on when the others were out.

In the semi-darkness, she upended her purse on the floor. Everything came out, and she pawed her phone away from the other things and snatched it up. She dialed 911, hoping she would have a voice when someone answered. She felt like terror was shutting her body down, bit by bit—like the darkness was really just her vision failing, and the fact that the screams had diminished was not because she had shut out the noise when she closed the door, but because deafness was overtaking her. The pounding of her heart was like a sprinter's footfalls, and she knew that fear-spawned adrenaline was coursing through her but didn't feel like it gave her any strength. She could barely manage to hold the tiny phone to her ear.

"Nine-one-one, what's your emergency?" a voice asked with startling suddenness. Maryann hadn't even heard it ring.

When she spoke, her voice had a quiver she hadn't heard in years, although it had been fairly common her first years of high school. "I'm at the mall, and—"

A banging sounded at the door. "Oh God!" Maryann shrieked.

"Hello?" the 911 operator said. "Are you there, ma'am?"

"Yeah, I'm . . . hold on." Maryann shifted her position so she could peek out the back room door and up the store's central aisle. The banging continued, and Maryann saw Saleem Jennings, her friend from the Pro Sports sporting goods store across the way, his palms beating on the glass, evident terror etched on his face. People thought Saleem was gay, because he dressed nicely and was a little effeminate, but she had gone out with him a couple of times and knew he wasn't.

All he looked now was scared.

"Ma'am, what's your emergency, please? Are you still there?"

Maryann had almost forgotten about the phone in her hand. "Yes. Yes, I'm here, it's just that my friend Saleem—"

"Has he had an accident?"

"No, it isn't that. It's . . . someone's attacking the mall, killing people I think."

"There's a shooter at the mall?"

"No, not a shooter. It's—"

Maryann paused, waving to Saleem with her free hand. He saw her, and she expected relief to show on his face. It didn't.

If anything, his fear grew and he pounded on the glass with new ferocity. His mouth worked but Maryann couldn't hear anything he was saying. Tears streaked his face and saliva glistened on his chin.

"Please, ma'am, tell me what's going on," the operator said.

"It's—hang on, I have to get the door."

"If there's a shooter, you should stay out of sight, and keep the door locked if you can."

"It's not a shooter! Saleem's out there, and I have to let him in."

She was halfway to the door when they came.

Saleem must have heard their approach, because his eyes went wide and his mouth opened in a scream that the glass only partly muffled, and then he turned away from the door like he was going to run.

But he didn't have a chance, because two of them caught him there (one looked like a child, no more than eleven or twelve, the other a biker type with a gray beard and ponytail). The child grabbed Saleem around the hips and slammed him up against the store's display window. Maryann thought for a second that he would go right through the glass, but he just crashed into it and blood spurted from his nose, and then the biker guy had a hand caught in Saleem's hair and he shoved Saleem's face into the window over and over. Blood smeared the window with a thick red film.

Maryann uttered a strangled cry and dropped the phone. The operator's voice came through, sounding very far away. Much too far to help.

The biker guy yanked Saleem's head backward. He must have snapped Saleem's neck, because suddenly his body went limp in the man's hands. The biker lowered his head to Saleem's broken neck, and the little girl—and this was the worst part, the worst thing Maryann had ever seen, the part that made her lose control of her bladder and soak the snug black pants she was wearing—the little girl pressed herself against the window and a snakelike tongue emerged from inside a mouth bristling with teeth and lapped the blood hungrily from the glass.

Maryann screamed then, screamed good and loud, a cry of pure horror.

And the little girl heard her, sucked that monstrous tongue back into her mouth, stared through the glass, and saw Maryann standing there in the middle of the store, illuminated by the emergency light.

She said something to the biker. The biker replied. Maryann couldn't hear them, but she got the gist of it.

Had there been any doubt, it would have vanished when the biker guy used Saleem's body to smash through the window. He left Saleem there, draped over the glass, and used him like a carpet to walk inside the store. The little girl followed. Maryann was rooted to the spot.

She couldn't make her legs work until they were just feet away, and by then it was too late. They closed the distance in seconds, and then Maryann learned what terror really was, terror and pain, and they both stayed with her until the moment she died.

"Let's go, everyone! Move out!"

Rocco had given them five minutes. The authorities would be on the way, and he didn't want full-scale war. Not yet. Not tonight. They had to get out now, while they could make a clean escape.

Shiloh was curled over a young woman who had been working in a mobile phone kiosk. Rocco had seen her briefly at the beginning—short dark hair, nice build, glasses, kind of Goth-looking but not too much. He had been interested in her himself, but Shiloh had been positively smitten so he'd let her have the girl.

Now he shook Shiloh's shoulder. "Babe, we have to boogie."

Shiloh looked up at him with sad eyes and ran the back of her hand across the crimson slash of her mouth. "I'm not finished yet!"

"Yes you are. It's time." He closed his fingers on her shoulder, drawing her to her feet. "Come on."

She went along, reluctant but ultimately obedient. One of the things he appreciated about her. He clapped his hands, whistled, and called out for the others again. Finally, they all came. The mall was a wreck of shattered windows, overturned benches and trash cans, and bloody corpses.

They left it all behind, running back to the RV. When they piled in, they brought the scent of carnage with them, the steely bite of fresh blood, and they were laughing, happy, fed.

Rocco's children.

As he drove away, police cars barreling past, pride swelled his chest, and he squeezed Shiloh's hand and knew the world waited to hear more from him.

Very soon, it would hear plenty.

37

LARRY GREENBARGER STOOD HALFWAY across the Michigan Avenue Bridge, looking down at the dark water of the Chicago River. Moonlight sparkled on the surface in spots, and the lights of nearby high-rises, but most of it was black. It was, he thought, like peering into a vein as it carried blood through the body, bringing oxygen, nutrients, and life. A breeze off the water touched his face like cool, fast-moving fingertips.

He had been to Chicago a couple of times, as a human. He had enjoyed the Field Museum of Natural History, Shedd Aquarium, and especially Adler Planetarium, at which he never failed to learn something about the universe that he hadn't known before.

It was a different city now, or *he* was different, or both. Museums and the like were mostly off-limits to him now, and meaningless anyway. His intellectual pursuits had narrowed in focus. He no longer cared about the world humans inhabited and how they related to it, except to the extent that a rancher might be interested in environmental sciences so he could maximize the output of his grazing lands. When he passed people on the sidewalks, he no longer felt the comfort of familiarity he once might have, or that tingle of fear, never knowing if this one or that might secretly harbor a knife or gun and homicidal thoughts. All he thought was that they were meat, beneath him, and should be showing more respect.

They would, soon enough. When *nosferatu* could inhabit these same streets and sidewalks by day, things would change. Instead of *undead,* vampires would have to be thought of as *formerly dead*. They wouldn't need affirmative action programs or special handouts, because they would take what they wanted. From legends to the dominant species, overnight—such an evolutionary leap had never before happened. Never before didn't mean never would, though.

Larry Greenbarger was on the cusp of history—history that he would make, by doing what he had always done. Only now, his efforts would be appreciated.

He left the river behind, walking north on Michigan. Although the hour was late, there were people around, and cars rolling past, steel cocoons in which humanity felt safe and protected. He watched them go, hungry but not famished. He heard blood flowing, smelled sweat and salt and flesh. The world was a restaurant and nearly everyone in it was on the menu, and they didn't know it. The thought made him laugh out loud. A man sitting with his back against a building averted his gaze. Once Larry might have feared him, but no more.

Not that Larry didn't still know fear. On the

contrary. He had only met one other vampire, and he had never walked into a den full of them. When he met the group the next day, he had no idea what would happen. They might embrace him as a brother, but they might just as easily decide that he was a threat, competition, and try to destroy him.

He was stronger than he had ever been, but that strength was in contrast to humans. He didn't know how he compared to other vampires. And once they had taken his formula, if somehow he had miscalculated, and the rage took them over . . . what might happen then?

Another possibility nagged at him. What if Walkin_ Dude wasn't a vampire at all, but another group of hunters, like the band he had destroyed before? Over the internet, he couldn't be certain. This time, meeting in an enclosed place just before daybreak, he would be trapped. He could escape into the daylight from ordinary vampires, if it came to that, although because he took the stuff in its earlier incarnation the rage would certainly overcome him before long. And if they didn't attack him until after they took it, or if they were human all along, then the daylight would offer him no advantage.

The whole situation was a sticky one, but he had to face his fears and keep the appointment. The whole point of his experimentation was to allow him to meet others and to share his findings. Without wide distribution, his work meant nothing.

He looked up at one of the tall buildings, feeling like a rube, just in from the country. *Look at that, Maw! That's what you call a skyscraper!*

But his mind was racing. Wide distribution—that was the key.

In case something happened to him, in case the meet didn't go as he had planned, he needed a backup. And he knew what it would be.

Vampires read the message board and websites. So did humans, and wannabes. But if they read about his discovery and spread the word, understood its potential, then his work was half done anyway. And the vampires who came across it could put it into practice, with or without Larry's presence.

All he had to do was get back to his computer and upload the formula to as many sites as possible, until he had to leave for the meeting.

Whether or not he survived the next twelve hours, his work would live on.

Really, that was what mattered the most.

38

THE VAN WAS REGISTERED to a guy named Walker Swanson, who lived in a dump out in Harvey that needed yard work and a coat of paint, or maybe just a good roaring fire.

It was outside jurisdictional boundaries for Alex and Larissa, and for Greg Fielding, but because they were the ones who had broken the case—Alex knew it had been him alone, but he was willing to share credit with his partner, and she insisted on including Greg—they were the ones to follow up on it. They sat outside Walker's house in two separate unmarked cars, because although Alex didn't think Walker was any kind of criminal mastermind, multiple-vehicle surveillance was both easier and safer than single vehicle. So far all they had on Walker was that his van had been parked near a homicide scene, but from what little he'd been able to find out, Alex liked him for the killings. He had gone to high school with the first victim, and he had turned up on surveillance video at the fast-food joint Wanda Case worked at. He was antisocial, a loner who worked from his home, a white guy in his twenties. None of it was definitive, but it fit the profile Alex had been developing.

Alex wanted to catch him in the act of breaking into a house or abducting a victim. Once they had something serious on him, they could break him. A search of his house would reveal clues. His DNA would match that found at some of the crime scenes. They would have their "vampire," and he would prove to be just another garden-variety, human psychopath, as Alex had insisted from the start. He wanted to build an airtight case, one that would persuade the most recalcitrant jury, so they would sit outside his place as long as necessary, until he went out for another victim.

"Good thing about a creep like this is he doesn't have much of a social life," Larissa said, as if reading Alex's thoughts. "So we probably don't have to worry about him going to a lot of parties or anything."

"If he goes out at night," Alex agreed, "it's probably to kill someone."

"Sooner the better, far as I'm concerned. I want to put this one to bed."

"You and me both."

She leaned back against her seat's headrest and blew out a breath. She sounded frustrated.

"What's up?" Alex asked.

"Hey, I'm gonna go keep Greg company for a little while," she said. "No reason he should be the one to sit around alone."

Alex started to respond, but caught himself. *You should stay with me, because you're* my *partner, not his,* he wanted to say. *Because it's not our fault his department's too cheap to assign him a partner of his own. Because I don't know how far things have gone between you two, but I don't want you sitting in a dark car with him, with nothing to do. I need everybody's attention on Walker Swanson's door, not Greg Fielding's zipper.*

But he couldn't make himself give voice to any of those arguments, so instead he swallowed his anger and his fear. "Whatever," he said, his voice close to breaking. "Fine."

"Cool," she said. She opened her door—the dome light had already been disconnected—and started out, but then stopped, leaned back in and touched Alex's thigh. "Thanks, Alex," she said.

Then she was gone, but her touch lingered on his lap like a hot coal, and Alex wondered if there was a way to set Walker Swanson loose on Greg Fielding before they brought him in.

Walker and Mitch stayed inside most of the night. Mitch had suggested the location for the meet, an abandoned motor court between home and the city, and the time had been set for just before sunrise so when the Light of Day formula worked, as its maker swore it would, they could test it by going out into the sun.

To Walker, that was a double blessing. Not only would he and Mitch be turned, but they would be a new breed of vampire. Advance soldiers of the new era. The later the hour, the more anxious he became. All of their work, all the people they had killed, led to this moment. And none of it had made him more anxious than this, the culmination of it all.

He tried to sleep, but every time he drifted off he would snap awake again, tingling with anticipation. Finally he gave up and spent some time working on uploading auction items.

About five-thirty, Mitch cleared his throat. "Walker, it's time to boogie."

Walker looked away from the monitor. "Finally."

"No shit."

Walker shut everything down. "Let's motor." He pulled on a jacket against the early morning chill, then went to the refrigerator and took out a Nalgene bottle of blood. With trembling hands, he unscrewed the lid. "One for the road," he said, and he took a drink.

The motel was empty when Larry approached, or it looked that way. There was a monument signpost by the sidewalk, but the sign it had once held had blown down or been torn off long ago. Words could still be seen, faded but legible, painted on the office wall. ROOMS BY HOUR DAY OR WEEK. WATER BEDS. XXX MOVIES. LO-RATES. A hot-pillow joint, then, the kind of places blue collar guys took women they were having affairs with, or streetwalkers. The white-collar guys would spring for decent hotel rooms. Then there were guys like Larry had been, who had never interested the sort

of women who would come to a place like this, but still
dreamed about it when he drove past one.

The place had eight square concrete block buildings,
each with two recessed doors, arrayed around a parking
lot of cracked asphalt with weeds growing up through
it. Most of the windows were broken and boarded over.
Larry observed the place as he drove by, then parked
down the street in the lot of a two-story office building,
and walked back carrying a duffel bag with his things
inside. A few cars passed, but he saw no sign of motion
or life at the motel.

Walkin_Dude had promised that the door to Room
14 would be unlocked, and that's where they would
meet. Larry stepped into the shadowed doorway of
Room 4 and observed for a few minutes. He didn't see
or hear anyone, and more important, he didn't smell
anyone. If this was a human-laid trap and vampire
hunters waited inside, he would be able to sniff them
out.

He had spent most of the night online, uploading
his formula to every place he could think of. Emails had
poured in asking for more information, and he had answered what he could. Finally, he had shut off the computer. He left it and his other equipment in a motel
room on the north side of the city, fully aware that
he might never make it back there. But he had done
what he could. If things worked out as he hoped this
morning, he would go back to that motel to collect his
things—but he would go back as a recognized prophet,

a prince of the undead. In life he had been nobody, a nameless scientist working alongside his fellow drones. But in death, he would be so much more.

And it would all begin soon, here in this no-name motel, where humans had mated and sweated and spawned more meat for the taking.

Smiling, Larry crossed the pitted parking lot and pushed open the door to Room 14, ready to meet his future.

39

LARRY HAD BEEN IN the room for about fifteen minutes when he heard footsteps outside. He went to the window, where a sheet of plywood had buckled out just enough to offer a strip through which he could see, and looked out toward the lot. Dark forms moved toward him. A lot of them. He heard whispered conversation. He tasted the air, but didn't detect human.

This had to be the group from New York, then. They had indicated that they were a much larger group than Walkin_Dude's; the latter had been reticent about how many his den really had, but Larry got the impression that it was just a handful, if that.

He moved into the darkest part of the empty room. Spider webs were thick, as was the stink of old piss. The walls were coated in grime, oily and streaked. As the door started to creak open, Larry tensed, ready to run or attack.

"Hey?" A male voice, young sounding but with a bit of a rasp. Then the door opened wider and Larry saw the speaker, tall and lean, with long dark hair and a goatee. He wore black clothes. At his side as he came through the door was a heavy young woman, a hippie type with flowing, straight hair. "I'm Rocco," the man said.

"Larry."

"You're the guy. Light of Day."

"That's right."

Rocco came forward, leaving the woman at the door and the others outside. "It's an honor," he said, extending his hand.

Larry took it, felt his cool, firm grasp. "Thanks."

"If this works . . . man."

"It works."

"Excellent."

"You should get your . . . them . . . out of the parking lot."

"Yeah," Rocco said. He crossed his arms and rocked back on his heels. He was a good-looking guy, Larry thought, charismatic. "They're good at blending in, but inside is better." Rocco stuck his head out the door, gave a low whistle and a beckoning motion, and then bodies filed in, blocking light from coming in the doorway. They came into the small room, their scents filling the space with a pleasant musk. Rocco introduced them: Shiloh, Angel, Chip, Winston, Brick, Goldie, Dragon Lady, and Nightmare, who looked like a Hell's Angel, only worse. From having been around only one vampire, Larry was suddenly surrounded, and it felt wonderful.

It felt like home, like a family reunion.

* * *

When Walker pulled up at the old motel, he was surprised to see an RV in the parking lot. The joint was deserted, or should have been. He parked near the RV, which appeared empty and silent.

"What do you think, man?" he asked Mitch.

"Maybe it belongs to the dude. The Light of Day guy. He said he's been on the road, right? And with a bunch of scientific equipment or whatever."

"I guess. I just don't tend to think of vampires as RVers."

"Maybe that's because you've never met any. All you know, RV parks around the world could be full of 'em."

"Could be," Walker admitted. "Should we go in?"

"We didn't come this far to sit in the van playing with ourselves."

"You're right." Walker tried to pull on courage, like drawing a cape over his shoulders. "Let's get in there." Before he could think it over any longer, he threw open the van's door and stepped to the broken asphalt. He straightened his shoulders, tried to suck in his gut, and took purposeful strides to the Room 14 door.

He was about to knock, then changed his mind. He was the one who had picked the place, who had come out here a couple of nights ago and pried out the nails holding the door shut. The Light of Day guy, if he was inside, was *his* guest, not the other way around. Instead of knocking, he pushed the door open with the flat of his palm. A wave of some sour stench met him halfway in, a smell of rancid meat and old blood.

The room was mostly dark, with just some light filtering in from outside, and that went away as the door swung shut. But before that happened, Walker saw enough to know that he and Mitch were seriously outnumbered.

"I thought we were meeting one guy, not going to a convention," he said. His voice quaked in spite of his efforts to control it.

"You must be Walkin_Dude," someone said.

"That's right. You can call me Walker. This is Mitch."

"I'm Larry." Someone came through the crowd, which parted for him—Walker could hear it more than see it. "I'm the one you came here to meet. These others—they came for the same reason, so they could try out my Light of Day formula."

He emerged from the pack, stopping in a shoe-string-thin band of light filtering through the crack of the door from the street lamps outside. He was an older guy, with thin hair and a big gut. He clapped a hand onto Walker's shoulder and reached for his hand. As he did, a strange expression washed over his face, and Walker almost lost control of his bowels.

"You're alive!" Larry said.

A hush fell over the crowded room.

"I thought you were one of us!"

"I want to b-b-be," Walker said anxiously. "*We* do. We've done everything we can—we've killed people, we've been drinking blood nonstop. We just haven't been able to find anyone to turn us."

"I don't know about turning," someone said from the midst of the crowd. "But I know where you can find someone to kill you."

"Whoa, hold up!" Walker shouted. "We . . . we don't mean anyone any harm. None of you, I mean! We hate people. We just want to be like you . . . *guys*. More than anything."

"You keep saying 'we,'" the one named Larry said. "What do you mean? Who else is with you?"

Walker jabbed a thumb over his shoulder. "Me and Mitch here."

Larry peered past Walker. "What are you talking about? There's nobody there," he said. "Just you."

Walker spun around. Mitch stood there, right in front of the door, but he had a strange half-smile on his face and his eyes were sad. "Dude, he's right here!"

"They're not buying it, man," Mitch said.

Larry kept his hand on Walker's shoulder. His grip was strong, his fingers like rebar rods. When he spoke his voice was soft, tinged with concern. "I think maybe you have some problems that being undead won't solve, Walker."

"I don't know what you mean! Are you blind or something? He's right . . ."

Mitch shrugged, but he seemed less substantial than he had a moment before.

"Mitch, for Christ's sake! Tell them you're there!"

Larry's hand pressed on his shoulder like a five-ton

weight. Streams of sweat rushed down Walker's sides and coated his upper lip; he tasted salt. His legs were rubber, barely supporting his bulk.

"There's no one there, son," Larry said.

"You're seeing things," someone else offered.

"No, I'm not! Mitch and I . . . he's my best friend!" Hot tears stung Walker's cheeks. Mitch had faded more. He blinked back to full life and color for an instant, then faded again, until he wasn't much more than a shadow covering part of the door.

Walker didn't understand. Mitch was flickering in and out, as if a strobe light was flashing on him. He had known Mitch for . . . well, he couldn't remember how long. Mitch was his best friend.

His only friend, really.

And if Mitch didn't exist, then . . .

. . . then fuck, he didn't know. He just didn't know.

Walker shut his eyes. When he opened them again, this would all be some nightmare. He would have fallen asleep at the computer, and Mitch would be sitting in the other chair, and none of it would be real, all the craziness with Andy and vampires would never have happened. Maybe he'd still be in high school, in bed with a pillow wrapped around his head because he didn't want to get up, didn't want to hear the alarm or Mom's screech telling him he'd be late, didn't want to face the taunts and insults from the guys, the looks of disapproval or disgust from the girls. Maybe he would be in grade school, before he had understood that he would always be the fat kid, the unpopular kid, the guy other kids pointed at, laughing.

And he opened his eyes.

And he was in Room 14 of a motel closed so long he didn't know its name, a joint he had passed a thousand times and never thought about until a few days ago, inside a room where people fucked strangers, where emotions ran more toward loneliness, even hate, than love. He knew what that was like, and the loneliness seemed to collapse in around him even though he wasn't alone, he was here with a dozen or so people—no, not people, *vampires,* that smell surrounded him still, and he knew now that some of it was him, the flop sweat sticking his shirt to his fleshy ribs.

They were vampires, the undead, and he was not, and Mitch wasn't real, had never been real. His life was awful, so sad and lonely that he had made up a friend who was closer to him than anyone had ever been. Terrible clarity shone on him like a spotlight.

"Look," Walker said. "I . . . I guess I made a mistake. Some mistakes. I'm sorry, I didn't mean to bring you here under false pretenses. I never meant to lie or—"

"It's okay, Walker," Larry interrupted. "You do want to be a vampire, right? One of us?"

"I . . . I thought I did, but—"

"I can take care of that, Walker. *It's easy.*" That iron grip clutched Walker's shoulder again, making Walker feel like crying out, but he wanted to maintain some measure of his dignity, even though the front of his pants felt hot and wet and tears had laid down tracks from cheeks to chin. Larry leaned in close and his teeth were terrible, his face hideous, monstrous, his open mouth stinking like a vat of slow-simmering meat in a slaughterhouse. A lazy fly came to a brief landing on Larry's lower lip, then took off again. "The thing is," Larry said quietly, "I've never turned anyone yet. You've never been turned and I haven't turned anyone. We can help each other, okay?"

Walker wanted to run away, wanted to scream, wanted to drive his thumbs into his eye sockets and force his eyes from his head so he wouldn't have to look at the monsters anymore.

But it was too late for that. Anyway, his life was nothing he wanted to return to. Like Mitch had said— Mitch who wasn't, who had never existed outside of his own head, but was still better than nothing—Mitch had told him: *Out is out, right? Done is done.*

"Y-yeah," Walker said. "We can . . . we can help each other." He tilted his head back. "You want my neck? Is that how it works?"

40

MARINA WATCHED THE DOOR close behind the last guy to go in. This one had been a fat guy, young, and something hadn't seemed right about him.

What was worse was that two cars had pulled up right behind him, only the occupants of those cars hadn't gotten out, they just sat inside watching the motel with as much interest as she was. Their cars were American-made sedans. One guy sitting alone in one, a man and a woman in the other.

"Jesus," she said. "Are those cops?"

"Look like it to me," Monte said.

"What are they doing on Greenbarger?"

"They didn't come with Greenbarger," Tony O. said. "They followed that last guy in."

"God, this is getting all fucked up," Marina said. "Larry's in there, and then all those bloodsuckers from the RV, now some chubbo, and the local law's on his ass."

"We knew it'd be crowded," Kat reminded her. "All those emails about the Light of Day."

"Yeah, but I thought we'd be able to handle it by ourselves. I didn't know the freakin' *gendarmerie* would be along for the ride."

"Maybe they can help."

"Maybe they can blow me before they get hurt. I'm going to talk to them."

"You want backup?" Jimbo asked.

"I think I can manage." She took off her night vision goggles and got out of the van. She had to wait for a couple of trucks to barrel past before she could cross the street. Place was supposed to be good for a quiet meet, but only compared to the track at the Daytona 500.

She went to the car with the single occupant. Maybe he was the boss. He spotted her coming and got out before she reached the vehicle. He was tall and rangy and he looked as happy as a funeral. Marina was reaching for her badge when he showed his.

"Chicago PD," he said. "I'm Detective Alex Ziccaria."

"FBI. Special Agent Marina Tanaka-Dunn."

"This is federal?"

"You have no idea."

Doors opened in the other car, then shut again with a bang. "Can you keep your people under control?" Marina asked.

"They're not my people. What are you doing here? This is a Chicago PD/Cook County joint task force. We've got a serial killer suspect in there, and—"

"You have no idea what you've got in there, Detective." Remembering her cop manners, she added, "All due respect."

"What do you mean?"

Marina looked toward the east. A band of pewter showed at the horizon. Daylight soon. The bloodsuckers would either come out in a hurry and get into their vehicles, or they would be trapped inside the room.

Unless that whole Light of Day process Larry had been promising worked. The thing had hit the internet during the night, spreading like mad. Operation Red-Blooded researchers were all over it, trying to figure out if it had any legitimacy, and if it did what they could do to counter it, take the links down.

Killing Larry Greenbarger wouldn't stop it, not anymore.

But that didn't mean it wouldn't feel good.

"Look, Detective, that information is classified. Way above your pay grade. Why don't you just get in your car and—"

"What's going on, Alex?" The female cop, small and fit, with short blond hair, strode toward them. Behind her came a muscular, thick-necked guy who looked about as solid and smart as a brick wall.

"That's my partner, Larissa Dixson," Alex said. "Behind her is Greg Fielding from Tinley Park."

Marina badged her before she got any closer. "This is a Bureau operation, Detectives. I'm going to have to ask you to roll out."

"We're not giving up our suspect," Larissa said. "We've got half a dozen corpses, and we're going to have to talk to him."

"Was there anything unusual about those corpses?" Marina asked.

"Unusual? What do you—"

"Yes or no? You'd know it if it was there."

Alex rubbed his forehead, as if he had a bad headache. "The blood," he said. "They were drained of blood."

"There you go."

"You know about that?" Greg Fielding asked.

"Like I told Detective Ziccaria here, there are levels of classification on this sort of op. I can't talk to you about it."

"Have you been on this for a while?" Larissa asked. "Why weren't we informed? If we had a known serial killer in our city, we should have been told."

"That's even above *my* pay grade," Marina said. "Look, this is under control." She waved a hand toward her van. "I've got a strike team in there. Nobody's walking away from that motel room unless they're in handcuffs."

"We can stick around," Greg said. "Offer support."

"I have all the support I need."

"But—"

Anger flared through Marina and she let it show. "Look, standing out here arguing might just compromise a Bureau operation and blow months of work! Any of you want to take the heat for that?"

"Let's step away, Larissa."

"That's a good idea. You should listen to Detective Ziccaria."

"This isn't over, *Special Agent* Tanaka-Dunn. I'm making a call. I'll get the mayor of Chicago on the line if I have to, but we're part of this until it's over."

"Is that how it is?" Marina asked. "You want to see whose dick is biggest? Because I guarantee you—"

"I'm just telling you."

"Fine. Make your call. But not from here. I want you off this block before I arrest you for obstruction."

"Let's go, Larissa."

Larissa Dixson looked at Alex, and then she looked at Greg. Marina saw at once what was going on, but it was personal between the three of them and she couldn't help saying it. "Go," she said. "Go with your partner or the guy you're sleeping with, but get off this street."

Larissa gave her a murderous expression, but she got into Alex's car. Greg hesitated a moment, then walked back to his alone and slammed the door.

Child, Marina thought, cringing at the loud bang. *Willing to blow the whole thing just to make a point.*

Both cars started up and cruised slowly to the corner, then around it. Marina had no doubt that they were already calling their superiors, and those people would call their superiors, and on up the chain of command.

She hurried back to the van, pulling her own phone as she did. She had programmed Senator Bobby Harlowe's numbers in. Home, cell, and office.

Chicago's mayor would find that she had allies, too. Mayors were a big deal on the local level, and

Chicago's mayor probably had the president's number on his phone. But so did Bobby Harlowe. And Bobby Harlowe sat on the Homeland Security and Appropriations committees. If it became a contest of length, his honor the mayor would find that Bobby carried a tape measure.

When she finished her call, she put the phone away and turned to her people. "Suit up," she said. "We're going to go kick some ass."

"There are a bunch of 'em in there," Monte pointed out.

"That just makes it harder to miss."

"How do you wanna handle it?"

"Handle it? I want to kick open the door and fill the place with UV and phosphorus. I want to smell vampire barbecue. Clear enough for you?"

"Clear as day," Monte said. "Sorry, bad metaphor. Simile. Whatever, I barely passed English."

"I don't care if you only speak ancient Greek," Marina said. "Long as you can handle a gun."

41

"HELP ME FIRST," Larry said. "I wasn't anticipating such a crowd, and I have to inoculate everyone."

"Not everyone," the one who had introduced himself as Rocco said firmly. "Sun's almost up. Start with one or two and we'll see how they do, then if everything's okay you can do the others."

"Any way you want it," Larry said. "I know you'll be happy, though. I distributed the formula online, too. Any vampire who wants it can re-create it easily now."

"Has it been thoroughly tested?"

"Tested enough. It works."

"How can I help?" Walker asked.

"Apparently I'm not injecting everyone just yet. I'd like you to be conscious to help me when I do, though. Then you'll have earned your way, and I'll be glad to turn you."

"Do me," Shiloh pleaded. "I want you to do me!"

"How many times have you said that?" Chip asked. "Millions?"

"Bite me."

"I think you've used that one too," Brick said.

Shiloh raised her middle finger toward both, and laughed. Then she caressed Rocco's arm. "Can I?"

"It's safe?" Rocco asked Larry.

"It's safe. Look, you've got me way outnumbered. If I'm wrong, you'll tear me apart."

"Got that right."

"So I'm staking everything on it."

"Staking?" Brick repeated. "Word choice, dawg."

"Sorry."

"Can I, Rocco?" Shiloh asked again.

Rocco gave her a concerned look that would have sickened the old Larry Greenbarger, human Larry, because he would have known that a woman like her would never look to *him* for guidance or protection.

Now, in this new unlife, everything was different. Who knew what he would have when word of his discovery spread? Vampire females might flock to him like some sort of undead George Clooney.

"I suppose," Rocco said. He sounded reluctant, as if he still didn't quite trust Larry but didn't want to deprive her of something she wanted so much.

"Very well," Larry said. "Will there be anyone else?"

"You can do me," Rocco said.

"If you're sure . . ."

"You do her, you do me."

Chip came forward. He was a heavyset black vampire with a thick salt-and-pepper beard. "Rocco, what if something goes wrong?"

"If something goes wrong," Rocco echoed, "do what good ol' Larry suggested. Tear him apart."

Larry was pretty sure nothing would go wrong, but

that didn't keep him from being nervous, just in case. He prepared a syringe, tapped the needle, squirted a little of his formula out. "You know how to give a shot?" he asked Walker.

"Not really. I usually don't look when I get one."

"These are easy. You don't need a vein, just jab the needle in and press down."

"Okay."

"You can watch me do these first ones, then help when it's time to do everyone else."

"Then you'll turn me?"

"Then I'll turn you."

"Okay," Walker said again.

Larry took Shiloh's forearm in his hands. Her flesh was as pale and cool as a marble statue. Her eyes were deep green, the color of a pond he had fished in a few times during his life. Full lips curled at the corners in the faintest smile, and he guessed she must have been devastating. Still was, for that matter; she had stopped aging at death, had never deteriorated. He could see falling in love with a woman like this.

"Are you ready?" he asked.

"Whenever, just do it."

Larry pressed the needle into her flesh, shoving it deep, and pressed down on the plunger. Shiloh didn't flinch. Her eyelashes fluttered a little, but she showed no other reaction. When the syringe was empty, he withdrew the needle. "Are you okay?"

"Fine."

"You're good to go, then."

Her head swiveled toward the door. "Outside? In the sun?"

"That's right."

"Wait, Shiloh," Rocco said. "Wait for me."

Larry was already back at his case, refilling the hypo. "I'll get you done in just a second," he said.

Rocco stood, waiting calmly. His shoulders were straight, his spine rigid. He watched Larry with dark eyes that missed nothing. He *was* the George Clooney of the vampire world, Larry decided, or one of them. All these vampires followed him because he projected strength and certainty, and the fact that he was tall and handsome didn't hurt.

Larry injected the formula into Rocco's corded forearm. He used the same needle he had on Shiloh. Infectious diseases were not, he reasoned, something the undead had to worry about. And from the looks of things, even if they were, Rocco and Shiloh would already have shared all of theirs.

"You're done," Larry said.

"Let's go outside," Shiloh said anxiously. "Come on, Rocco."

"Rocco, I don't know about this," Goldie said.

"It'll be fine," Larry promised.

"Better be," Brick said.

"If there's a problem, we'll come back in," Rocco said. "If there's not, we'll stay out for a little while, just to see."

"I know you'll be thrilled. It'll seem bright at first, and hot—you're not used to it. But you will be, and your eyes will adjust soon."

"I can't wait to see what it's like," Shiloh said.

"We're going, Shiloh." To Brick and the others, he said, "Watch him."

Larry went to the door and opened it just a hair, peered out. The sun had crested the horizon. There was no full sunlight in the motel's parking lot yet, but plenty of indirect sun. Most vampires wouldn't survive it.

"You others should move back away from the door," he said. "I'll open it, and leave it open so you can watch them outside."

"You've taken the stuff, right?" Rocco asked.

"Of course."

"Then *you'll* go out first."

Larry had hoped to avoid that. He had taken the early version. If he stayed out for more than a couple of minutes, sun-rage would overtake him. He didn't think that would be a problem for Rocco and Shiloh, but he wouldn't know that for sure until they went out.

He didn't see any way to refuse Rocco, though.

"Fine," he said. "Everyone clear?"

The other vampires moved deep into the room. None of them wanted to risk early morning sunlight slanting inside. Larry opened the door and stepped out, leaving it open.

He took several steps into the parking lot, stopped, turned back to the door. Indirect sunlight warmed his back and shoulders. "The water's fine," he said. "Come on in."

"I'm coming," Shiloh said. She started for the door, but Rocco stopped her, moved past her until the doorway framed him. He stood there for a few moments, blinking, then stepped out. He raised his arms to shoulder height and held them there, offering the largest possible surface to the light.

"It is bright," he said.

"You'll adjust," Larry snapped. Rage starting to build already. He had to get back inside. "Come on, Shiloh."

"It's all right," Rocco said.

Shiloh gave a girlish squeal and flounced out. She bobbed up and down in the light. Larry rushed back inside, felt the cooling shade. The rage began to dissipate immediately, but it had been close. Another minute or two out there and he might have lost control.

"This is fantastic!" Shiloh shouted.

"Everything okay, Rocco?" Angel asked.

"Fine," Rocco replied. "Bright, like he said. Warm. But it doesn't hurt. Doesn't burn."

"Of course," Larry said. Now that he was safely inside, excitement over what he had accomplished began to set in. Rocco and Shiloh were out in the sunlight, and they weren't losing control of themselves. Both were smiling. Walking in the sunlight was a pleasant experience for most humans, and it could be for vampires, too.

"You should also be stronger than ever," Larry reminded them. "Test it."

Rocco flexed his arm. His muscles were always impressive, but they wouldn't have changed in appearance, Larry knew. Only in function. Rocco turned slowly, looking for something to test, and his gaze settled on Walker's van, parked beside the RV. He went to its rear, crouched down, got a grip on the undercarriage, and straightened his knees. The van's rear end lifted, seemingly without effort. Rocco shifted his grip, raising the thing to his chest, then got under it and pushed up. The van raised higher, until Rocco held the rear end over his head and the nose scraped asphalt.

Walker watched with awe, not complaining about the damage done to his vehicle. After holding it there for several seconds, Rocco lowered it gently back to the ground, then dropped it the last couple of feet.

"You're right, Larry," Rocco said. He grinned broadly. "I am stronger."

"I knew you would be."

"Me now!" Shiloh said. "I want to try something!"

Rocco pointed to a wrought-iron railing alongside a ramp leading to the office door. "How about that?"

"Okay!" She dashed over to it, palms up as if collecting sunflakes on them. When she reached the railing, she gripped it in both hands. She pushed with one and pulled with the other. The iron gave easily beneath her efforts.

"This is awesome!" she cried. "I love it!"

"I knew you would!" Larry called.

She raced across the parking lot and back into the room, ran straight to Larry and threw herself against him, pulling him into a close embrace. She pressed those devastating lips against his. There was none of the warmth he would have expected from a human woman, but the pressure was there, the press of firm breasts against his body, the feel of her hands on his back. "Larry," she said, her lips barely an inch from his. "You are awesome!"

"Thank . . . thank you, Shiloh." He hoped Rocco wasn't a jealous type. He had already learned that vampires could get erections, but he was starting to be reminded of that fact, and unless she let go of him soon she would notice.

She did. "Later," she whispered. "I'll do whatever you want. You're like a . . . like a savior or something." Then she released him and spun back to Rocco, just now coming into the room. "Rocco, I'm gonna do Larry later."

"Have fun," Rocco said, smiling. "He deserves it."

Larry guessed he still had a lot to learn about vampire social rituals, but he liked what he had seen so far.

"How is it, Rocco?" Winston asked.

"It's great. It's everything he said it would be."

"So we can all do it?"

"If he's got enough juice."

"I have plenty," Larry said. "Walker, come on over here and help me."

42

"THAT'S GREENBARGER!" MARINA GRABBED binoculars and looked at the man again. "That's definitely him."

"You said he had gone over," Kat said.

"He has."

"But he's outside, in daylight."

"Then his stuff works."

"I guess it does."

Monte sighted down the length of his weapon. "You want me to take him out?"

"The place is full of bloodsuckers," Marina said. "I want to take Larry, but I want the rest, too. And if we can get Larry alive, that might be helpful—I'd like to know what he's learned since he changed."

"Long as you're not runnin' us through hoops just to show off."

Marina stared at Monte. He had said it with a smile on his face, so she guessed he was only giving her a hard time.

"Let's wait until he goes back in," she said. "Then take them all."

"Fine," Monte said. He lowered the weapon.

Marina didn't blame him for wanting to move. So

did she. So did everyone else. It was what they got up for every morning. She could feel the pent-up energy pinballing around the van, and holding it back was hard.

But she was in charge, and one of the responsibilities that came with that was deciding which tactics and strategies made the most sense for the overall mission. Like it or not, there was more to consider than simply killing vampires.

"Here come some more," Kat said.

Marina tensed as a young-looking woman came into the light, followed by a dark, muscular man. As soon as they were out, Larry Greenbarger dashed back into the room.

The two of them appeared hesitant, then almost ecstatic.

Then things turned terrifying.

The man hoisted half a van over his head. The woman twisted wrought iron like it was aluminum foil. She ran back inside, and the man followed at a more dignified pace.

"Jesus Christ," Jimbo said.

"No kidding." Marina could barely contain her unease. Vampires were plenty powerful, but sunlight? That was supposed to kill them. Here they were performing feats of strength that should have been difficult under any circumstances, even as the sun rose in the sky.

The sun was the best weapon humanity had against

their kind, as effective a deterrent as nuclear bombs against the Soviet Union. If this spread—and it already had, at least online, although she supposed there was some small degree of skill involved in mixing the chemicals that might leave some vampires out—then there would be no holding them back.

Marina had not always taken the job as seriously as she should have, but it was more than a job to her just the same. It was a mission, and as close to a sacred one as she could imagine. The bloodsuckers were unnatural, an incomprehensible threat, and now, suddenly, that threat was growing geometrically.

"Let's put these animals down," she said, afraid that if they waited another minute, Greenbarger would dose more of them.

Her people responded with enthusiastic grunts, restrained versions of the shouts they would have given if they weren't hoping to sneak up on a motel room full of potential supervampires. They shoved open the van's doors, and were just stepping out when two Chicago PD vehicles rolled up to the end of the block and stopped. One was a truck full of cops in assault gear, who spilled onto the street. The other was a long black limo, from which emerged an older gentleman wearing a black suit, striped tie, and an air of self-importance. He eyed the Operation Red-Blooded van and stalked toward it, his SWAT team backing him up.

"Can we maybe move this off the street?" Marina

asked. "We have a federal operation going on here and I'd hate for our surveillance subjects to look outside and see all this." She nodded toward the assault team. "And really, I think we have it under control, but if your people want to wait around—out of the way—in case we need backup, that's all right with me."

The man wiped his ruddy face with a handkerchief. She got the impression he did a lot of that, and as soon as he moved it away, sweat was beading on it again. "Apparently you misunderstand the situation," he said. "I'm Andrew Tenko, special assistant to the mayor for law enforcement. He wants this to be a Chicago operation, not federal."

"Maybe he does," Marina said. "But that's not a call he gets to make."

"You might want to check in with your boss about that. The mayor has been on the phone with the Director of National Intelligence for the past fifteen minutes."

Marina fought back a curse. She would have to call Kleefeld and see if he had been leaned on. But every minute that ticked by was a wasted one in which who knows what might be going on inside. And every second they stood out on the street, someone might emerge from the motel room again and spot them.

She took the man's arm. "Sir, I don't care if you're the president of the United States—we have to get off this street. Now." She led him around to the back of the van, waving the SWAT team away at the same time. The man was stocky, but inside his suit he felt like a mass of loose skin with a few bones inside it, no muscle mass or serious fat.

Her team understood the stakes, and they took cover behind the van. She saw them scoping the motel room with weapons at the ready, and she knew they were professionals, trustworthy and ready for anything. She wished she had as much faith in the Chicago cops.

"Do you understand what you're getting in the way of here?" Tenko asked her. "There's a man in there we suspect of killing half a dozen people and draining their blood. My detectives tell me that they're sure this is their man, but they need to catch him engaged in a criminal act. Therefore I can't have you blowing their cover."

"With all due respect," she said—police manners—"you and your cops have no clue about what's really going on in that room. And if you don't want to blow their cover, why bring a whole assault squad and park them on the block in question? You don't think anybody inside might hear that?"

"I'm not a policeman," Tenko said. "I don't set police procedure, I simply try to ensure that the men and women of law enforcement have the resources they need and the leeway to take the measures that need to be taken."

"If you don't let us handle this our way," Marina insisted, "then you'll be sentencing a bunch of your officers to their deaths. How will you feel about that?"

Tenko wiped his face again, blinked at her. "I suggest you call your boss."

"I'm going to do just that," she said. "While I do, I don't want you to move an inch." She turned to Monte. "If this guy tries to go anywhere, break his knees. But quietly."

"It'd be my pleasure," Monte said. He was smiling again. Marina was glad that particular smile wasn't directed her way, but she was glad to see that Tenko looked uncomfortable about it. She went into the van to call Kleefeld—to beg, if necessary. She needed to get this settled, and it had to be done now.

43

WATCHING ROCCO AND SHILOH outdoors had encouraged the other *nosferatu,* so they mobbed around Larry and Walker to get their shots. Rocco brought order, not by raising his voice but by lowering it to a near whisper. The vampires hushed to hear what he had to say, and they lined up where he told them to. Once that was settled, filling the syringes and getting everybody injected took no time at all.

Then it was Walker's turn. "After he does this," Rocco said, "we can all go outside. But this guy helped us, and apparently he's been trying to join us for a long time. Let's give him the respect and attention he deserves."

Rocco's den mates gathered in a circle around them. Larry felt a surprising pressure, as if he was on stage and couldn't risk getting a line wrong or missing a cue. He approached Walker, who once again tilted his head back, exposing his pale, thick neck. It was impossible to say which was more nervous, the one who had never turned another human being, or the one so desperate to forsake his humanity.

The flesh of Walker's neck reminded Larry of pork rinds, a treat he hadn't even thought about once since waking up dead. But Walker had that same greasy, salty sweetness. He trembled in Larry's grasp, flinching away from his long, probing tongue. A blue vein throbbed in Walker's temple, and Larry was tempted to pluck it out and pop it in his mouth.

But he had a purpose, and killing Walker outright wouldn't further it.

Although he had never turned anyone, he thought he knew how to do it. Bite him, but don't drain him. Make sure plenty of his own bodily fluids mixed with Walker's. That was the key; he had to transfer the Immortal Cell into Walker's body. Walker would die, but not for long. The cell's properties would bring the body back to life—only better. A new, improved Walker would be the result.

"You're sure about this?" Larry asked. Even as the words escaped his lips, in a kind of hiss, he knew it was too late. He couldn't resist any longer. He opened his mouth, held tightly to Walker's shoulder and arm, and let his teeth close on Walker's neck.

That pork rind flavor sprang into his mouth as though he had put one on his tongue. Then he tore into meatier flesh and muscle, and blood rushed in, sweet and sticky. He let it flow for a minute, swallowing quickly, but even so some escaped his mouth and ran down his chin, hot and wet.

Walker shuddered and moaned and tried to yank away, but Larry's grip on him was too firm. Walker thrashed and kicked. After a short while he settled down, then went limp. Larry lowered him gently to the ground.

The vampires from New York crowded around, and Rocco bent over to watch.

"How long should it take?" Larry asked him.

"It takes a while," Rocco said. "The fluids have to inter—"

Walker interrupted him by spasming furiously, spinning across the floor. Larry and Rocco jumped away; other *nosferatu* cried out in alarm.

"Is he supposed to do that?" Larry asked.

"No way!" Angel said. "That's messed up!"

Larry felt panic setting in. "What do I do?"

"I don't know!" Shiloh cried. "That's totally jacked up!"

Larry crouched beside the thrashing Walker, put a hand out to try to calm the young man. He snatched it back abruptly. "He's burning!"

"Our kind don't get fevers," someone said.

"Not a fever—it's like he's on fire!"

"This is bad," Goldie remarked. "I don't know what it is, but it's bad."

"None of you have ever seen this?" Larry asked desperately.

No one answered in the affirmative. Walker's uncontrolled heaving and rolling around was slowing, but his skin was turning red, his eyes bulging from their sockets. Pink-tinged drool flowed from his mouth and bloody mucus from his nostrils. He whimpered with pain, and his limbs shook like thin branches in heavy wind.

Larry had to do something. He was a scientist, not a medical doctor, and he didn't know if there was a doctor in the world who could do something to save a life in this situation. He didn't know if there was still any life to be saved. But all the vampires were looking on. Judging him. If he was to take his place at the forefront of a new vampiric society, he had to look competent.

Ignoring the heat radiating off Walker's body, he placed both hands on the man, trying to hold him still. Walker's back arched twice in quick succession, then a third time, and his head snapped to one side, tendons standing out like steel bars even through the fat of his neck.

Then Larry felt something bubbling, through Walker's clothing, through his flesh. He yanked his hands away again. "He's . . . I don't know . . ."

Walker's head whipped back and forth a couple of times, and then stopped with his mouth hanging open.

Smoke issued from his mouth. Larry passed a hand through it. Not smoke, *steam*. The whites of Walker's eyes were bubbling now, boiling, Larry realized. They burst and bubbled like steam pots in a geothermal region. Underneath his skin, his blood was boiling, too. Larry could smell it, could see the undulations in Walker's veins.

"Oh God," Larry said. "Oh God, he's . . . he's *boiling*!"

"What do you mean?" Rocco asked.

"I don't . . . I don't know!" Blood seeped through Walker's pores now, the body still twitching but probably from the activity taking place inside it, not from any vestiges of life. As it reached open air, it sizzled and smoked. "I don't know," Larry said again. "Maybe something about the vitamin D entering his system so suddenly, inside my blood . . . it seems to be cooking him from the inside out."

"So what you're suggesting," Rocco said, "is that now that you've given us that crap, none of us can ever turn anyone again?!"

"I . . . I'd have to do more studies. Research."

"I'm not asking for scientific certainty, Larry. Your best guess."

Larry looked at Walker. Boiling blood bubbled up from his ruined eye sockets, out his nose and mouth, pattered onto the floor from his ears. "I'd have to say yes, that's right. I don't know why it would be any different for you than for me. Or why Walker would have reacted differently than any other human."

"So we can go in the sun, but we can never reproduce?" Shiloh asked.

"If I'm right, that's correct."

"And you spread this formula all over the internet?" Rocco asked. "Where anyone can see it?"

Larry had almost forgotten about that. "Yeah . . ."

"And you thought, what, that you were helping us?"

"That was the idea."

"Only now you understand your mistake."

"I guess so . . ."

"Spreading this around before it was completely tested. Getting so carried away that instead of helping us—your own kind—you've doomed us."

"Yeah . . ."

"Not just us in this room, who you injected, but anyone else who has tried your formula. Even if we can let our kind know the risks, there will be some for whom it's too late, others who will take the risk because they want to walk in the sun. To see—how did you put it?"

"The Light of Day."

"Yes. The Light of Day. That's right."

"I know," Larry said. "I'm sorry. I'm so sorry, you guys. I didn't . . . I just didn't know."

"But you understand something has to be done."

"I'll keep working. I'll make it better. I—"

"No, you won't," Rocco said. He didn't sound like he was negotiating.

Larry noticed that the vampire ring had tightened. He couldn't see any of the walls through the legs and bodies surrounding him. Walker had stopped moving, only a little sizzling blood issuing from him. Larry rose, tried to straighten his spine and square his shoulders, but in this crowd he was still out of shape, heavy, old.

He didn't stand a chance, and he knew it.

. His knees were trembling so much he could barely stand.

Brick came first, lashing out with sharp claws that sliced through Larry's shirt and chest. Then Nightmare, then Chip. Larry flopped from one to the other as the flesh was peeled from his body, the limbs torn off.

He had never thought of his newfound strength as a disadvantage before, but it took them a very long time to finally destroy him . . . time, and a great deal of pain.

44

"I HOPE TO GOD this is some sort of joke, Marina," Kleefeld said.

"Do I sound like I'm laughing?"

"You don't."

"See, generally, jokes are meant to be funny. This isn't funny in the least."

"I've got that." Kleefeld went silent. Marina had just told him what she had witnessed, and what she believed it indicated about the success of Larry Greenbarger's "Light of Day" formula, and about the city of Chicago's objections to a full-on assault. She figured it would take him a few minutes to process, so she didn't rush him. Outside the van, Tenko paced, keeping a wary eye on Monte the whole time.

"You're sure about what you saw," Kleefeld said after a moment.

"Sure that three vampires walked around in the sun? And two of them were scary strong? Yeah, I'm pretty sure."

"Move in."

"Really?"

"I don't care about Chicago's serial killer. If he's

been draining bodies, he's a vampire. If he's a vampire, he's our business anyway, not theirs."

"Will you call someone who can drag this paper pusher off my ass so we don't have to worry about him getting in the way?"

"I'll call, but don't wait for that. You have a green light to go."

"Thanks, boss." Marina ended the call. "Let's hit it," she announced.

"Really?" Kat asked.

"Really. Lock and load." She grabbed her weapon and pushed the door open. "Come on, Monte. All hands. Sorry, Mr. Tenko, but we've got to cut our conversation short."

"What? But . . . you can't—"

"Can and are," she said. "No time to chat, see you."

He sputtered some more, sweat popping out all over his florid face, but Marina ignored him.

At least they didn't have to worry about night vision goggles. Fighting vampires in broad daylight would be a new experience, but it would also make things easier for the humans in the long run. They raced across the street and into the motel's parking lot. At one end of the block the SWAT team watched, waiting for instructions. At the other, the Chicago cop, Ziccaria, was running forward, awkwardly drawing a service automatic. Behind him, the other two detectives hurried to catch up.

Then she snapped her attention forward. That motel

room was the target and she couldn't let anything distract her. Twenty yards from it, she stopped. Her team, disciplined and trained, stopped when she did. Every weapon was trained toward the room's door and boarded-over window. The little buildings were angled in such a way that if there were a back door or window, anyone emerging from those would still be visible from here.

"Let's give 'em a taste!" Marina shouted. The concrete walls would block much of their fire; but the door and the boards over the window wouldn't stop any of it. She figured the walls would trap the bloodsuckers inside, and once her people started laying down fire, ricochets off the inner walls would do some of their work for them. She pointed at the window and opened fire.

Phosphorous rounds streaked into the board, shredding it like paper. The door offered no greater resistance. The interior lit up, revealing a room full of screeching, hissing bloodsuckers.

But they didn't stay in the room.

They emerged, growling and slavering, straight into the full-throated assault of weapons *and* sunlight.

And they didn't stop.

Alex was halfway across the street when the government agents halted, just past the edge of the parking lot. The agent in charge of the op, Marina something, shouted a command and opened fire on the building,

and the other agents followed suit. He could hear
Larissa screaming at him to wait up. But he wanted
Walker, and if there was a chance to get him out alive
then he had to take it. Walker was his case, his killer,
and he wanted the guy in Chicago custody.

It didn't look like the Feds wanted *anyone* in custody.
They laid down fire on the building as if they were in
a war zone and the occupants were known hostiles. No
warning, no announcement, just the roar of sudden
gunfire splitting the morning peace.

Alex's mouth went dry. His weapon sat in his hand,
useless. The agents were riddling the room with some
kind of tracer rounds. Fires were already breaking out
inside.

The room's occupants charged out, directly into
the barrage. Alex saw one of those tracer rounds
streak into a man's neck and out the other side,
spraying gore, but the guy was hardly slowed. He
staggered a moment, shook his head angrily, then
resumed his advance.

Which was when Alex realized that he wasn't looking at human beings after all.

Humans didn't have teeth like that, or claws,
or long, distended jawlines. He didn't know what
these . . . these creatures were, but they resembled no
humans he had ever seen.

Something touched his shoulder and he jumped, letting out a startled bark.

"What the hell are those things?" Larissa asked.

"I have no idea," Alex said, trying to make his heart stop bouncing around in his chest. "But they're not natural."

Her hand tightened on his shoulder. "My God, they're vampires."

"What?"

"They're *vampires*. Everyone was right all along."

"Get real, Larissa."

"Look at them! Tell me if you can come up with a better explanation!"

Greg Fielding reached them. Alex noted, in spite of the distraction, that when Greg arrived, Larissa moved her hand off his shoulder. "I don't know what they are," Greg said. "But they're ugly bastards."

Two more of them shook off direct hits like they were nothing. "They're strong, too," Alex said. "We'd better move back."

He didn't have to say it again. He, Larissa, and Greg started to retreat. Alex waved the SWAT officers in as they went. They had the big guns and body armor the detectives lacked.

The Feds kept firing, but even they were starting to retreat a little as the creatures—the *vampires,* Alex admitted with reluctance—came on.

Three of them swarmed over one of the Feds. The other agents directed their fire toward those three, which created enough of a pause for more of the things to race from the motel room.

They ran out into morning sunlight. Alex had

always thought sunlight was fatal to vampires—in the movies, anyway.

Apparently this was no movie. The screams of the agent sounded real enough.

As the SWAT team moved in, Alex fell back farther, and allowed himself a moment of relief. Whoever or whatever those things were, the Feds and the SWAT cops would wrap them up.

Or so he fervently hoped.

45

PHOSPHOROUS ROUNDS CUT THROUGH the bloodsuckers like hot steel through ice cream. But it didn't stop them, and the TRU-UV lights were just as useless as the genuine sunlight.

Marina had known a lot of frightening moments during her career as a vampire hunter, but none quite as chilling as the realization that the old ways of killing them no longer applied.

"Fall back!" she screamed as the vamps swarmed toward them. Whether anyone heard her over the racket of gunfire, the boots of the SWAT cops, and the shrieks of the attacking vampires, she couldn't tell. Her team held their ground, guns blasting, so she stayed with them. She picked one of the vampires, aimed at its head, and squeezed off a long burst. The thing's head exploded, and it went down, momentum carrying it another several feet before it collapsed. At least that still did the trick.

Then four of them gathered around Jimbo. His gun rocked and flared but his shots were missing their heads, firing low into groins, bellies, and chests. The bloodsuckers were hurt but not destroyed. Jimbo's eyes went wide, his mouth falling open, and Marina could see the precise moment at which he realized he wouldn't be walking away from this one. She opened fire, hesitant at first because she didn't want any of her shots to accidentally hit Jimbo, but once it looked like he wouldn't live without the assist, she had to risk it.

She hit one vampire in the back of the skull, sending fragments and bits of brain sailing in an arc over the others. Claws raked across Jimbo's nose and cheek, slicing into his left eye and trailing ocular fluid and blood in its wake. Jimbo screamed. Marina shifted her aim and blasted that one's head into jelly.

"Look out!" Kat shouted. Marina caught a glimpse of a shape rushing toward her and swung her weapon around. Too late, though—the bloodsucker plowed into her and drove her to the pavement, slavering fangs snapping just above her face.

Brick down, Dragon Lady down, Angel down. New strength continued to course through Rocco, and he was sure the others felt it, too. But the meeting had turned into an ambush; Larry's fault, or Walker's, he wasn't sure which. Fixing blame didn't matter as much now as getting out in one piece. Rocco cared about everyone in his den, the new ones as well as the long-timers, and seeing even one fall was like a stake to the heart.

He couldn't stop to mourn, though. Once the barrage on the motel room began, they all knew their only hope was to get out, scatter and re-form later.

Or else to kill their attackers.

The initial assault had been carried out by a group of men and women without uniforms, but with high-tech weaponry, including lights that probably would have killed them fifteen minutes earlier. Operation Red-Blooded, Rocco guessed. Rumors about them had spread through the vampire community over the past couple of years. Behind them came what appeared to be local law enforcement in assault or riot gear—heavily padded, with visored helmets, but with traditional weapons that were largely meaningless to the *nosferatu*.

Chip, Goldie, Ciara, and Kenton teamed up against one of the bigger attackers, a man holding his automatic weapon in both hands and strafing them like a madman. The woman who seemed to be in charge, slight but fierce, took out Ciara and Goldie almost immediately, but then Shiloh charged her and the two of them crashed to the ground.

Rocco moved to help Shiloh, but one of those assault-clad cops shot him in the upper chest and the impact knocked him back several steps. The guy fired again and hot pain tore through Rocco's shoulder.

The cop might get lucky and get in a head shot, Rocco knew. Enraged, he vaulted one of the non-uniformed people and sailed across fifteen feet of parking lot, landed, sprang off his toes, and flew another eight feet toward the cop. Another shot scraped Rocco's back but did little damage. When he got his hands on the cop, he yanked the man off the ground and raised him above his head, spinning him around several times, then hurled him into the others. As he flew away, the cop dropped his machine gun. Rocco scraped it up and pulled down on the trigger, holding it, feeling the gun stutter as bullets churned into the other cops.

When he had cleared some space, he turned and aimed it at the woman Shiloh wrestled with. Shiloh would want the kill herself, of course, but at this point Rocco was impatient and anxious enough to be willing to use human weapons against them. He waited for Shiloh to give him an opening, and as soon as she did, he would take the shot.

"My God in heaven," Greg Fielding said.

Alex didn't speak, but inwardly, he echoed the sentiment. Those things were almost unstoppable. Four of them had surrounded one of the government agents, in spite of what must have been dozens of bullets biting through them. Blood and flesh were thrown into the air. The last time Alex saw the agent, a guy who looked as sturdy as an oak tree and as tall as a skyscraper, he had someone's teeth shredding his neck and was being dragged to the ground, flailing and crying out for mercy.

A female vampire—Alex had decided to stop denying the evidence right in front of him—bowled over Marina. Another male had taken one of the SWAT officers' guns and used it on some of the cops. Yet another engaged one of the Feds, who was shooting him with his weapon's muzzle pressed right up against the vampire's chest, but the vampire was ignoring the shots and bringing his open maw close to the agent's face. A tongue like a long strip of shoe leather flicked out, scraping the horrified man's cheek.

"We have to get out of here," Larissa said.

"Yeah," Greg agreed. "There's nothing we can do. Call in an air strike, maybe."

Alex didn't offer an opinion, but he started to back away, afraid to tear his gaze away from the carnage. The vampires were impossibly strong—a single leap could clear the distance between them. As long as the three detectives didn't present an immediate threat, he thought the vampires would leave them alone, but the second they became a problem, they were dead.

That was his theory, anyway. He no longer cared about Walker, about anything but getting safely away from this slaughter, and he believed that the three of them could make it to shelter if they kept their cool.

But now one of the vampires spotted them—he could feel its gaze burning into him—and called out something, and then it was tearing across the parking lot toward them.

"Run, Larissa!" Alex shouted. He put his body between her and the vampire and raised his duty weapon. *Head,* he told himself, *hit it in the head.* He had been watching, and that was the only thing he'd seen that worked.

Greg was backing up, not looking behind him, and he bumped into Alex just as he squeezed the trigger.

Alex's shot went wild, and Greg jumped at the report, startled by the sudden bang.

And a thought flashed through Alex's head, just a glimmer of one but it might work, might allow him and Larissa to reach safety. It was wrong, it was dirty, and he didn't care. Before he had even thought it all the way through, he was acting on it.

Greg was still off balance from being startled, from running into Alex as a shot was fired. It didn't take much to trip him; a sweep of Alex's right leg, behind Greg's left and in front of his right. Greg lost his balance, tumbled headfirst onto the asphalt. He caught himself on his palms, but his gun skidded from his hand.

"Run!" Alex cried again. He turned—had already been in motion as he tripped Greg, so it would look like he didn't even know the detective had fallen, and moved to grab Larissa's arm, to drag her along as he hauled ass out of there. This part he also hadn't worked out ahead of time, just taking each moment as it came. The only thing that mattered was leaving Greg as a sacrifice, to slow the vampire down—and at the same time, to eliminate him from Larissa's life, and to make sure he didn't go out as a hero but as a klutz, someone who had fallen on his face and lost his weapon.

It was cowardly.

Alex couldn't remember ever claiming not to be a coward, as long as he had lived. It wouldn't be a claim he could ever make after this.

But he would live, and so would Larissa. Those were the important things.

Maybe he would lose a night's sleep or two over Greg, but he had never liked the guy anyway.

And Larissa would need some comforting, a shoulder to cry on, strong arms to hold her through the nights, right?

46

MARINA DIDN'T THINK SHE would ever stop hearing Jimbo's screams. They were high pitched, horrified, scraping at her brain like rusty nails being tugged from hard wood. Marina was wrestling with a female vampire, but Jimbo's cries seared their way into her attention in spite of her immediate situation.

The bloodsucking bitch was strong. She had knocked Marina down backward and straddled her. Marina couldn't bring the gun around to any useful position, so she abandoned it. She tried to wriggle and writhe, but the vampire had her pinned down and was leaning forward, trying to close those nasty teeth on Marina. Marina had her left arm raised, elbow bent, forearm against the vampire's upper chest to hold her back. It wouldn't work for long, though. Already the strain on Marina's arm and shoulder was intense, her arm ready to snap under the vampire's pressure.

She refused to let the bloodsucker beat her. Jimbo was gone, she was sure, and she heard cries of pain and terror from other quarters—maybe her people, maybe cops, she couldn't tell. She had lost too many people to the bloodsuckers. A mission that had been fun and games had taken on a new, more serious nature, and losing now would mean her people would never be avenged, the deaths on her conscience for whatever eternity waited for sinners.

Her gun useless, Marina's right hand snaked a knife from its scabbard: eight-inch blade, blood grooves, serrated top edge. Sharp as a surgeon's favorite scalpel. It had worked back in New York; maybe it would again. The bloodsucker was leaning hard on her, snapping at her. Drool dripped from her fangs, splashing hot against Marina's face. Marina twisted her head away, kicked the vampire in the back. Anything to distract her from the knife hand.

"Just hold still," the vampire hissed. "Surrender is so sweet . . . you have no idea."

"Surrender . . ." Marina replied, "just pisses . . . me . . . *off!*" As she spoke, she arched her back, bucking up, and lashed out with the knife. She slashed at the vampire's left forearm, the hand holding Marina's shoulder against the ground, nearly severing it.

The vampire squealed, cursed, and fell forward, off balance from the sudden attack. Marina brought her left elbow up and smashed it into her teeth, and at the same time drove the knife into where her heart should have been. The knife wasn't silver or wood or anything like that, just steel, but it would hurt just the same. The vampire threw her head back and released a mournful wail. Marina took advantage of the moment to swipe the blade across her throat.

Vampire blood showered her skin and clothes. She twisted out from under the wounded vampire, gained her feet, twined her fingers through the beast's long hair and yanked her head back, loose on its damaged neck.

"Your turn to surrender, bloodsucker," Marina said as she brought the knife forward to cut the rest of the thing's head off. "Oh, wait . . . I'm not giving you that chance!"

"Greg! Oh God, Greg!"

Alex caught the look in Larissa's eyes and realized his mistake. Greg Fielding wasn't just a boy toy for her. She genuinely *liked* him, and if Alex was responsible for his death, even by accident, she would never forgive him.

Greg was trying to scramble to his feet, but his palms were bloody and they weren't supporting his weight, and his stupid hard-soled cop shoes wouldn't gain traction on the crumbling asphalt. One of the vampires had almost reached him. She looked like a little old lady, but her hands were hooked into gnarled claws and her mouth was full of wicked teeth, and her wrinkled face was twisted into a ferocious rictus.

She was about two seconds away from tearing Greg's head off.

And forever destroying whatever friendship Alex and Larissa might have had.

Alex darted back to Greg's side, getting to the fallen detective at the same time the vampire did. She was reaching for Greg's head. Alex thrust his weapon out until it was almost touching her forehead. She stopped, noticing the barrel just before tearing into Greg, and hissed. She brought a hand up to swat the gun away, but Alex squeezed the trigger.

The .38 slug tore a compact, nickel-sized hole between her eyes, but it blew a chunk out the back of her head as big around as the mouth of a juice glass. She stopped short, her claw just missing Greg's face, the hand reaching for Alex dropping to her side. A surprised look settled on her face. Alex fired twice more, through her right eye and the center of her forehead. She took two unsteady steps back, like she was fighting a wave of dizziness, and then she keeled over sideways.

"Thanks, man," Greg said, finally regaining his feet. "I thought she had me."

"Get your gun," Alex said. He didn't want the man's thanks, didn't want to be reminded that he had saved Greg's life at all. He turned back to Larissa, who had watched the whole thing in something like shock, her own weapon held loosely at her side. "You okay, Larissa?" he asked.

She started to move. He thought she was nodding, or shaking her head, but then her body shuddered and started to fall, revealing the vampire behind her, a skinny kid who looked about fourteen, and his hand was drenched in blood, holding a still-beating heart, and as she flopped down Alex saw the hole in her back where the kid had punched in and taken it, taken the heart that was the only thing in the world Alex had truly wanted to possess.

Rocco looked up from the bloody throat of a government agent and saw the small one, the woman, holding a dripping knife in one hand and Shiloh's hair in the other, about to sever her head.

He was twenty feet away. Twenty-five. The battle raged between him and them. He had been so certain Shiloh would take her he hadn't bothered to watch their struggle. "Shiloh!" he cried, his voice thick with anguish and rage.

He poised to leap the distance. But Kenton got there first, driving his shoulder into the woman and knocking her a dozen feet away. Shiloh slumped to the blacktop. Rocco reached her in an instant. He scooped her into his arm, tucking her against his shoulder, holding her head steady on her savaged neck with his other hand. "Help me!" he called. "Someone help!"

Winston appeared at his side, then Nightmare and Goldie. "Start the RV! We need to get her out of here!"

"On it," Nightmare said. He dashed off toward the RV, ignoring the bullets that struck him. The attackers, Red-Blooded and local police, were fewer in number now, and mostly tending to their own wounded, but a few kept trying to shoot the *nosferatu*, either not realizing or not caring that their efforts were largely fruitless.

"Protect her!" Rocco commanded. He rose to his feet, hoisting her with him. A bullet struck him in the lower back and he staggered but held on to her and kept his balance. Then his den closed ranks around them and they rushed to the RV's open door.

The sides were bullet riddled, and one tire was shredded. No doubt the authorities would be able to find it again, even track it with one of the helicopters Rocco heard chattering through the sky toward them. He didn't care about any of that. All that concerned him at the moment was giving Shiloh a safe place to lie still and recover. Their kind healed quickly, but a wound this bad would still take time. He could fashion a bandage of some sort in the vehicle. He just needed some breathing space.

Inside, he took her to the bed in the main cabin, laying her down carefully, then sat beside her to hold her head in place. "Drive!" he screamed. "Get us out of here!"

Nightmare, behind the wheel, shouted an affirmation, and the RV's big engine rumbled as he shifted gears. They started rolling, bumping over the curb and onto the street. More bullets thwacked into the body, and a window shattered. The damaged tire flapped, then came off and the thing tilted left, scraping on that side. They couldn't go for long like this, but if they could escape from the immediate battle scene, Rocco would be happy with that. He would improvise from there. Play things by ear.

That had worked for him so far, and for a long time. He and his den had dodged police, Elder Death Squads determined to thin the vampire herd, and except for that one disastrous raid, the agents of Operation Red-Blooded. It would work again. He wouldn't lose Shiloh.

He couldn't say if he loved her or not. He only knew that he didn't want to be without her.

When he imagined walking in the sun, it was always with her. Hand in hand under a sparkling blue sky, feeling the warmth denied them for so long.

It was a dream, a beautiful, improbable dream, but he wasn't about to give up on it now.

He held Shiloh's head on her neck and felt the unsteady rocking of the RV as it raced away.

47

ONE OF THE VAMPIRES started screaming, clutching another one to his chest like a father carrying a daughter
with a twisted ankle. Alex's awareness of this was only
incidental; he stood in frozen silence watching the beast
who had killed Larissa hold her heart to his lips like a
juicy orange and drink from it.

This vampire turned toward the other one's screams,
and that shook Alex free from paralysis. He raised
the .38 and as the vampire started to run toward its
fellows, he unloaded the magazine into its skull. The
thing dropped, Larissa's heart rolling from its grip onto
the pavement. Bits of grit and asphalt stuck to it, coating it with gray.

The rest had taken refuge inside the big RV. Alex
aimed at it, pulled the trigger, and remembered that
he had just emptied the gun. He was running a couple
of steps behind himself. He found another magazine in
his pocket, ejected the first one and rammed the second
home. The RV was on the street now, sparks flying up
from where it ran on one rim. Alex fired at it, aware
that he couldn't stop it from here. But the effort, the
boom of his gun and the *thock* of bullets striking the

vehicle's shell, made him feel like he was at least making an effort.

Greg Fielding knelt beside Larissa, tears coating his face, holding her hand in his and patting it gently. *He has to know she's dead, doesn't he?* Alex wondered. *Of course he does, that's what the tears are for.*

She couldn't feel his touch on her hand, then.

But he could.

In the end, Alex guessed, that was all that mattered.

Marina scraped herself off the pavement. If that vampire hadn't summoned the others to help him with the one she had almost decapitated, she would have been done for. As it was, she was bruised and battered, but alive. She couldn't say as much for her team. Kat had made it, and Monte. Tony O. had been bitten and needed to be put down before he could turn. Jimbo was dead.

She found Monte sitting on the ground pummeling a fallen bloodsucker, smashing its skull and brains into jelly with his big, knobby fists. She had to shake him hard to get his attention, and when he looked up at her, there was hatred in his eyes, like a film preventing him from seeing past it. Marina kept shaking him, saying his name, until he blinked her into focus and his face softened.

"It's over, Monte," she said. "The vampires are gone."

"We didn't get all of 'em?"

"Not all. Some. Most, maybe. But they hurt us, too.

They got Tony and Jimbo. Kat has a broken arm, but I don't think she's compromised. We'll get her into medical. They fucked up the Chicago PD, too. The bloodsuckers are in an RV that's short one tire—I don't think they'll get far, and I'll get eyes on it ASAP. But we're going to have to let it go for now, get someone else working on it."

Kat joined them, crouching down and propping the knuckles of her right hand on the ground. Her left arm rested against her legs. Pain showed in the creases around her eyes and the lines at her mouth. "They were out in the sun," she said. "Our UV didn't do squat."

"Out in the sun, and stronger for it," Marina added. "We'd have taken them otherwise."

"You think?" Monte asked.

"I know it."

"But . . . this is bad," Kat said. "Vampires who aren't afraid of the sun? How do we . . . ?"

"I don't know," Marina said. "But we'll figure something out. We have to, right?"

"I guess," Kat said.

"Sister, we need payback. They can't do that to Jimbo and the Tonys, to R.T., Spider John. They can't do that and just walk away."

"I'm ready," Monte said. "I had to watch Jimbo die and I couldn't do shit about it, and if I had one of 'em here I'd . . . I'd . . ."

He looked down at his hands, the knuckles bruised

and swollen. Marina hoped he hadn't cut them open, because if he'd got vampire blood in the cuts then she would have to shoot him, too. She had been drenched in blood as well, but mostly on her uniform—she had avoided getting any in her mouth or eyes.

She was sick of killing her own. Sick of the whole thing, the struggle between alive and undead. It never ended, probably never *could* end. Progress was made and lost in the space of a heartbeat. It was a quagmire, Vietnam style, from which there could be no extrication because the enemy could be temporarily defeated, but never vanquished.

The parking lot glistened with blood, its metallic smell hanging heavy in the air. This was all about blood. Who had it, who wanted it. It could have been land, or gold, or oil—it was the wanting that was trouble, not the thing itself.

Marina didn't know what else she could do. Nothing, probably. She was no longer suited to civilian life, and if she tried it, she would no doubt find that she missed the action. Besides, as the cliché went, by now she knew too much.

She was trapped, as locked into her place in the war as the vampires themselves were. There would be another battle, and another, and more after that. She would walk again on ground sticky with spilled blood, smell the pungent odors of injury and death, hear the whimpered cries of the barely living. This wouldn't be the last time she looked upon a scene of chaos and carnage. If she closed her eyes, she found, she could imagine the next one.

The only saving grace was that the next battle would give her another chance to kill vampires. And if that was all she had left in the world, then she would take it. Cling to it.

It wasn't much, but it was better than nothing.

Epilogue

ALEX ZICCARIA WALKED UP the sidewalk, arms swinging loose at his sides. Cars and trucks rushed up and down the street, their wakes buffeting him, the growl and roar and rumble of internal combustion engines all but ignored. Sunlight splashed upon his face. He squinted against it but otherwise paid it no mind.

Around him were the ghosts.

Everywhere he looked, ghosts. Those he had tried to save and couldn't. Those he didn't know of until after they had died. Those who had died before he was even a cop, before he was born. The victims of human beings who were willing to kill other humans.

He didn't know where vampires fit in. He didn't know enough about them to make that judgment. But even if they weren't human, they had been once. They left behind ghosts, too. Diaphanous figures moving through the sunlight even as the light moved through them. No spark in their hollow eyes, just a lost, lonely stare from which Alex couldn't look away.

He would have to write up a report at some point, but not now. Not today. He didn't know what it would say. That something was loose on the streets of

America, something terrible? He had no idea what they really were or how to stop them.

So he walked, slowly, unsteady on his feet, an old man's walk. And he watched the ghosts, flickering in the sun like characters from one of his precious silent movies. He checked each face in case it was hers. And it never was.

He could, however, walk for a long, long time. He could walk forever. Or so it seemed.

So it seemed.

ABOUT THE AUTHOR

JEFF MARIOTTE is the award-winning author of the supernatural thrillers *Cold Black Hearts, River Runs Red,* and *Missing White Girl* (all as Jeffrey J. Mariotte); horror epic *The Slab;* teen horror quartet *Witch Season;* and many other novels, including three previous *30 Days of Night* novels written with Steve Niles. His comic book work includes *Desperadoes, Graveslinger, Zombie Cop,* and much more. A co-owner of specialty bookstore Mysterious Galaxy, he lives on the Flying M Ranch in southeastern Arizona.